Outstanding praise for the novels of Elizabeth Thornton

Almost a Princess

"Well written . . . this book will appeal to fans of Amanda Quick, Candace Camp and Lisa Kleypas."

—*Booklist*

Cherished

"A glorious, wonderful book! I defy anyone reading the opening chapter not to feel compelled to read the whole book. I consider Elizabeth Thornton a major find."

—Mary Balogh

Tender the Storm

"Fast paced . . . filled with tension, danger and adventure . . ."

—*Rendezvous*

The Perfect Princess

"A joy to read!"

—*Romantic Times*

Princess Charming

"Delightfully entertaining."

—*Philadelphia Inquirer*

Strangers at Dawn

"Thornton has been a long-time favorite thanks to her well-told tales of intrigue peppered with sizzling romance and *Strangers at Dawn* is among the best."

—*The Oakland Press*

Whisper His Name

"Thornton creates appealing characters and cleverly weaves in familiar Regency settings and customs."

—*Publishers Weekly*

The Bride's Bodyguard

"This witty Regency romance/mystery will keep you up all night."

—*The Atlantic Journal/Constitution*

Books by Elizabeth Thornton

*Published by Zebra Books

ELIZABETH THORNTON

A VIRTUOUS LADY

ZEBRA BOOKS
KENSINGTON PUBLISHING CORP.
http://www.kensingtonbooks.com

ZEBRA BOOKS are published by

Kensington Publishing Corp.
850 Third Avenue
New York, NY 10022

All Kensington titles, imprints and distributed lines are available at special quantity discounts for bulk purchases for sales promotion, premiums, fund-raising, educational or institutional use.

Special book excerpts or customized printings can also be created to fit specific needs. For details, write or phone the office of the Kensington Special Sales Manager: Kensington Publishing Corp., 850 Third Avenue, New York, NY 10022. Attn. Special Sales Department. Phone: 1-800-221-2647.

Zebra and the Z logo Reg. U.S. Pat. & TM Off.

First Printing: March 1988
10 9 8 7 6 5 4 3

Printed in the United States of America

Chapter 1

The faint strains of the orchestra wafted up the wide well of the imposing, marble staircase and invaded the quiet seclusion of Briony Langland's fourth-floor chamber as she prepared for bed.

"A wicked waltz," said Nanny reprovingly. Her lips pursed in displeasure, and she glowered at Briony's pale reflection in the oval mirror of the polished mahogany lady's dressing table. But Nanny's arm never wavered for an instant in its habitual labor of brushing Miss Briony's long, fair, soft tresses until they shone like silk.

"One hundred," she said at last, laying down the silver hairbrush.

That a ball was in progress in the nether regions of Broomhill House in the village of Richmond near London and she banished to the Olympian heights of her uncle's mansion disturbed Miss Langland's equilibrium not one whit. Briony did not like balls. She had never been to one, but she knew that dancing was frivolous and so, by conviction, if not by inclination, Briony detested balls.

Nanny nimbly braided Briony's hair and wove the plaits into a neat coil, securing them with pins to the crown of her fair head. The final touch to this toilette was a scrap of Nottingham lace, euphemistically called a "night cap," which was gingerly placed on Briony's braids and tied securely under her chin with ribbons. Briony glared distastefully at the reflection in the mirror, which, as was to be expected, glared distastefully back. She looked to be nearer a child of twelve than a full-grown woman of nineteen years.

"Now into bed with ye," said Nanny peremptorily. Her charge hesitated. It was on Briony's mind to ask Nanny if she might read for only a few minutes before snuffing out the candles, but something in the resolute stance of Nanny's buxom figure made her change her mind. She climbed posthaste into the high, four-poster bed and pulled the blankets up to her chin.

"Skin and bone, that's what ye are," said Nanny. "Ye're wasting away before my eyes. It's porridge and fresh cream for ye every morning before ye even sit down to table to eat yer English breakfast." Nanny was Scottish.

"Yes, Nanny," replied Briony meekly. Briony had no intention of eating such unpalatable fare.

Nanny came closer to the bed and subjected Briony to the closest scrutiny. "And dark circles under yer eyes like rings o' soot!" Her voice softened. "My wee lamb, ye must have done with this grieving. Can ye no see that it's not what yer mammy and yer pa, God rest their souls, would want for ye? It breaks my heart to see ye like this. 'Tis more than a year since the terrible tragedy. Now that ye've put off yer mourning and come to bide with yer aunt and uncle, can ye no find a little contentment? Are ye no happy here, Miss Briony?"

Briony swallowed. "Of course I am happy, Nanny. As happy as I can be under the circumstances. I am merely a little homesick for Langlands and Aunt Charlotte, nothing more."

Nanny stood looking pensively at her charge for a few moments longer. "Give it time, my wee lamb," she said gently. "Ye've been here for only a sennight, and ye could not remain longer at home in the care o' yer father's aunt. It was not fitting for a lass o' yer years to be so cut off from society, and the poor woman could scarce take care o' herself, never mind the likes o' ye and Master Vernon. Here at least ye have yer cousin Harriet to keep ye company. Sure London is no like being in the wilds o' Shropshire, but a body can get used to anything after a while."

"But Richmond isn't London, Nanny!"

"Near enough." Nanny sniffed. "I have not noted any lack o' fine ladies and gentlemen with their top lofty ways! See that ye don't become one o' them."

Briony chuckled. "Aunt Esther is going to have her work cut out for her if she thinks to turn a Quaker girl into a fine lady. I give you your own words, Nanny. 'You cannot make a silk purse of a sow's ear.'"

"Yer mammy raised ye to be a *real* lady, not one of them simpering misses. Was she no a lady herself before she became a Quaker?"

"Mama was always a lady," agreed Briony readily. "After all, she was Uncle John's sister."

"Then see that ye remember all that she taught ye, even though ye must learn new ways o' doing things now that ye're wards o' yer grand relations."

Nanny bustled about shaking out Briony's garments—dull, gray, Quaker garments—before sorting them and storing them in the large, mahogany press which stood against the wall. Briony watched her movements from under gold-tipped lashes and in a burst of affection broke out, "Oh, Nanny, what ever would I do without thee? I do love thee."

Nanny turned on her mistress roundly. "Miss Briony! Mind yer tongue." She softened her rough tone. "Ah my wee lamb, it was ever yer wont to express yer affections in the Quaker way. But ye must be careful now. What would yer grand relations think if they could hear ye? I thank the Lord that yer pa never allowed ye and Master Vernon to speak in that foolish Quaker way of yer mammy's."

Briony's face dimpled with mischief. "Shame on thee, Nanny! Dost thou not know that the Bible is written in the Quaker tongue—and thou a Puritan?"

"Enough, I said!" Nanny was not amused. "And," she went on primly, "I am not a Puritan. I am a Scottish Presbyterian."

"Same thing," teased Briony.

"Ach—Sassenachs!"

Briony's eyes fairly sparkled. "Nanny, is it fair to indulge your own foolish whim to talk in that incomprehensible Scottish tongue of yours whilst denying me the privilege of conversing in my peculiar, Quaker way?"

"It's not the same thing, my wee lamb, as ye well know. Yer uncle is yer guardian, and what he tolerates in me, he would not abide in you! And what yer aunt would say, I hardly like to think. No doubt she would take it into her head to have a fit of the vapors."

No, admitted Briony inwardly, her uncle and aunt would not be favorably impressed to find themselves addressed in "thees" and "thous." The Quaker mode of speech was one that their father had not tolerated in his children although he had always appeared to find it charming in his wife. But even Mama did not always remember to speak in her plain, Quaker mode, for as the daughter of the first Baron Grenfell, it had never been part of her upbringing.

Briony's expression grew thoughtful. "Nanny, you know what Aunt Esther intends for me—fine gowns and dresses, parties and balls, concerts, theaters and outings, and oh, a dozen other things. She means for Vernon and me to take our places in Polite Society. I don't wish to seem ungrateful or rebellious, but how can I permit it? How can I be true to all that I believe in—to be true to everything Mama taught me?"

Nanny MacNair stood at the bottom of the large four poster, surveying the sweet face of her "wee lamb." It did not surprise her in the least that Briony, who had always been somewhat intractable as a carefree youngster growing up in a loving, and sometimes permissive, Quaker home should now take it upon herself to honor the memory of her dead mother by conforming to what she had in the past dismissed as merely irrelevant. Nanny chose her words with care.

"Yer mammy, as a good Quaker woman, raised ye in the fear and love o' the Lord. No woman can do more for her children. But yer father, too, was a god-fearing man although no Quaker. Ye must honor his memory also. Yer uncle is yer guardian now. It is yer duty to obey him. Let yer conscience be yer guide. Do everything ye are asked to do, but do it without sin.

Briony's eyes filled with tears. She wished with all her heart that she had paid more heed to her mother's instructions, that she had been more biddable, more tractable, that she had cherished more the sweet hours of companionship that they had shared as a family.

But on that warm July morning brilliant with sunshine, as she and her brother, Vernon, had lazily watched their parents boating on the calm waters of Lake Windermere and had waved to them negligently from the sunbaked shore, who could have foreseen the tragedy that was too soon to overtake them? Who could have foreseen the sudden squall that had blown ferociously in from the west searing the sky with tongues of forked lightning and whipping the waves to a raging whirlpool? Who could have foretold the awful horror of that day?

Briony, watching terrified and soaked to the skin from the shore, had seen it all. She would never forget it. It had been her constant nightmare.

Blinking back the hot, sudden tears, she managed a tremulous smile. "Good night, Nanny, and thank you . . . for everything."

Nanny MacNair picked up an armful of mending and came to kiss her charge on the brow. "May God bless ye, my wee lamb," she soothed, "and sweet dreams to ye." Briony was left to her solitary reflections.

She and her brother, Vernon, had been raised by strict Quaker tenets, even though their father had remained of the Anglican persuasion. She knew that there were "gay" Quakers who enjoyed music and dancing and who wore garments of every color of the rainbow. But her mother had not been one of those. Jane Langland had been a conservative and had raised her children in the conservative, Quaker tradition. And since they were Quakers, they were not judgmental of their neighbors but ever ready to see the best in everyone. If they were strict, and they were, it was in adhering to their principles in their own conduct. Towards others' foibles they were gentle and forbearing. At least, thought Briony, they were supposed to be. But theory and practice did not always coincide, leastways not in some of the Quakers she had met at the quarterly and half-yearly business meetings to which she had accompanied her mother. Her father and brother, naturally, had always absented themselves—not their dish, so they said.

Briony grew restless. The room was hot and stuffy. She threw back the blankets and moved to open the sash window. A cool, late, autumn breeze sent her hurrying to don her dressing gown. Her chamber was at the back of the house and, from the window, she could see the

River Thames glowing with a mysterious luster. She imagined the river, as it had been in Tudor times, filled with long barges of laughing courtiers and their ladies being conveyed to Hampton Court. Sir Thomas More had traveled this river coming from his manor downriver in Chelsea, past the old Palace at Richmond to Henry VIII's magnificent new residence.

The orchestra was playing the second waltz of the evening. She would have to learn the steps of all the dances, but she had not the least intention of ever dancing anything as vulgar as the waltz.

Briony did not censure her uncle and aunt, Sir John and Lady Grenfell, for holding a ball in their splendid palladian mansion. Nor was she envious that her cousin, Harriet, was at that moment decked out in dazzling finery and hanging on the sleeve of some dashing blade. Briony Langland did not choose to go to balls—not yet. And her uncle and aunt were content for the present to give Briony her head. But Master Vernon, at seventeen and two years younger than his sister, had no such scruples. He had accepted his invitation to the ball with alacrity.

No, Briony did not like balls. But she did like books, and there was nary a one to be found in the room that her Aunt Esther had assigned to her. Her own books were in transit from her home in Shropshire and could not be expected until the end of the week. If she only had a book to read, she thought desperately, she could postpone the persistent nightmare which haunted her sleep. Somehow she must procure one.

Being a redoubtable lass, as Nanny would say, and not in the least shy or lacking in initiative, Briony determined to make her way unobtrusively to her uncle's library, which was well away from the assembled guests, and choose something at her leisure.

Avoiding the cantilevered, public staircase on which she might meet some stray guest, she moved with her usual, unhurried grace along the uncarpeted landing, her little high-heeled slippers clicking sharply on the newly sanded floor, and she passed through the doorway leading to the servants' staircase. In a matter of a few minutes, she had descended to the ground floor.

Pulling her dressing gown more snugly around her, she removed her satin slippers and, clutching them securely in her free hand, tiptoed through the deserted hall. From the floor above could be heard the chatter of the merry throng. Briony retrieved a candelabra from the hall table and crossed into the cavernous book room, shutting the door firmly behind her.

Chapter 2

Within the sheltering confines of her uncle's favorite
Queen Anne wing armchair, Briony stirred. As she struggled from the dark, slumberous depths to wakefulness,
her eyes flickered open, and for a long moment she
gazed uncomprehendingly at the candles sputtering
halfway down their sprockets in the silver wall sconces
flanking the gilt-edged mirror above the fireplace. The
muffled whisper of a moan, low and drawn out, on the
other side of the book room door slowly penetrated her
consciousness, and she made an effort to rouse herself,
her silky lashes blinking rapidly to banish the vestiges of
sleep from her eyes.

"Hugh?" The disembodied voice was soft and sultry.
"Don't you care that my reputation may be in tatters?
Our absence is bound to be noted."

The thread of girlish laughter which followed divested
the remark of any real censure. Briony heard the rustle
of some piece of feminine apparel, then a soft protest
which was cut off by a low bark of wicked, masculine
laughter. Her brows drew together. She was not such an
innocent that she did not understand the significance
of what was transpiring on the other side of the library
door. The door knob rattled, and Briony came fully alert.
She had no wish to come face to face with the couple who
were intent on . . . she let the thought die half formed

in her mind. The situation was too distasteful to contemplate. When she saw the doorknob turn, her hands tightened on the book in her lap, bringing it to her bosom, and she rose swiftly to her feet. The door was pushed roughly open, and Briony squared her shoulders and lifted her chin a fraction, prepared to brazen out the inevitably embarrassing interview. Nothing happened. For some inexplicable reason, the owners of the throbbing voices delayed their entrance.

"Hugh! Not so fast!" Another soft protest which the gentleman did not hesitate to disregard. Then after a moment, Briony heard the bemused tones of the thwarted lover.

"As I recall, Adèle, you were the one who suggested this rendezvous. If you wish me to retire to the card room, you have only to say so."

Evidently, the lady demurred, for Briony could tell by the sounds of their labored breathing that the passionate embrace had been resumed. The delay gave her the few moments she needed to look around for some means of concealing herself. It was then that she remembered the newfangled contraption her uncle had so recently acquired. The idea had come to him when he was visiting Osterley Park, the grand house of their near neighbors, the Earl and Countess of Jersey. He had taken one look at the modern convenience in George Villiers' impressive library and nothing would do until he had installed one in his own abode. It was his pride and joy.

Briony glided soundlessly to the far wall. At the edge of one shelf of books, her fumbling fingers found a bolt. She drew it back and pulled. The wall of shelves became a door and Briony passed through, pulling it softly behind her. Her place of concealment was not one that she was happy to occupy for it happened to be her uncle's private water closet, reserved for the gentlemen when they wished to relieve themselves when business or brandy had kept them too long at their ledgers.

As the darkness closed around her, too late, she realized that she had left her high-heeled slippers on the floor beside the commodious wing armchair in front of the fireplace. But not for the world would she return to retrieve them. There was nothing she could do but exercise a little patience. She determined to wait it out until the couple in the library took it into their heads to remove to some other part of the house. She hoped it would be soon, for the frigid marble floor beneath her naked toes had brought the goose bumps quivering along her arms and shoulders. She shivered and pulled her dressing gown closer to her slender form in a vain attempt to stave off the cold.

The long minutes dragged by, and Briony's teeth began to chatter. The chill in that dark, tomb-like vault was fast becoming unendurable. She put her ear to the wall, but heard nothing save her own ragged breathing which the arctic temperature had induced. She grew impatient.

With the greatest circumspection, she opened the door the merest crack, hopeful that the unwelcome intruders had taken themselves off. She was to be disappointed. Her ears were assailed by the soft grunts and groans of the besotted lovers. Briony swung the door wider and peeped out. The shameless pair had ensconced themselves on her aunt's best satin brocade sofa, which held pride of place, flanked by two long windows, on the opposite wall. The gentleman, if such he could be called, had pinioned the writhing lady beneath him on the couch. Briony drew back, deeply disgusted by such a show of unseemly behavior. Another soft protest from the lady, and Briony decided that she had had enough.

She raised the leather-bound volume high above her

head and tossed it with all her strength against the fireplace wall, where it rebounded with a crash. Adèle emitted one long, shrill scream and then there was silence.

"Damn!" exclaimed Hugh Montgomery, Marquess of Ravensworth.

With shaking fingers, Briony secured the door to her hiding place, clamping her teeth together to stifle the gurgle of nervous laughter which sprang to her lips.

The Marquess raised on one elbow and with feline grace uncoiled himself from the clutches of his frozen companion. He got to his feet slowly. As he straightened his cravat, his lazy glance roved around the shadowy room, missing nothing. It came to rest on the rug in front of the empty grate, and a smile, slow and devilish, played across his generous mouth. He glanced down at his silent partner and his smile faded.

"Tidy yourself, woman!" he growled, his insolent eyes taking in her blatant déshabillé.

Adèle pushed to a sitting position, one hand smoothing down the hem of her crushed, silk gown, the other adjusting the fine Brussels lace which barely covered the swell of her ample bosom. "What was it?" she asked on a thread of a voice, her amber eyes wide with apprehension as they glanced around the gloomy interior. They came to rest on the hard-chiseled features of the man who towered above her, and her gaze lingered, then swept over him, savoring the powerful sweep of his broad chest and shoulders and every corded muscle of his lean flanks and thighs. Hugh Montgomery's leashed sensuality was evident in every spare line of him. She watched as the aristocratic features relaxed into a grin at some private reflection, and Adèle's breath tightened in her throat. He was so unconsciously virile. His air of unshakable confidence had a calming effect on her ruffled sensibilities. She reached out to pull him down. Long fingers grasped her wrist and she was unceremoniously yanked to her feet.

He chuckled softly. "Not now, Adèle, or hadn't you noticed? Our secret tryst is no longer . . . secret." He placed a warning finger against his lips. "Be a good girl and run along. I'll catch up with you later."

The lady opened her mouth to protest her dismissal, but one glance at Ravensworth's cocked brow, so eloquently sardonic, and she suppressed the impulse.

"Is that a promise?" she asked hopefully.

"I beg your pardon?" It was obvious that Ravensworth had already lost interest in her.

She made an effort to control her rising pique. "I collect that Viscount Avery is playing a trick on us. Your friend doesn't much care for me, does he?"

Ravensworth's tone was perfectly amiable. "Since you ask, no. But don't let it trouble you. *Chacun à son goût*, and Avery's palate is known to be a trifle . . . fastidious."

Adèle was not quite certain that Ravensworth had paid her a compliment. As she puzzled over the problem, trying to decide whether she should act insulted or come back at him with some devastatingly witty rejoinder, if only she could think of one, she found her elbow in an iron grip and she was led uncompromisingly to the door.

But the lady was not about to give up so easily. She had used every feminine wile she could think of to lure him back to her bed, and she had almost succeeded. Not that the Marquess ever pretended to be constant as a lover. He had a roving eye which he never made the slightest attempt to conceal from the bevy of titled ladies and opera dancers who coveted the privilege of warming his bed.

His frankness in that respect was not only outrageous, but an offense, albeit a forgivable one, to a woman of her rank and fortune. She, an acknowledged beauty, a countess, widow of her late husband the Earl, could not even claim so exalted a title as Ravensworth's mistress. He showed no preference for his string of women, but enjoyed what each had to offer with a casualness which, in other men, would have been regarded as positively depraved. But Ravensworth was Ravensworth, a rogue, a roué, a rake, but an irresistible charmer for all that. There were few women who could resist an invitation to his bed. Adèle St. Clair was not one of them.

She laid a restraining hand against his chest. "You know where to find me? I've kept on the house in Duke Street."

"Yes, I remember," he responded noncommittally. He opened the door and pushed her firmly across the threshold.

"You'll join me later?" she persisted.

Ravensworth hesitated for only a fraction of a second. "If it is convenient." His level look was inscrutable.

A spate of angry words rose to tremble on her lips but died unspoken when she observed the implacable set of his mouth. She inclined her head in gracious acquiescence, but before she could utter the words à *bientôt,* the door was shut inexorably in her face.

The Marquess turned back into the room, and a few lithe strides brought him to the wing armchair so hastily vacated by Briony. He eased himself into its soft, cushioned depths and crossed one silk-stockinged calf over the other, bringing his black patent evening pump to rest casually at the knee of his gray satin breeches. His gold signet ring with its lion rampant crest flashed in the soft glow of candlelight as he bent to retrieve the book which lay abandoned in the empty grate. When he determined that what he held in his hands was a gothic novel of the type favored by the romantic young miss of the day, he grinned, showing a flash of even white teeth against his swarthy complexion. One long hand trailed to the floor to recover the flimsy, feminine slippers at his feet. He dangled them from one hand in front of his face for a moment or two, then his grin deepened.

"You can come out, now, chérie. I know you're here somewhere."

In the depths of her cavernous, dark tomb, Briony quailed. She pulled on the door of her icy refuge to ensure that she was beyond the gentleman's reach. It was her undoing. A pencil, poised perilously at the edge of the shelf, rolled forward, balanced on the precipice momentarily, then toppled to the uncarpeted floor. Ravensworth heard the crack and was instantly before the concealed door. In a moment he had flung it wide. In his hand he held a candelabra, the better to see the jealous wench who had spoiled his sport with the wicked widow. When he saw the slip of a girl with her solemn gray eyes looking warily up at him, his smile froze. He had never before in his nine and twenty years set eyes on the chit.

After a moment's baffled silence, Ravensworth's ire began to rise. He had expected something different.

"Who the devil are you? And what do you mean by spying on me?"

As Nanny could have told his lordship, Briony, appearances to the contrary, was not faint of heart. She refused to be intimidated by his threatening manner. Gathering the shreds of her dignity about her like the folds of her threadbare dressing gown, she swept out of the water closet and brushed his lordship aside.

"I beg your pardon. Have you been waiting long? The water closet is unoccupied now."

"The what?" asked Ravensworth in some perplexity as she sailed past him. He deposited the candelabra on the nearest table.

Briony had no wish to engage the irate, young gentleman in idle conversation. She saw a clear path to the door and hastened toward it. Ravensworth was before her. He reached the door in two long strides and cut off her escape. Briony halted in her tracks.

In other circumstances, she might have admired the virile beauty of the dark-haired Adonis who barred her path. But Briony scarcely noticed it. She became suffocatingly aware of the leashed power of her adversary, and she stilled like a hapless doe who has inadvertently roused a sleeping tiger.

The man towered above her. Even if she screamed, who was there to hear her? The ballroom was on the floor above, and there was no reason, save one that she could think of, why her uncle's guests would wish to trespass to the floor below. She forced herself to relax. The man was her uncle's guest and therefore, by implication, a gentleman—more or less. Cool logic prevailed. Safer by far to humor the ill-tempered philanderer.

"Who am I? Would you believe . . . a guardian angel?"

Briony knew by the tensing of his jaw that her halfhearted attempt at levity had failed.

"A guardian angel?" he encouraged. When she remained mute, he went on with glacial politeness, "Would you be so kind as to explain that remark?"

"A guardian angel . . . for a damsel in distress?"

"Guarding what, may I ask?"

There could be no turning back now. "Her virtue, of course." She schooled herself to meet the blaze of his eyes with unflinching composure but his expression, she noted with some relief, remained impassive.

He propped one arm against the door and leaned the full press of his weight against it, and Briony's breathing became a little easier.

His lordship's measuring stare took in the slight form

of the quivering girl who faced him so resolutely. The scrap of lace pinned at a ridiculous angle to her braided hair and the voluminous, wool dressing gown buttoned high at the throat and low at the wrist gave her a decided grandmotherly air. Miss Prim and Proper, he conjectured. Her accent was cultured but her garments shabby. A governess perhaps, or a paid companion. Damn if he wouldn't like to crack that cool exterior.

"Who gave you leave to judge the morals of your betters?"

Briony's calm, gray eyes looked reproachfully up at him. "Was I being judgmental? I think not. And I believe, if you but consider it, you will acquit me of that particular vice. The lady protested, but you would not listen. She told you 'no,' but you insisted. What kind of woman would leave a sister in such peril?"

"What a child you are!" the Marquess exclaimed, shaking his head at the picture of wounded innocence she presented. Then, in a gentler voice, "The lady was not unwilling."

"I heard her refuse you." Briony was obstinate.

"Tell me, Miss Virtuous," he asked in a controlled tone, "does your 'no' always mean 'no' and your 'yes'— 'yes'?"

"Invariably."

"You cannot be serious."

"But of course I mean it. How is it possible to communicate if we say one thing and mean another? Imagine the confusion!"

"Miss Virtuous," said the Marquess of Ravensworth with a touch of asperity, "you are either the most ingenious wench that I have ever encountered or the most ingenuous."

"Why? What do you mean?" she asked, her brow wrinkling.

The Marquess laughed and shook his head. "Don't be ridiculous, girl! You know what I mean. What would happen to . . . well . . . gallantry, flirtation, flattery, and so on, if one told only the unvarnished truth?"

Briony looked slightly contemptuous. "Such things, I suppose, would die a natural death."

"And wouldn't you be sorry?"

"No! Why should I?"

Ravensworth looked incredulous, then puzzled, and finally disbelieving. "Do you stand there and tell me that you never fib, never tell an untruth, never practice even the smallest of deceptions when you find yourself in an impossible situation?"

"Never!"

"I don't believe it!"

"Try me," she replied recklessly.

This was going too far. The Marquess was not one to refuse a challenge. A lecherous gleam kindled in his eye.

"With the greatest of pleasure."

In one swift movement, he pushed himself from the door and tumbled Briony into his arms. She opened her lips to voice her protest at such manhandling, but before she could utter a word, his mouth swooped down and he kissed her.

Hugh Montgomery was a practiced lover. He knew to a nicety how to break down the resistance of the most reluctant female. His mouth slanted across Briony's shocked lips, moulding them with slow, deliberate, tender ardor, tasting, savoring, drugging her with persuasive pleasure.

It was Briony's first real kiss and she was captivated. She relaxed against him and opened her mouth to allow him freer access. The Marquess was not slow to avail himself of the unconscious gesture. His lips moved over hers, drinking in the sweet taste of her. He felt her innocent response as she trembled in his arms, and he was enthralled. His tongue slipped easily between her teeth, stroking, teasing, awakening her to a man's desire. He was thoroughly enjoying the novel experience of having an untried wench in his embrace when passion, blazing, all consuming, and so unexpected rose like a hot tide in his veins. His kiss deepened; his arms tightened around her small, warm body; he pressed her closer, closer, demanding everything that she had to give, and a whirlpool of emotion, of exquisite, tormenting sensation, caught them both in its irresistible eddy.

It was the Marquess who brought the kiss to an end. He drew back his head and looked searchingly into Briony's velvet gray eyes. Damn if the chit hadn't seduced *him!*

There was wonder and surprise in his voice. "Why did I kiss you?"

"I think you were trying to prove something," Briony managed when she caught her breath.

"Was I? Ah yes, I remember! Now truthfully, mind!" he softly admonished. "Do you wish me to kiss you again?"

"No," she breathed on a strangled whisper.

"Liar!" The word was a caress. He bent his head to capture her lips again, but Briony struggled free of his arms.

"You don't understand. I don't deny that I enjoyed the experience. How could I? But I don't think kissing is . . . well . . . healthy."

"Why ever not?"

She extended both arms and held them up for his inspection. "My fingers are tingling."

Ravensworth found her candor enchanting. "You win. You really are without guile. And now that you have proved it to my complete satisfaction, I think I want to kiss you again."

But Briony had regained a modicum of her Quaker discretion. She refused his offer politely but firmly.

"Who are you?" he demanded. "And don't fob me off with that 'guardian angel' drivel."

"Then perchance I am your nemesis?"

"My nemesis?" He laughed shortly. "There isn't the woman born, m'dear, who can get the better of Hugh Montgomery."

"I did!" Briony smiled shyly up at him and Ravensworth's heart missed a beat. The sweetest, most adorable dimples had appeared on her kissable cheeks. "However," she continued, and gave him one of her clear-eyed gazes (the dimples, regrettably, instantly departed), "I don't wish you any harm. Indeed, I wish you well."

"Do you? Why?" he asked, truly interested.

"Why not?"

"You don't know me," he said simply, then added as an afterthought, "yet."

Briony missed the implication. "What an odd thing to say! As if wishing someone well depended on personal acquaintance. I wish the whole world well."

"Even rogues and murderers?" He was mocking her.

"Of course. I don't mean that I wish them to achieve their hearts' desire. That would be mere foolishness."

"Oh quite!"

"Now you are laughing at me."

"I wouldn't dare."

His eyes were warmly appreciative. Briony did not venture to let her gaze linger. She glanced at her bare toes and remembered her slippers. With a show of gallantry, he fetched them for her and slipped them on her feet. His hands were warm but she shivered. A burst of laughter sounded close at hand and introduced a sense of reality.

"Who are you? At least tell me your name."

Briony demurred. She had no wish to have her name become the butt of a roué's ribaldry. He opened the door to let her past. His smile was endearing.

"Then Lord Ravensworth's nemesis, be warned! I shall never permit you to get the better of me again."

He watched her retreating back until she disappeared through what he rightly supposed was the door to the servants' staircase. He allowed that his interest was piqued, but only slightly. She was an unusual wench, but what of it? His nemesis? The devil take her! She was only moderately pretty and he had no time for wenches who played hard to get. There were plenty more blossoms on the tree and none of them the least distinguishable from the others. He had only to stretch out his hand and take what he wanted. Still, he conceded reluctantly, it would be some time before he would forget that kiss.

Chapter 3

Lady Esther Grenfell was a handsome matron of eight and forty who in her youth had been accredited as one of the Great Beauties. She was, at the present moment, sitting up in bed placidly sipping her first cup of coffee of what gave every evidence of becoming an intolerable morning. Sir John, her lord and master, and a devoted husband, did not appear to be in an amiable temper. Like a caged tiger, he paced back and forth before her bed, casting the blackest looks in her direction.

"Esther," he said accusingly, "your daughter has gone too far. She is incorrigible! Have you no control whatsoever over her deportment? What she needs is a good horse whipping, and if she don't mend her ways from this day forward, that is exactly what she is going to get."

Lady Esther nibbled on a piece of dry toast. "My dear," she began in a soothing tone, "Harriet is merely young and inexperienced. I know that sometimes her behavior appears to be . . . outrageous, but she is a good girl at heart."

"*Appears* to be outrageous? Madam, it *is* outrageous." Sir John was not to be placated. "Do you understand, my dear wife," he went on severely, "that our youngest child is gaining the reputation of a flirt, a high flyer, a hot at hand, hoydenish out and outer?"

"You exaggerate, dear."

Sir John held up his index finger. "Item one—a broken engagement; item two—smoking a cigar, quite brazenly, in the gardens of Carlton House—of all places; item three—a disastrous curricle race to Twickenham in which she nearly broke her neck; and last but by no means least, item four—imbibing at Almack's—*Almack's* I say—and insulting Lady Jersey while she was in her cups."

"Do you tell me that Sally Jersey was foxed too?" Lady Esther smothered a giggle.

"Madam, you deliberately mistake my meaning. This is no time for levity. Your daughter's lack of conduct brings shame to our family name."

Lady Esther swung her shapely legs out over the bed and went to stand before the cheval mirror. "It's true," she agreed amicably. "Harriet's behavior is not all that one could wish."

"It isn't *anything* like what I would wish," went on Sir John in querulous accents. "She drags herself from one sorry scrape into another. Where did we go wrong? Of our other five children, not one has ever given us a moment's uneasiness."

"Yes, they certainly spoiled us with their easygoing, tractable dispositions."

"Why can't she be more like them?"

"Because, my dear," replied Lady Esther giving her husband an affectionate look, "as you know perfectly well, your youngest child takes after you."

"You are referring, I collect," he responded stiffly, "to what you are used to call my 'misspent youth'—the follies of a mere boy. But let me advise you, madam wife, that conduct which is tolerated in the male of the species is regarded as an abomination in the softer sex."

"Do you say so?" Lady Esther asked, raising one quizzical, elegant eyebrow. She put up her hand to push back a straying silver lock at his temple. "Why you hypocritical, aging reprobate, your sister Jane—yes, Briony's mother of impeccable propriety of *later* years—was not one whit better. It was the unsavory reputation of the scapegrace Grenfells which made my father hold out against our nuptials for so long. You never cared a fig for family name until you started your own nursery."

Sir John made as if to say something but Lady Esther went on in a rush.

"Oh, you reformed, I know it, if that was what you were about to say. And I have no doubt that Harriet shall reform too."

"And when are we to expect this auspicious occasion? Today? Tomorrow? Next year?"

"I expect that she will follow in her father's footsteps, dear. When the right man comes into Harriet's orbit, she will do everything necessary to win his regard."

Sir John appeared to be stymied until he remembered that he had one more card to play. "You do realize, Esther, that your daughter's subscription to Almack's has been canceled?"

"Well, what of it?"

"What of it? I cannot believe that you miss the significance of such an unprecedented action. She has been ostracized."

"Pooh!" Lady Esther slipped out of her nightdress and began to don a cotton chemise that was all but transparent. Sir John surveyed his wife's slim form with an appreciative eye.

She gave a dismissive wave of her hand. "These patronesses of Almack's have too high an opinion of their powers. We Grenfells are quite above their touch. I really don't care to spend my Wednesday evenings with such dull—but oh such pattern cards of propriety—ladies.

What hypocrites! It is common knowledge that Sally Jersey's own mother-in-law was Prinny's lightskirt not so long ago, yes, and would be so still if he were to give her the nod. And Sally thinks to set herself up as a pattern of morality for girls like Harriet?" Lady Esther's voice shook with indignation.

Sir John, very wisely, kept his counsel to himself. After a thoughtful pause, his wife continued in more moderate tones, "However, for Briony's sake, if for no other reason, Harriet must be made to see the error of her ways."

Lady Esther struggled into her blue gown of fine cambric and Sir John moved to do up the fastenings at the back. Blue had always been her color, he thought idly, as he watched her run a comb carelessly through her short, dark curls. Even now, after thirty years, he still wondered at his good fortune in having captured the Incomparable Lady Esther Woodward, the belle of her first and only Season before she had succumbed to his persistent attentions and accepted his suit. He rested his hands lightly on her shoulders and eyed her with mock suspicion.

"Madam wife, you know that I am putty in your hands. Tell me what you have in mind." She moved toward the adjoining dressing room, which they had, for convenience and privacy, turned into their own quiet place of retreat. Lady Esther plumped herself down on one comfortable armchair and indicated to her husband where he should sit. He retrieved a cigar from a box of inlaid ivory on a nearby table and lit it before joining her. "Well," he said at last, "I await your pleasure."

"John dear, our daughter Harriet is not our only problem. In her own way—a very different way, I grant you—your niece Briony is going to pose just as great a dilemma."

"Nonsense!" interposed Sir John emphatically. "Briony is a virtuous lady and everything she should be. She has a sweet disposition, is not frivolous, her word may be relied upon, and she isn't ever likely to embark on the sort of hair-raising larks which seem such a deuced attraction to our headstrong daughter."

"My dear, she is a Quaker."

"What has that to say to anything?"

"I'm not sure. But don't you find her somewhat . . . straitlaced?"

"How so?"

"Well, for example, the gowns which we ordered arrived this week, unexceptionable, very pretty, modest gowns for a young lady about to embark on her first Season. They suit her admirably. But do you know, I figured there was something not quite right about them when she began to wear them."

"And?"

"It took me some time to deduce that any gown which was cut lower than here"—Lady Esther indicated halfway down her bosom—"had been filled in with a scrap of lace."

"It simply shows that my niece has a proper degree of modesty in one of her tender years."

"My, you have changed," retorted Lady Esther. "But there is more. Briony is honest to the point of incivility. One daren't ask her opinion on any subject for she gives it—without considering the consequences."

"Now that is ridiculous. If you ask for her opinion, why shouldn't the gel give it to you without wrapping it up in clean linen? She sounds very straightforward to me!"

"Oh quite, but it isn't the way one goes about things in Polite Society. She has much to learn. Now this is where I believe that I have hit on the perfect solution." She smiled in obvious satisfaction.

"Which is?" he encouraged.

"I have asked our daughter if she will act as Briony's mentor and show her cousin how to go on in Society."

Sir John looked to have lost the use of his tongue. Finally he sputtered, "Have you lost the power of your wits, madam? Our daughter couldn't show a rag-mannered fishwife how to go on in Society. Briony don't need Harriet's advice."

"Don't be so obtuse, you silly blockhead." The words were harsh but her manner mild. "Harriet will show Briony by example. And she is hardly likely to set Briony a bad example, is she?"

"Esther, I hope you know what you are about. I have grave misgivings about this cork-brained scheme. It seems to me that you should have done it the other way round."

"But John, Harriet is too headstrong to take correction from such a proper girl as Briony."

"Precisely!"

"Do you have such a low opinion of your daughter, sir, that you condemn her out of hand?" There was an unfriendly sparkle in Lady Esther's eye.

"Of course not, my love," said Sir John in a mollifying tone. "No need to protect your cub from me. It's simply that I wish her to be more like her mother."

"But she is like *you*. How many times do I have to say it? And it is precisely because she is like you that I find her the most—oh—attractive and yes, adorable of all our children."

"Esther!"

"No, don't rebuke me, I am being honest, a virtue you have just confessed that you admire. Harriet may be a trifle unruly—well, perhaps that is an understatement—but she is such a high-spirited, vivacious girl. Those were the qualities that I so much admired in you when we first met.

Oh John, you were so . . . alive." She put a hand out impulsively to touch his arm. "I won't have her spirit broken."

"Nor shall it be, my love," he soothed, covering her delicate hand with his own strong one. After a moment, his grip tightened and he pulled her onto his lap. "And do you believe that this aging, reprehensible reprobate is less alive than formerly?"

"Only a trifle!" She gave him a saucy look.

"Then, madam wife, I shall correct *that* misapprehension on the instant." And he gathered his lady wife to him in a lingering embrace.

"Pay attention," said Miss Harriet Grenfell. Two pairs of eyes watched her every move intently.

"All must be done with the greatest finesse. Take the snuffbox with your right hand"—she produced a slim, oval container of beaten silver—"and pass it to your left, like so. Then rap the snuffbox with the index finger of your right hand." She rapped smartly on the lid of the box. "Now Vernon, watch carefully. This is the tricky part. Open the snuffbox with a flick of your left thumb." She opened it with a practiced movement. "The wrist must be relaxed. If you open the snuffbox too hastily, you may spill the contents of the box and become a laughingstock. Now offer the box to your nearest neighbors." She extended the open snuffbox. "Take some," she encouraged.

Briony looked into the box. "It looks like cinnamon. How am I to take it up?"

"Like this," replied her brother, proud of his superior knowledge. "Just a pinch between the thumb and forefinger." He looked for confirmation to Harriet, who nodded her approval. Briony followed his example. "I watched Lord Ravensworth take snuff at the ball," Vernon said by way of explanation. At the name, Briony's ears fairly pricked.

"No. Don't put it directly to your nose," Harriet admonished. "Rub it between your fingers first. Now sniff delicately with each nostril like this." Harriet demonstrated. Her audience obeyed.

"Quite pleasant," said Briony, and on the next breath gave a violent sneeze. She smiled sheepishly. "What did I do wrong?"

"You took too much." This was from Vernon, from his superior knowledge.

"I'll learn by practice," avowed Briony.

"Oh no you won't, sis. Snuff taking is a gentleman's pastime."

"How so?" She looked to Harriet for guidance. Harriet shrugged.

"One of these incomprehensible customs that prevail in Polite Society and which must be obeyed. Some ladies disregard the rules, but they are generally elderly duchesses and not bound by the edicts that apply to debs like us."

A clock on the mantlepiece of the marble Adam fireplace chimed the hour and alerted Vernon. "Drat! My tutor will be waiting and I can't delay. I'm having trouble with my Greek—the abominable Aeschylus, you know. If you will excuse me, ladies." He turned to leave the small yellow saloon, which was never used by any save the younger members of the household. At the door he turned back. "Briony, do you think you could spare me an hour or so this evening to reinforce what Mr. Keith takes such pains to teach me? You explain things so much better."

"I shall, if you feel it will do any good, but I collect that the language and I shall continue to suffer," Briony teased.

He ignored his sister's banter. "And cousin Harriet, may I ask you also to instruct me further in the fine art of snuff taking?"

"Certainly," replied his bemused cousin, still reeling from the discovery that the slip of a girl next to her was a scholar.

The door shut with a click and Briony returned to the subject at hand.

"Harriet, you made those movements so beautifully. Surely I am not mistaken in thinking that yours is a practiced hand?"

Harriet smiled conspiratorially. "I would never dream of doing it in public. It's just not done. But if I take snuff in private, who is to know? Who cares even? Sometimes I have seen a lady take snuff from a gentleman's wrist, but that is as far as she dare go. Try it." She placed a pinch of snuff on the back of her wrist and proffered it to Briony. Briony sniffed delicately. This time, there was no sneeze.

"The novice always take too much," Harriet continued. "The trick is to extract only the smallest pinch that you can manage. If one sneezes or grimaces when one inhales, the effect is ruined."

"May I try it?" Briony asked.

"By all means." Harriet passed the snuffbox to her cousin thinking that this mild-mannered girl had far more spunk than she had at first given her credit for.

Briony went through the movements several times until she had perfected them. "I like it, and I don't see any harm in it, do you?"

Harriet concurred. "None whatsoever."

"Then, cousin Harriet, in the privacy of the boudoir, perhaps we may partake of snuff together?"

"I should be delighted," returned an enthusiastic Harriet.

Briony proved to be an agreeable companion and Harriet was delighted with her newfound friend, for her cousin, although in no way forward in her own behavior, was not at all censorious of some of the more questionable practices that Harriet indulged in. If Harriet should partake, on the rare occasion, of a glass of wine, Briony declined without giving the least offense. Cards she refused to play on the grounds that she had no wish to deprive her friends and acquaintances of even a farthing, but when Harriet asked her to participate "just for fun," Briony consented. It soon became evident to the Broomhill household that as long as their young relative "could see no harm in it," she became as fun-loving as any other girl.

On the question of telling the truth, the whole truth, and nothing but the truth, however, Briony was immovable. In the confines of the Grenfell family, there was nothing objectionable in this trait, since Briony never ventured her views on any subject uninvited. Only those who truly desired a disinterested opinion ever requested Briony to express her sentiments. Few did.

In Society, however, such candor could only be regarded as an unmitigated impertinence, and Harriet, in her role as mentor, used all the charm at her command on more than one occasion to extricate Briony from an awkward situation.

Lady Grenfell kept a watchful eye on her two young charges and observed with pleasure their growing intimacy. She was gratified to see that under her daughter's tutelage, Briony's solemn manner had become much more relaxed. Nor did she fail to note that association with Briony was having a beneficial effect on the more wayward Harriet. She felt justifiably proud that in the space of only a few weeks her "cork-brained" scheme was beginning to bear fruit. And since, in her father's eyes, Harriet had "at last" begun to comport herself in the style of a true lady, he waived his objection to her use of the curricle in which she had almost broken her neck.

Chapter 4

The Marquess of Ravensworth had his rooms on the second floor of Albany House on Piccadilly in Mayfair. Two gentlemen in restrained but elegant costume of black coats and yellow pantaloons were lounging in his study in two comfortable though old-fashioned armchairs on either side of a blazing fire. Each was drawing deeply on his Havana cigar. After a few minutes of companionable silence, the dark-haired gentleman uncoiled his long, muscular torso from the depths of his chair and moved to open the window.

"Bit foggy," he mumbled by way of explanation.

"Quite so," absently observed his fair-haired companion. Ravensworth returned to his place. It was Viscount Avery who took up their conversation where he had left off.

"It's not as though I wished to break her spirit, but surely a future husband has some voice in the conduct of his betrothed? I merely wished to curb Harriet's wilder excesses."

"Oh, I'm in complete agreement," concurred Ravensworth. "For a delicately nurtured female, Harriet Grenfell's conduct leaves much to be desired." The Marquess drew steadily on his cigar. "In a female of a different class," he continued pensively, "such behavior need not damn her; one might even find it taking in a provocative sort of way. But in a wife, it would be inexcusable. How did you persuade her to break the engagement?"

I didn't," the Viscount responded morosely. "It was her own idea. I simply told her that she would have to choose between Originality and me. She chose the former."

"You surely don't regret it?" asked Ravensworth, surprised to hear a note of disappointment in Avery's voice.

"Well, of course I do! D'you think I want to shackle myself to any of these spiritless misses whom my mama keeps throwing at my head? Marriage is a life-long sentence, my friend."

"But a gentleman, if he finds his wife not to his taste, can always acquire other interests," Ravensworth emphasized.

"No, no," said Avery with an apologetic shrug. "The thing is, I've completely lost interest in every other woman, even the beauties. So you can see what a devil of a coil I am in."

"My God!" exclaimed Ravensworth. "This is serious! I had no idea, dear boy, that you were completely *bouleversé.*"

"Oh completely," responded Avery with a halfhearted attempt to shake off his despondent humor.

A lackey entered and quite unnecessarily banked up the fire with a shuttleful of coal. When he had withdrawn, Ravensworth continued.

"But this puts a different complexion on the problem. You did not tell me that you love the lady."

Avery shrugged. "What of it? Harriet won't make the least push to conform to my wishes and I have no intentions of giving in."

"Marry her, then, and *make* her conform to your wishes!"

"Are you mad, Ravensworth?" Avery demanded incredulously.

"No, my friend," said Ravensworth in a superior tone. "Merely using the gray matter between my ears. Think for a moment! Why is Harriet Grenfell's behavior so outlandish? Why doesn't she conform to Society's standards?"

"It's inbred. Her father, I hear, was exactly the same."

"You're getting closer. It is because Miss Harriet Grenfell is adept at managing her two doting, indulgent parents. But when Harriet marries, whose authority does she come under then?"

"Her husband's, of course."

"And if *you* were that husband?"

"Ravensworth, what are you getting at?" A hint of impatience edged Avery's voice.

"Only this. A husband, if he has the will, has it in his power to manage his wife. He can threaten her with all sorts of dire consequences—deprive her of her dress allowance, her liberty even. You can send Harriet to oblivion, if you wish, to one of your northern estates, if she don't conform."

"Harriet wouldn't like it."

"Of course she wouldn't like it, you blockhead. That is the whole point of the exercise. A woman is just like a filly. She must be broken to the bridle, not given her head."

Ravensworth's words revolved slowly in Lord Avery's mind. "Is that how you plan to manage your wife when you get shackled?" he asked doubtfully.

"Indubitably! If I have the misfortune to marry a wench who thwarts me. But that day is far off."

"What? Haven't you encountered anyone at all who has taken your fancy?"

"A score or more but no one who has tempted me to

offer more than my illustrious—bed." Ravensworth's smile verged on the self-congratulatory.

Avery laughed wryly. "One of these days, Ravensworth, you are going to meet your nemesis, and I hope that I am there to see it."

Ravensworth's shapely hand, about to bring the stub of his cigar to his lips, abruptly arrested itself in midair.

"What did you say?" He appeared to be startled.

Avery repeated his observation.

His lordship slowly exhaled a ring of smoke which trailed a lazy path to the high-coved ceiling. He watched it for a moment or two before replying.

I think I have met her." His voice was expressionless.

"Have you indeed?" Avery's eyes were alight with interest. "And?"

"Nothing! Just a slip of a girl whom I met at the Grenfells' ball. At least, not at the ball, but in the library."

"What were you doing in the library?"

"I was with Adèle."

"That explains it. Go on!"

"Mm?" Avery's words had broken into what appeared to be a pleasant reverie. "She told me that my kiss made her tingle."

"You must be funning! You kissed another woman when you were with Adèle?"

"Of course not! She got rid of Adèle."

"What? Is she a brazen hussy, then?"

"Rather ingenuous, I thought."

"Who is she?" demanded Avery.

I thought you might know of her. Have the Grenfells engaged a new governess or a companion of late?"

"Not to my knowledge. Wait! Harriet has a cousin staying with her. A Quaker girl from Philadelphia in Shropshire."

"Never heard of it." After a moment's reflection Ravensworth asked, "What's a Quaker?"

Avery considered. "Damned if I know. From what Harriet said, I collect they are dreadfully virtuous."

"Mmm . . . pity!"

"Why? Are you interested?"

"Only mildly! Is she the proverbial poor relation?"

"I can't say. Probably. But her background is impeccable. Would you care for a peek at her family tree? I can arrange it if you wish." Avery's face was wreathed in smiles.

Ravensworth was rattled. "No need. *I'm* not thinking of getting married."

"No? Then better forget her."

Ravensworth cocked a sardonic eyebrow and Avery chortled.

"I mean it, Ravensworth," he warned. "This girl is not one that will accept a slip on the shoulder. Don't even think of it. I told you, she is virtuous."

"You forget, she let me kiss her. Besides, virtue won't give her all that I can offer."

"She don't want anything you have to offer if it comes without the blessing of Mother Church."

"Avery, you are an incurable romantic," said Ravensworth in a deprecating tone.

"And you are a fool as well as a cynic," retorted the Viscount.

Ravensworth was silent. At length he muttered, "We'll see." Lord Avery said nothing.

After a moment, Ravensworth negligently flicked the ash from his cigar into the stand by his elbow. He leaned his head against the back of his chair and regarded the fog in his study with a frown of distaste. "The atmosphere in here is intolerable. Why don't we get a breath of fresh air?" He stubbed out the cigar and stood up with resolution.

"Where to?" asked Avery, collecting his overcoat from his lordship's valet, Denby. "Hyde Park?"

"No," mused Ravensworth, rearranging his impeccable neckcloth. "Farther afield. How would you like to tool my team around Richmond? I have some friends there I haven't seen in an age."

Lord Avery grinned broadly. "I'm game. Are your friends related to the Richmond Grenfells by any chance?"

Ravensworth clapped him on the shoulder. "One and the same, dear boy, one and the same."

Richmond Park, that vast tract of land which Charles I had set aside as a Royal Chase, was within a few minutes' drive of Broomhill House. It was not to be expected that any member of the beau monde would be encountered so early in the day, for Richmond was a full seven miles from London and only the most enthusiastic town whips and riders ventured so far afield and, in general, not before late of the afternoon.

Briony and Harriet did not precisely have the park to themselves, for the residents of Richmond and neighboring Twickenham were not slow to avail themselves of so attractive a wilderness, but in an area of over two thousand acres, riders and equipages were few and far between.

After a protracted drive in Harriet's curricle, with each girl taking her turn at the ribbons under the watchful eye of the mounted groom, they came to a halt beside a stand of poplars, and Harriet instructed Evans to put Duster through his paces for a good half hour. The groom obeyed with alacrity, leaving the two girls in the stationary curricle enjoying the sight of a herd of timid deer in the near distance.

"Do you mind if I smoke?"

Briony was not sure that she had heard aright. "I beg your pardon?"

Harriet repeated the question.

"Well, I don't see any harm in it," Briony replied cautiously.

"Good," said Harriet, withdrawing a slim cheroot from the depths of her reticule. "I don't indulge in the house because Papa disapproves. But on occasion, I enjoy the luxury. Would you care to join me?"

Briony demurred but watched with keen interest as her friend rubbed the cheroot between her mittened fingers and put it to her ear. The sound seemed to satisfy her, for in the next instant she had lit it and was inhaling deeply. Briony watched the cloud of smoke issuing from her cousin's mouth as she exhaled.

"Blowing a cloud!" said Briony knowingly.

Harriet laughed. "You know the gentleman's cant, I see. Vernon, I suppose?"

Briony nodded.

A curricle approached and Harriet and Briony watched its progress with mild interest. Briony observed the occupants idly—two young gentlemen of quality, she noted, one as dark as the other was fair. As the curricle slowed and drew to a halt, her eyes focused on the dark-haired stranger. He seemed vaguely familiar.

A many-caped driving coat was slung negligently over his broad shoulders, and as she watched, he discarded his hat and gauntlets and ran a careless hand through black curly hair. His face was tanned deeply by the sun and his lips, which began to smile in greeting, softened what might otherwise have been a forbidding countenance.

Briony was not vain but at that moment she knew that in her modest but spanking, up-to-the-mark green velvet pelisse and matching bonnet trimmed with ribbons she had never looked prettier, and she was glad.

"It's Avery," wailed Harriet, referring to the fair-haired gentleman. "Here, take this!" The next instant, Briony found the smoking cheroot thrust into her hand. She held it gingerly between thumb and forefinger.

Lord Ravensworth called out, "Miss Grenfell, how do you do? I take it Sir John has forgiven your last disastrous drive? How do you manage to twist him round your thumb?" He glanced at Lord Avery and grinned.

Briony recognized the voice and felt her heart beat just a little faster. She watched as Ravensworth tooled the curricle closer, his eyes quite openly appraising her person. Briony was a modest girl but she was not a prude. Since she was an innocent, blushes very rarely stained her cheeks. Nor did she feel compelled to drop her gaze when a gentleman stared boldly at her. Her lack of experience with gentlemen of a predatory nature ensured that Briony's manners were natural and lacking in affectation. She was conscious of Ravensworth's regard and gave him back look for look.

"May I introduce . . ." began a flustered Harriet.

"My nemesis," interrupted Ravensworth, suddenly recognizing Briony's clear-eyed, unabashed, steady gaze. "I would recognize those eyes anywhere."

"My cousin, Miss Briony Langland," finished Harriet. "Are you acquainted?"

"We have not been formally introduced. Ravensworth, at your service, ma'am. And this is my friend, Lord Avery."

Briony gave a civil nod in their direction. Ravensworth, remembering the night of their first encounter and her confession that his kiss had set her to tingling, smiled a slow smile. It was wasted on Briony. She was acutely conscious of only one thing—the cheroot which was burning steadily between her fingers. Her hand gave an involuntary twitch.

"Blowing a cloud, Miss Langland?" Ravensworth inquired on a note of censure. "D'you know what you're doing with that thing? Have a care, or you'll set yourself on fire."

The note in Lord Avery's voice was nothing less than churlish. "I presume that Miss Grenfell has been instructing you in all the accomplishments of a lady of quality?"

Briony observed the mounting color in her cousin's cheeks and a sense of injury on Harriet's behalf rose in her breast. How dare these gentlemen condemn in Harriet what they condoned in practice? There was no harm in it; no need for guilt or shame, she reasoned.

"Would you care to join me?" she asked politely, remembering what she supposed was the correct etiquette for smoking.

"Thank you, no," responded Ravensworth with exaggerated civility, "but don't let us interrupt a pleasure which you obviously enjoy."

Briony felt compelled to continue. She pursed her rosy lips and with the elegant motion of the wrist which she had observed in Harriet, brought the cheroot to her mouth. She inhaled and exhaled almost on the same breath. Smoking, she discovered, was not to her taste, but she was not about to give her opinion unless invited. She tried again.

"Well done, Miss Langland," said Ravensworth blandly.

"At least for a first try. Now that you have proved how audacious you are, why don't you get rid of that ridiculous thing?"

The remark goaded Briony into further indiscretion.

She tried again. Unfortunately, she made an error in judgment and inhaled too deeply. She gave a little cough, and then another. Once started she could not stop. She sputtered and gasped for air until the tears ran down her cheeks. How Ravensworth happened to be in the curricle with her and Harriet on the grass verge she could not tell. But she gratefully submitted to his ministrations.

"Th—thank you," she croaked hoarsely, still wracked by the occasional cough.

"Don't mention it," he replied, all politeness, drying her wet cheeks with his large, linen handkerchief. "Harriet, be a good girl and ride with Avery," he instructed. "Someone has to be responsible for you girls. Avery!" he addressed his friend. "Let's get these damsels home."

Briony retained Ravensworth's mangled handkerchief and held it firmly to her watery nose. By the time she had fully recovered her breath, she was conscious that Avery's curricle with Harriet in it had disappeared. The foul-tasting cigar was still clutched tightly to her bosom. She stole a glance at Ravensworth and was relieved to see that he was smiling.

"Now, Miss Langland, oblige me, if you please, and rid yourself of that odious object."

Briony smiled shyly up at him and wondered at the stricken look which suddenly came over his lordship's face. She hastened to obey, and carelessly flicked the offending object out of the curricle. The cheroot made an arc high in the air and Briony watched in horrified fascination as it came to rest on the rump of one of the impatient, fretting horses harnessed to the curricle.

For a moment, nothing happened. Then all was pandemonium. The startled horse reared in its traces and set the other one off. With a terrified bray they bolted, dragging the rocking curricle furiously in their wake. Ravensworth hung desperately to the reins with one hand and with the other grabbed wildly for Briony to prevent her from falling out.

The carriage swayed dangerously from side to side as it bumped over every rock, rut, and pothole, and looked to Briony as if it were on the verge of breaking up. She clung blindly to Ravensworth's protective arm and closed her eyes in terror. Briony prepared to meet her Maker.

Many miles later, when she felt the violent motion of the curricle slacken, she slowly opened her eyes. The horses were running themselves to a standstill, and Ravensworth, grimfaced and stern, finally reined in. She waited, white-faced, for his fury to descend upon her. With trembling fingers, she adjusted her bonnet and straightened her pelisse. She clasped her hands together to still their involuntary shaking.

When he spoke, his voice was gentle. "Are you all right, Miss Langland?"

"A bit shaken, nothing more, thank you," she replied breathlessly, willing her breathing to a more regular pace.

He removed his cape and flung it over her shoulders. "Here, this will keep you warm. You've had a shocking experience. You're a brave little thing."

Briony spoke through chattering teeth. "It's not the first time I've been in a runaway carriage. Please, see to the horses first. I feel responsible, and would not want them to suffer further on my account."

Ravensworth disregarded her request and extracted a small flask from the inner pocket of his coat. He removed the cap and put the flask to her lips. "Drink it," he ordered. Briony hesitated. "Drink it," he said in a tone that brooked no refusal. Briony obeyed. She felt a searing heat in her throat and sputtered. In a moment her teeth stopped chattering.

When Ravensworth saw that she was quite recovered, he gave the reins into her hands and, jumping lightly from the curricle, went to examine the steaming animals. He was back in a moment. "Not a scratch on 'em. We've had a fortunate escape. Better let them rest for a while."

Briony began, with some dignity, to offer him her apologies and thanks but he cut her off abruptly and she fell silent.

"Do I understand, Miss Langland, that you are a Quaker?"

"My mother was a Quaker," corrected Briony, "and I try to follow Mama's . . . principles."

"I wonder at your smoking. Do Quaker ladies smoke?"

"Oh there are no rules and regulations. We each must follow our own conscience in matters of conduct," she explained seriously.

"How very convenient!"

She smiled shyly at the jibe. "No, not for Quakers. Oh, for those who have not taken the trouble to develop a conscience, perhaps it is convenient. But not for me."

"I see. Are you implying that I have no conscience?" he asked quizzically.

"Have you?" she returned boldy, remembering the scene of seduction in the library.

"Not much! Does that trouble you?"

There was a pause. "Yes, it troubles me," said Briony gravely.

"Oh? Why?" He saw her doubtful look and he chuckled. "Don't wrap it up in clean linen for my benefit. I know you to be a lady who is frank to a fault."

Briony was goaded into a reply. "If what you say is true, and I can scarcely believe it, you would be a scoundrel. Are you a scoundrel, Lord Ravensworth?"

He laughed. "What do you think?"

"I?" said Briony, surprised at his question. "I do not know you. How can I say?"

"Miss Langland," began Ravensworth more seriously, "I beg you will not form a hasty opinion of my character from our first, unfortunate meeting." He coughed to cover his embarrassment. The young lady beside him, he noted dourly, gave no indication of being in the least embarrassed by a subject which all gently nurtured females ought to find highly indelicate.

"Yes, go on," she said encouragingly.

"It was not as you think. The lady knows me for what I am and she was not unwilling."

Briony was silent, and Ravensworth began again.

"I may not have much of a conscience, Miss Langland, but I am not a scoundrel! I am a man of honor."

"I see," said the lady noncommittally.

"Will you accept me as such?"

"A man of honor? I will if it satisfies you."

"It does not satisfy you?"

"Since you ask, no!"

"Why not?"

She shrugged dismissively. "Honor! What is this code of honor you gentlemen live by, my lord? Whom does it serve? Who devises the rules? How can honor be satisfied by duels and vendettas and so on? Yet that is what you gentlemen believe. No, I do not think a man of honor is to be compared to a man of conscience.

Ravensworth was taken aback at the scorn in Briony's voice. "What it means, madam," he said curtly, "is that if I give you my word, you may rely upon it."

Briony began to fuss with her gloves and Ravensworth perceived that the lady had no wish to pursue the conversation further, but some devil in him goaded him on. He could not let it rest.

"Do you believe in fate, Miss Langland?"

"Why do you ask?" she inquired curiously.

"Because I am beginning to believe that you *are* my nemesis. Did the gods send you?"

Briony chuckled. "Why should the gods send retribution on you?"

"For my misdeeds!"

"Are you the only person to regret misdeeds?"

"Did I say I regretted them?"

Briony looked frankly into his eyes as if to read his mind. Blue, honest eyes, she noted, fringed by long, thick, curling lashes; expressive eyes, with warmth, amusement, and something else concealed in their depths.

"Come now, Miss Langland, a man with no conscience cannot be expected to regret his misdeeds."

"And a man of honor?" she asked quietly.

"A man of honor doesn't have any."

Her gray eyes never wavered in their close scrutiny of his expression. He watched her brow wrinkle in puzzlement.

"Well," he finally demanded, "have you nothing to say in reply?"

Briony's tone was reserved. "I don't understand."

"In plain terms, Miss Langland," said Ravensworth, impulsively taking her hands into his, "I wish you to know that although I may not be as . . . virtuous as some gentlemen, I am not unscrupulous. You may depend on my word as a man of honor."

Briony was deeply troubled but she managed a polite, "Thank you," before lapsing into another of her reflective silences.

Ravensworth retrieved the reins from her hands. "I think the horses are recovered enough. Shall we find the others?" He spoke in a conversational tone.

On the drive back, not another word was said about Conscience or Honor, but Briony meditated on his words. Logic told her that Lord Ravensworth was dangerous, but her instincts gave her an entirely different message. She decided that there could be no harm in allowing him to pursue the acquaintance, if he wished it, for whatever might be the state of his lordship's Conscience, hers was as lively and as sensitive as it had ever been.

Chapter 5

The freezing temperatures of a bitingly cold spring did little to dampen the high good humor of Sir John and Lady Esther in the year of our Lord 1814. With the little Corsican, Napoleon Bonaparte, safely confined on Elba, England was enjoying a period of unalloyed peace with Europe for the first time in over twenty years. Public confidence had reached such heights that many of Wellington's units had been disbanded and others had crossed the Atlantic to join forces with loyalists in Canada against the United States of America.

Although news from the colonies was far from reassuring, the Grenfells had a particular reason for their mood of self-congratulation. They were celebrating the birth of their latest grandchild to their eldest daughter and her husband, who lived a mere two days' journey away in the Georgian city of Bath, and Sir John and Lady Grenfell proposed to spend an indeterminate number of weeks in the tranquil company of one of their offspring whom they averred had never given them a moment's unease.

In the normal course of events, nothing on earth would have persuaded such dutiful parents to desert their troublesome, scapegrace daughter but there had been what Lady Esther was pleased to call "A Transformation" in her youngest child. Miss Harriet Grenfell had changed. No one would deny it. Whether this conversion had come about because of the influence of Lord Avery, whose suit looked to be prospering, or whether her Quaker cousin had exercised a beneficial effect on Harriet's character, Lady Esther could not say. Nor did she care. It was enough that Harriet's manners, whether in public or in private, were conformed to the highest standards of a genteel lady of quality. Lady Jersey, that lioness of Almack's, had even hinted that one of the coveted vouchers to the assemblies might be forthcoming. Harriet's parents, not unnaturally, were quite overwhelmed.

Such was their conviction in Harriet's metamorphosis that they saw no reason, when they removed to Bath, why Harriet and Briony should delay their enjoyment of their London Season when people were beginning to trickle back to town. It had been their intention from the first to take up Great Aunt Sophy's generous offer to accommodate the Grenfell family in her commodious townhouse in Half Moon Street for those few months when the Season was at its height. In the circumstances, Aunt Sophy allowed herself to be more than willing to act as chaperone to the girls. Broomhill House could not be faulted in proportions and situation for a year-round family residence but it was conceded that Richmond was a tad out of the way for two young debutantes who would wish to be in the center of the social whirl.

Perforce, it was with an easy conscience that the assembled members of the household said their farewells to Briony and Harriet as the girls set off in the family coach on the short drive to town. Since there was little to occupy one of Nanny's particular abilities in a childless household, she had consented to accompany the Grenfells as nurse to the new babe. But she made it perfectly clear that this was to be a temporary arrangement since her loyalties lay with the Langland branch of the family and, although it remained unspoken, it was Nanny's fondest hope that her ample arms would be nursing the first child of her "wee lamb" in the not too distant future.

Vernon was to remain in Broomhill House temporarily. The Oxford Entrance would be upon him all too soon, and he desperately needed the time to perfect the intricacies of Greek grammar and syntax. It was with a wistful smile that he said his adieus to his sister and his cousin, promising that as soon as he was over "this infernal hurdle," he would be punctilious in presenting himself at Half Moon Street. Briony was uneasy in her mind about leaving her younger brother for it seemed to her that in the months since they had taken up residence in Richmond, Vernon had thrown off the moderating influence of his temperate parents and gave every evidence of becoming as dandified and as indolent a gentleman as any of the young bucks of his new circle of friends. She was sadly aware that there was little to restrain the natural impulses of a callow youth inclined to levity, for a sister's influence was all but negligible.

On one person, however, Briony's proximity was having a profound effect. Harriet, in the months since Briony's near disastrous accident in the curricle, had been suffering from the worst pangs of guilt that she had ever experienced in her life. That Briony had never so much as intimated the least displeasure in having the fatal cheroot thrust upon her simply to save Harriet's face swelled that young lady's sense of remorse immeasurably. She felt that her conduct had been worse than reprehensible, but when she had tried to make her heartfelt apologies, they had been brushed aside as being quite unnecessary. To be forgiven so freely and easily made Harriet's iniquity weigh even more heavily upon her. Lord Ravensworth and Avery had wasted no scruples in calling her to account for her irresponsible conduct, but from Briony there had been not even a mild rebuke. Harriet's conscience smote her heavily.

She soon came to perceive that cousin Briony, in her own way, was as much an original and as unconventional as Harriet had ever aspired to be, but she took no pleasure in that knowledge. On the contrary, it worried her to death. That her own outrageous behavior had on many occasions scandalized the more august members of the ton had never troubled Harriet overmuch in the past. But she would tolerate no disparagement, no ridicule, no ostracism of the gentle cousin whom she had come so much to admire. Her mind was resolute. No outré act of hers should ever again lure Briony into committing a social solecism. Harriet resigned herself to becoming a Model Girl.

Harriet's pride, however, was deeply wounded. Lord Avery she had jilted in a fit of pique when he had had the effrontery to issue an ultimatum. He had summarily ordered her to mend her ways or to cry off from their betrothal. Well, she had sent him to the roustabouts with a flea in his ear, even although her heart had been breaking. Harriet had her pride. Since then, Avery had been, with his friend Ravensworth, intermittently in her company for the last number of months. Her feminine intuition told her that her erstwhile fiancé was not immune to her charms. Moreover, her present deportment was everything he had said he wished it to be, but there had been no renewal of those offers which she had in her fury spurned. Harriet was troubled.

Briony was no less troubled by the attentions of Avery's friend. As her acquaintanceship with Ravensworth progressed, it had occurred to her, on occasion, that his lordship was cherishing a tendre for her. That notion she had soon put out of her head when he had explained with a confiding air that the heir to His Grace, the Duke of Dalbreck, might not marry where his fancy lay but that he was expected to make a match of the first consequence. Briony heard these words with a ripple of regret for she found the Marquess the most attractive man of her acquaintance even though she freely admitted that he was not a suitable mate for a respectable Quaker girl. When, therefore, she began to suspect that she was becoming enamored of a man with whom she had little in common, a man who, moreover, was an openly confessed libertine and against whom every feeling of delicacy recoiled, she ruthlessly suppressed these tender emotions and directed her wayward thoughts in a direction more fitting for one of her gentle upbringing.

It was impossible to avoid his company altogether, however, for he and Avery seemed to have many acquaintances in Richmond and Twickenham and he was frequently in attendance at the small house parties which were assembled to pass the tedium of the long winter months. Briony was quick to perceive that even a man of Ravensworth's unsavory reputation was courted by eager hostesses, and when she queried Harriet, she was informed that whatever the state of his lordship's morals, his manners were impeccable and any hostess who had enticed him to her board could be considered to have a feather in her cap and something to crow about.

Briony could not fathom why Ravensworth sought out her company when he had frequently indicated that his autocratic father intended him for another, but she put it down to the incomprehensible ways of the ton in which she was a novice. She looked forward to the prospective sojourn in town, where she hoped that she might be so much in company that it would be less obvious that she was trying to avoid the man whom she found so unsettling to her usual tranquility.

The Marquess of Ravensworth smiled devilishly at his darkly handsome reflection in the cheval mirror in his dressing room in Albany House, and his lordship's valet, Denby, waiting patiently in the background to ease his master's broad back into a snug-fitting coat, noted the fleeting look and speculated on what devilment his master was contemplating.

With a delicate hand, the Marquess adjusted his fine lawn neckcloth which was intricately folded in a style commonly known as "à la Ravensworth" and he surveyed the result with a critical eye. His hair, which he wore rather long and disheveled, was in the "Titus" mode. Ravensworth's locks, however, owed nothing to art. His closely curled hair was honestly come by, for it was a distinguishing feature of all the Montgomerys.

He allowed a solicitous Denby to smooth his coat of blue superfine over his broad, muscular shoulders and he pulled the front open a trifle to reveal a white satin waistcoat heavily embroidered with silver thread.

"What do you think?" asked Ravensworth. "The diamond or the sapphire?" Denby considered. He appraised his master's figure from the top of his curled locks to the tips of his black kid pumps fastened with ribbons. He noted with approval the exquisitely tailored fit of the Weston coat, and the white satin breeches with matching waistcoat and silk stockings.

"The sapphire would be more noticeable, my lord." Ravensworth's hand reached out to retrieve a sapphire pin from a box which his valet had extended. "But so predictable! May I suggest the diamond?"

Ravensworth smiled in approval of his valet's sagacity

and adroitly positioned a large, square diamond to the folds of his immaculate neckcloth. Denby was highly gratified that his lordship, in matters of taste, invariably deferred to his superior knowledge. The Marquess moved to his dresser and from a flask poured some cologne, which he dashed generously on his tanned visage.

"Is this a special occasion, my lord?" asked the valet politely, wondering at his master's unwonted preoccupation with his looks.

Ravensworth smiled one of his endearing, slow smiles. "You could say that, Denby. Yes, I think that this may prove to be an *exceptional* evening." It was only later that Ravensworth remembered these heedless words and the irony of them was not lost on him.

Harriet Grenfell was playing lady's maid to her cousin Briony as she helped her dress for a small party which was to be their first dress-up engagement of the Season. She stood irresolutely with thick ropes of Briony's hair entwined in her fingers and tried unsuccessfully to pin them to the crown of Briony's head. The coils slipped out of her hands and cascaded over Briony's shoulders and back.

"Botheration," exclaimed Harriet in exasperation. "Briony, this will never do! Why don't we ask Aunt Sophy's abigail to shear this . . . stuff from your head. It's so unfashionable, dear. Now wouldn't you prefer to have short curls like mine?" Harriet put one hand up to pat her coiffured hair shaped closely to her head.

"Let me," said Briony, taking the offending strands into her own capable hands, and without as much as glancing into the mirror, she twisted them into a smooth chignon to lie neatly on the nape of her swan-like neck. Briony moved to a chest of drawers and retrieved a tucker of white Brussels lace, which she quickly fastened around her shoulders to cover the bare expanse of bosom which was revealed by the low neckline of her gown. Harriet groaned.

"Briony, my love, you cannot be seriously intending to grace an evemng party where there is like to be dancing *dressed like that?*"

"What is wrong with my gown?" Briony asked in consternation, examining the white slip of muslin closely.

"Nothing is wrong with your *gown,*" replied Harriet with some passion. "It is all the little extras which are ruining what might otherwise be a charming effect. Look at me. Do you find fault with my ensemble?" she entreated. "Do you think that I am dressed like a wanton?"

Briony appraised Harriet's gown, which was remarkably similar to her own except for the color. It was of pale blue muslin and suited Harriet's cornflower blue eyes and burnished gold curls to perfection. "Of course not," she answered. "You are everything you should be."

"Then why do you insist on making a dowd of yourself?" wailed Harriet. "Why don't you dress like me?"

"Because," replied Briony in patient accents, "I must be true to myself." Her cheeks dimpled as she smiled at Harriet, but that young lady was not to be so easily won over. She tried again.

"Briony dear, I am thinking only of your happiness." She hesitated to go on but anxiety on her friend's behalf compelled her. "I don't wish to see you mope. Please believe me! You will never find partners dressed in that fashion. I know what I am speaking of. Young gentlemen are . . . repelled by ladies who appear to be prudes."

Briony was amused. "Do you take me for a prude, Harriet?"

"Of course not! Who better than I should know that

you are no such thing? But it is the message that your whole demeanor tells."

"But when they come to know me better—"

"They will never come to know you at all," Harriet interrupted on a rising note. "Please forgive me for saying so," she went on bluntly, "but your appearance is positively eccentric. It is worse than eccentric; you look to be the veriest blue-stocking. No young gentleman would wish to solicit your acquaintance."

Briony was nonplussed. "But Harriet, this is the style I have customarily adopted, and the young gentlemen did not shun my company in Richmond."

"I daresay they didn't," responded Harriet. "But in Richmond—what did we attend? Nothing but family parties in neighbors' homes, or drives in the park—small fry. This evening is to be an assembly of the first stare—not so grand as a ball, I grant you, but grand enough for all that. Please, Briony," Harriet begged her cousin earnestly, "let yourself be guided by me in this."

No persuasion of Harriet's, however, could budge Briony once she had made up her mind. Nor would she believe that all the gentlemen were of such a frivolous disposition. It was with a heavy heart that Harriet accompanied Briony and Great Aunt Sophy to the Countess of Blaine's party at her house in Cavendish Square. It looked to be, thought Harriet, an evening of unmitigated disaster.

Chapter 6

Briony wanted only one thing—a dark, cavernous hole to creep into where she could be alone and cry out her misery in peace. At first, the evening gave every indication of being one that she should enjoy. That was until the dancing commenced in the adjacent apartment. One minute she was in the center of a group of bright, chattering girls, and the next moment they had deserted her, each of them captured by some graceful swain and carried off to the dance. Only Harriet stuck grimly to Briony like a limpet as if she feared to let her out of her sight. To ruin Harriet's enjoyment in the evening was the crowning mortification. But nothing that Briony said could persuade her cousin to accept one of the beaux who solicited her hand, not even Avery.

And so they had sat among the dowagers, or promenaded with Avery and appeared to be engrossed in their interesting conversations, but Briony was acutely conscious of the pity she saw in the eyes of more than one dowager glancing in her direction and her courage failed. She had never had any expectation that she would be really popular. All that she had hoped for was a small circle of congenial friends. But even that small wish was to be denied. Life in Society, Briony discovered, could be cruel.

It was well on in the evening when Ravensworth put in

an appearance and Briony, when she saw him, felt her spirits sink even lower. In her eyes, he was quite the most handsome and elegantly attired gentleman in the room, but she was by this time so convinced of the truth of Harriet's statement that she was a dowd and repellant to gentlemen that she shrank from seeing the pity which she was sure would be reflected in his eyes also.

She observed the confident ease with which he moved from group to group, but when he flashed her a roguish grin from across the room, she remembered Aunt Esther's admonition that it was rude to stare and she averted her gaze. She knew instinctively that he would seek her out. Nevertheless, when he appeared suddenly at her elbow and solicited her hand for the waltz, she was so taken by surprise that she gave it to him before she remembered her intention never to dance anything so vulgar.

The Marquess had been covertly observing Briony since he had first caught sight of her. He was, to say the least of it, taken aback by her prudish costume. For a full minute he had been angry that she should be so lacking in perception as to make herself a dowd. But after a moment's reflection his anger had abated. He could see that her society was shunned by all the young bucks but he did not pity Briony. It was, after all, her own doing. *No*, his lordship was reflecting on how such a circumstance could be turned to his advantage. It would make her, he mused, more receptive to what he was about to propose for her future. Once she was under his protection, he had every intention of choosing her clothes and jewelry and uncovering the loveliness she took such pains to hide. He saw her gazing at him and he flashed her one of his winsome smiles.

For the blades who ignored Briony's society, Ravensworth felt only amused contempt. While they pursued what they considered to be the diamonds of the first water, those beauties with unexceptionable morals and manners but little else to recommend them, he, Hugh Montgomery, was about to snatch the prize of victory from under their noses. He chuckled involuntarily to think of it. But it sobered him to remember that it was only an accident of fate that had thrown her in his path. In normal circumstances, he would never have given her a second glance, his Briony. He repeated the name under his breath. Even her name had the power to bewitch him.

He was sure that he had prepared her for what he had in mind. His conscience pricked him slightly when he thought of the half truth he had told her. It was true that his father would *like* him to marry a girl of his own station but he certainly did not *expect* it. Hugh Montgomery never allowed the wishes of others to influence him. He always followed his own inclinations, and his father, the Duke, knew it. In some perverse way, His Grace even approved of this wayward trait in his only son.

One day, Ravensworth conceded, he would probably marry and secure the succession. His wife would be, by birth and breeding, everything that was required to fill her exalted role as his consort. But he never expected to love such woman. That would be vulgar and quite unnecessary. His pleasures he would take elsewhere.

His liaison with Briony he intended to be a life-long commitment. She was, after all, no lightskirt, but a gently bred female and deserving of the highest consideration. Such an arrangement was not unusual for men of his rank. He would try to be faithful, but should he fail, there would be no question of discarding Briony. That would be a dastardly act and quite beneath the touch of a man of honor. Briony's place in his life would be unassailable.

The opening bars of the waltz broke into his consciousness and he sauntered confidently toward the row of dowagers to claim Briony for the dance and for himself. When he caught her eye, he smiled one of his slow smiles.

Briony could not for the life of her understand why his lordship was for the umpteenth time reminding her of the fact that he was expected to make a suitable match. She listened to him in mounting irritation as he led her with easy grace through the movements of the waltz.

"You see," said Ravensworth with a note of apology in his voice, "we Montgomerys are a very old family. We go back to the Norman Conquest."

"Really?" said Briony, mimicking the drawl she had observed in those members of the ton who wished to depress the pretentions of their inferiors. "The Langlands go farther back than that."

Ravensworth looked startled. "Do they indeed?"

"Oh yes," replied Briony, giving her voice just the right inflection of bland indifference. "We are one of the old, old families."

"Langland?" Ravensworth queried. "Is it Saxon?"

Briony shook her head in faint derision. "No, no, not Saxon. Farther back than that."

Ravensworth eyed her suspiciously. "Who was your antecedent then?"

A gleam kindled in Briony's eye. "I believe his name was Adam."

"Adam Langland?"

"No! Just Adam." Her cheeks dimpled. "You can find him in the Bible."

Ravensworth gave her a slight shake. "You irrepressible girl. You know perfectly well that it's a book I am not familiar with."

"That doesn't surprise me," she retorted dryly.

He caught her close and spun her around with such violence that he almost swung her off her feet. Briony gasped and Ravensworth smiled down at her. "I warned you not to try to get the better of me. If you don't mind your tongue, minx, I shall certainly make you regret it, one way or another."

"You're making me dizzy," gasped Briony.

He spun her round again and she clung to him to keep from falling. "I want to make you dizzy." His voice deepened. "As dizzy as you have made me."

The music came to an end and Briony swayed in his arms, trying to recover her bearings. He steadied her then, after a moment, tucked her hand into his arm and, without consulting her wishes, intimated that they should go in search of a bite to eat. Briony docilely followed his lead.

"Why have you brought me here?" The question came from Briony. One moment they had been in the chandeliered dining room brilliant with candles preparing to select a plateful of delicacies from the glittering, heavily laden table and in the next instant Briony had been unceremoniously ushered through a door into a small, dimly lit saloon.

Ravensworth closed the door gently behind him and Briony repeated her question. "Why have you brought me here?" She gazed up at him with clear, untroubled gray eyes.

"Because," said Ravensworth softly, "there is something of a private nature I wish to say to you and I have no intention of broaching the subject under the curious ears of the ton."

"What subject?" Briony asked innocently.

They were standing at the threshold of the door and Ravensworth caught her arm and directed her firmly to a sofa against the wall. "Please be seated," he requested in his familiar voice of authority. Briony sat down.

As he looked into the depths of her unclouded, trusting eyes, it was suddenly borne in upon Ravensworth that his proposal was more difficult to articulate than he had at first supposed. He began rather diffidently. "Miss Langland . . . Briony, you are no doubt aware that my father, the Duke, intends me to marry well."

"Oh quite."

Ravensworth made a deprecating gesture with his hands. "I owe it to my House and Name."

"Of course," said Briony in some mystification. "I believe you have mentioned the matter on several occasions."

His lordship then began, rather haltingly, to assure the lady that although she could never bear his name, his heart would be hers forever. Briony listened in growing confusion as the Marquess restlessly paced back and forth and enumerated all the benefits that would accrue to her if she consented to form "a liaison" with him.

"A liaison?" Briony tentatively reiterated.

The Marquess sat down beside her and impetuously drew her hands into his. "My darling girl, you know my circumstances. I offer you my protection. I promise that I shall cherish and take care of you. You shall be my own true wife in everything but name." He watched her closely, as if half fearful of her response.

Briony was sure that she had misunderstood. She turned upon him one of her steady, clear-eyed gazes and Ravensworth's own gaze faltered.

"In simple terms, my lord, tell me what it is you want of me," she said with deceptive calm.

The Marquess began again, trying to couch his thoughts in words that would convince her of the folly of refusing his offer. "And such an arrangement is not uncommon where there is a wide disparity in station between a man and the woman he wants. But think of your own happiness!" he went on persuasively. "You need never be the Poor Relation again. I shall make handsome provision for you, Briony, yes even a settlement. I cannot bear to think of you living out your life on the charity of others." Her calm manner emboldened him. "Briony, we could travel in Europe. I would take you to Greece, and when your relatives become accustomed to the idea, we could settle in England, in my house in Kent. You would like it there, I think."

An icy rage descended upon Briony. She could not believe the words she was hearing. "But if I should marry someone—"

He cut her off without a qualm. "That is highly improbable. I don't wish to appear brutal, my dear, but how is such a wish to be accomplished? You are a penniless orphan. You have no dowry. Your looks and manners are not such as are likely to 'take' in Society." His voice exuded confidence. "Come now, you observed this evening how small your chances are of catching a husband. It takes a man of discrimination to appreciate your singular qualities. I am that man. You will never receive a better offer than mine. For your own sake, I beg you to accept it."

"Do I understand, Lord Ravensworth, that you are asking me to be your mistress?"

The words were spoken quietly but distinctly, and for the first time Ravensworth felt a twinge of disquietude. "Briony," he replied sternly, "you must know that is not how I think of it."

"Then you are *not* asking me to be your mistress?" Briony queried politely.

He gave a little sigh of exasperation. "If you wish to

put it like that, then yes, I am. But in my mind you would be my own, true wife."

"Ah yes! A wife who is not really a wife. Should we have children?" she asked ingenuously.

He watched her closely. "If you wish it."

"Do *you* wish it?"

He brought her unresisting hand to his lips. "Yes," he said simply.

"You would wish bastards on me?"

His lordship flushed an angry red. "Briony. I wish you would refrain from using these coarse expressions! They offend every feeling of delicacy."

"Forgive me. It is a Quaker failing. I have always been in the habit of using plain speech."

She withdrew her hands from his warm clasp and stood up with a semblance of tranquility which she was far from feeling. Emotions of anger, wounded pride, and bewilderment seethed in her breast. When she addressed him, her tone was scathing.

"I am sorry to be so disobliging, Lord Ravensworth, but there are a number of reasons why I feel compelled to decline your . . . well-meant offer." Her voice shook with repressed rage.

Ravensworth's eyes narrowed to dangerous slits when he heard her words of refusal.

"In the first place, I have no vocation to be a mistress. Pray forgive me. I collect that such plain speech wounds your sensibilities."

Ravensworth's jaw clenched. "I do not want a woman who has a vocation to be a mistress," he retorted bitingly. "Why do you insult yourself and me like this? If I had wanted such a woman, do you imagine that I would have approached you?"

"In the second place," continued Briony, deliberately ignoring everything that his lordship had said, "I would not form a liaison with you, no, not even a legal one, should you be the last man on earth." Her voice rose on a note of hysteria and she dug her nails into her palms in an attempt to master their involuntary shaking. She found it difficult to breathe and wished only to be rid of his hateful presence.

Ravensworth reached out and captured one of her hands. He laughed softly. "You are angry with me. I have been too hasty. You need time to consider my proposal."

Briony choked back the hot words that sprang to her lips. She would not give him the satisfaction of discovering how much he had wounded her. She tried to disengage her hand but he held it more firmly.

"I need no more time to consider your proposal, my lord," she said stiffly. "You boasted, yes boasted, that you were a man of honor. I believed you. That for your honor!" She snapped her fingers under his nose and he recoiled. "You have insulted me in every possible way! You may take your honor, sir, and go to the devil."

Ravensworth's brow was black with anger. He stood up to tower over her, and she shrank back to see the menace in his eyes.

"Let me go," she cried, her self-control almost at breaking point.

Cruel fingers dug into her shoulders as he turned her to face him. "I shall release you," he said grimly, "when you answer one, simple question. Do you care for me? Do you?" He shook her angrily. "Tell me, damn you!"

Briony longed to deny it, but she could not. She gave him a stricken look and remained silent.

"Oh Briony, Briony," he said with a harsh laugh, "how unfortunate for you that you are incapable of telling a lie."

He took her face between his hands and drew her closer. Briony stilled in his grasp. Something in his coiled, pantherlike stance warned her that to resist would be fatal.

She was conscious for the first time of the sheer power of him and it frightened her. This was not the man who had been solicitous of her welfare in the foregoing months, the man who had placed himself in jeopardy to save her in a runaway carriage, but a stranger. She heard the soft, fearful panting in her throat and tried to stifle it.

"Briony," he said hoarsely as he bent his head to cover her trembling lips with his mouth.

Briony sobbed and hot tears spilled onto her cheeks. He brushed them away with an uncaring hand and his arms encircled her, pulling her hard against the whole length of him, compelling her to put her hands on his shoulders. She twisted her head to escape the hunger she sensed in his mouth, but he merely bent to kiss the soft depression between her breasts. Gently but inexorably his ardent lovemaking coaxed her to surrender to his possession, and Briony, trembling in his arms with an anticipation she did not understand, felt powerless to resist. When she parted her lips to allow his probing tongue to penetrate her mouth, she knew that she had lost.

"Tingling, my love?" he murmured provocatively.

Briony was dimly aware that his caresses had ceased. She looked into Ravensworth's blazing eyes and the look of triumph she saw reflected there moved her to shame.

"Let me go!" she entreated with quiet desperation. She averted her head as if his presence disgusted her.

"Briony, Briony, don't turn away from me," he chided, grasping her chin. He spoke softly. "You belong to me. You do understand that, don't you?"

She met his eyes squarely. "Once I thought we might be friends but now . . ." She left the sentence unfinished. Her voice vibrated with disdain. "I never thought to meet such cruelty from any man, least of all from a man of honor. You are contemptible. I despise you!" His hand dropped from her face as if it had been stung, and

Briony wrenched herself out of his arms and flung out of the room.

His lordship sat down in the depths of the sofa. He would wait ten minutes or so, he thought, before following her. No need to rouse the suspicions of the whole ton. Let her cool her heels for a bit. He reached inside his coat pocket and retrieved a cigar. He lit it absently and drew smoothly on it. He really had no idea how to proceed if he wished to capture this girl. He closed his eyes and considered. She was beyond reason. How could she believe that his offer was insulting? He was destined to be a duke and she, to put it plainly, a chit of no consequence. Is that what she was after? His title and fortune? Was she just another scheming wench after all? No. That was out of the question! Every instinct, every nerve recoiled from such a suggestion. Miss Briony Langland was simply a virtuous lady. Damn it, he didn't wish her to be *unvirtuous*. Why couldn't she understand?

It began to be borne in on his lordship that he had lost not only a battle but probably the war as well. What a devil of a coil to be in! The word "nemesis" came unbidden to his mind. He chewed on his lip unthinkingly. Avery, he thought, would die laughing.

Chapter 7

When Briony flung away from Ravensworth, her one thought was to be rid of all the cruelly indifferent people who had inflicted such wounding humiliation upon her from the first moment she had crossed the threshold of the grand house. She pushed her way roughly through the crowded dining room, half expecting to feel Ravensworth's hateful hand upon her shoulder, but nothing impeded her precipitous flight. A few startled glances alighted upon her fleetingly as she elbowed her way through the crush, but the ton took little interest in the doings of a negligible quizz.

When she reached the large foyer, she hesitated, unsure of how best to accomplish her escape. Her warm mantle was in the ladies' cloakroom and it took her less than a minute to retrieve it and hasten past the startled porter who was guarding the entrance.

It never occurred to Briony to apprise Harriet or Aunt Sophy of her intentions. Her emotions were in such a tumult that she was far from considering the matter in a rational light. Briony was beside herself with fury and shame. Clutching her mantle firmly to her, she struck out across Cavendish Square, having no clear idea of where she was heading, nor did she care. She wanted only to put as much distance between herself and the despicable Marquess as she possibly could.

A cruel wind whipped her small figure, and Briony put her head down to escape its icy blast, but her pace never slackened for a moment. She was half running in her delirium, oblivious to everything but the host of confused thoughts which chased themselves across her mind. She did not hear the approach of the carriage nor the furious oath of the coachman until she was directly in the path of the rearing, screaming horses. By the time she was alerted to her danger, it was too late. She tried instinctively to twist away, but the hooves of the lead animal lashed out and struck her a glancing blow on the back, sending her spinning. She fell headlong on the road, the breath knocked out of her. She was half conscious of the commotion coming from the coach as doors slammed and the passengers called out their alarm. Briony attempted to rise to her knees, but she had not the strength. She looked up to see three anxious female faces hovering over her—the most beautiful faces that she had ever beheld in her life. She gave a tremulous smile. "Are you muses or angels?" she asked weakly before a dizzying blackness descended upon her.

Briony's eyelashes fluttered. She really did not wish to be drawn out of the safety of her slumber, she thought drowsily. If she refused to waken, she need never face the cruel world again. A hand lifted her head from the pillow and a cup was pressed against her lips.

"Drink this," said a soft, sweet, feminine voice. Briony opened her eyes and gazed at the angelic, smiling face.

"Am I in heaven?" she asked haltingly.

She heard the low, musical laughter. "No, you poor girl. But if you try to run down any more coaches, you will soon have your wish. What is your name? Your parents, your guardians will be worried about you. I must inform them of your whereabouts."

"Briony. I am . . . Briony," she managed before slipping into a welcoming insensibility once more.

When Briony reluctantly awakened to full consciousness, the room was in semidarkness. Her head ached abominably and when she moved she felt a searing pain in the small of her back. She moaned softly. A cool hand was laid on her forehead and she recognized the charming countenance of the lady she was beginning to believe was her guardian angel. Briony pulled herself up to lie back on the pillows and groaned.

"Now, you *will* drink this," said the Angel firmly and she pushed a cup of warm broth to Briony's lips. Briony greedily drank down the hot soup.

"Where am I?" she asked. "How long have I been here?" The Beauty removed the empty cup from Briony's fingers and sat down on the edge of the bed. "You are in my home. Yesterday evening, you were run down by the hackney coach in which I was a passenger. You might easily have been killed, you know. You ran straight across the Oxford Road without a thought for your safety. I was on my way home from the opera with my two sisters."

"The three muses!" Briony suddenly remembered.

The lady bestowed a disbelieving smile on Briony. "My sisters and I are not in the least alike," she demurred.

"But you are all beautiful," responded Briony honestly.

"That's as may be. But you, young lady, have given us all a fearful fright! We might have killed you! Now will you please give me the direction of your parents or guardians so that I may put their minds at rest?"

Briony did so, and the Vision glided from the room. Briony heard her low, melodious voice giving someone instructions on the other side of the door.

She eased back into the soft, feather pillows and

winced. Her emotional pain was as tangible as the physical pain in her bruised back. The events of the evening came back to her in a rush—the humiliating rejection of her peers and the contemptible proposal which Ravensworth had put to her. Her cheeks grew warm with embarrassment when she recalled his tantalizing caresses and how shamelessly she had welcomed them. She hoped fervently that she would never set eyes on the ignoble nobleman again.

For the anxiety which Harriet and Aunt Sophy must be experiencing on her behalf, Briony reproached herself bitterly. It never entered her head that Ravensworth himself would be suffering worse agonies of remorse and reproaching himself even more bitterly for being the cause of her precipitous flight.

She blamed herself for having left the party unescorted, but she had been half delirious with wounded pride. The thought of it roused the same feelings of overpowering mortification and helpless fury. She repressed the sobs that rose in her throat and she began to hiccup softly. She wondered how she could ever again face the world, and tears of self-pity coursed down her cheeks.

The Angel returned and halted abruptly when she saw her patient's overwrought condition. "My dear," she said solicitously, moving toward a trembling Briony to take her hands. "Tell me at once what ails you. Perhaps I should send for Dr. Pemberton again?"

Briony, who was habitually a diffident, constrained young lady, was completely disarmed by the note of genuine concern in her nurse's warm voice. Before she knew what she was about, she had spilled out the whole sorry story, omitting only the part about Ravensworth. She told of her mother and how impossible a task it seemed to reconcile her conscience and the frivolities of life in High Society. The Vision held Briony comfortingly in her arms and listened in silence. When Briony came to the end of her tale, the lady spoke reassuringly.

"People can be very cruel, as I know to my cost. You are right to follow the dictates of your conscience, Briony. Yes, even I, such as I am, have made it my only rule. But do be sure, my dear, that they are *your* convictions. Then you need never hang your head in shame. Stare the world down if you must, or snap your fingers under its nose."

Briony gave an involuntary giggle. "I did!"

"That's better," the Vision said with a smile in her voice. "No more self-pity, if you please. It really is an unconscionable waste of time and effort. Be true to yourself and let the world go hang. But do be sure, my child, that it is yourself that you are true to and not someone else's notion of what you should be."

Briony let the soothing words wash over her as the Vision stroked her hair. She felt immensely comforted and was overcome with a rush of gratitude to the stranger who seemed to have taken her interests to heart.

"Come now," the Beauty said at last, "we must dress you for going home."

"But what reason shall I give my cousin and Aunt Sophy for my running away?" Briony asked, alarmed in spite of herself.

"Never enter into long explanations, my dear. Stick to the facts. It is the easiest way. You went for a walk and were run down by a carriage. It is, after all, the truth."

Yes, thought Briony, it is the truth, but not the whole truth and nothing but the truth.

She was putting the finishing touches to her toilette when she heard the wheels of a carriage on the cobblestones outside. She could not as yet walk unaided and waited patiently for her aunt's footmen to fetch her down. When the door to her chamber opened, the last man on earth she wanted to see crossed the threshold.

"Ravensworth!" Her breath was ragged. She saw the blinding look of relief in his eyes, but she would not look at him. She dropped her gaze and plucked nervously at the sleeve of her gown.

"I can manage now, Harriette," she heard him say in his familiar tone of authority. She looked up expectantly, supposing that her cousin had accompanied his lordship, but there was only the Vision smiling down at her. Ravensworth was acquainted with the lady then, thought Briony, her interest piqued.

She had already conveyed her thanks before Ravensworth's arrival. Now it only needed her to take leave of the stranger who had been so kind.

"I shall call on you one day soon, when I am in better fettle," she began, addressing the lady whom Ravensworth had called "Harriette."

"No!" said two voices in unison.

Briony looked inquiringly from one to the other.

"It is not necessary," the lady replied smoothly, moving to the door to hold it open. "Besides, I shall be removing from town very soon. This is only a rented house and I am giving it up at the end of the month."

"But when shall I see you again?" asked Briony plaintively. "I owe you so much. Surely you will give me the opportunity of renewing our acquaintance? At least tell me your name."

As she spoke, Ravensworth put his strong arms around her and lifted her easily against his chest. "Please, put me down," she entreated. "I am not an invalid. I can walk." Every nerve recoiled at his touch. He ignored her request and maneuvered her through the open door. He turned to the Vision.

"Thank you. What more can I say? If ever you should need a friend . . ." His voice trailed off as he sensed Briony's attentiveness. "Your obedient servant, ma'am," he concluded stiffly and carried a protesting Briony down the stairs to the waiting carriage. Her fury boiled over.

"But—but—but . . ." She struggled feebly in his arms. "I do not know the lady's name."

He refused to listen and handed her into the carriage to the welcoming arms of her cousin, then he climbed in nimbly beside her.

"Oh Briony, thank God you are safe." Harriet enfolded Briony in her arms. "We were so worried about you. What happened? Why did you leave the party without saying a word to anyone?"

Briony sensed Ravensworth's keen regard. She did not have the courage as yet to stare the world down. She was careful not to let her eyes meet his.

"I went for a walk and was run down by a carriage," she said simply.

Harriet cried and laughed on the same breath. "How like you, my darling girl! I swear you can get into more scrapes than I ever did in my life."

Briony was lost in thought. "How is it, Harriet, that you waited in the carriage? Why did you not come up to be introduced to the lady who has been so kind to me?"

It was Ravensworth who answered. "I was deputized to perform the necessaries. We did not wish to put the lady to further trouble on your behalf."

The answer was far from satisfying Briony but she held her peace. She was conscious that Harriet was deeply embarrassed. There was a mystery here and she intended to get to the bottom of it.

* * *

The Marquess of Ravensworth was slumped in a chair in a small saloon, normally used as a waiting room, just off the foyer in Aunt Sophy's house in Half Moon Street. A two days' stubble covered his wan cheeks and dark circles accentuated his black, troubled eyes. The Viscount Avery looked only slightly less haggard. The ladies of the house had been finally persuaded to take their rest.

"What a conundrum," said Avery, observing the amber liquid in the glass he held up to the light. "If word gets around that Miss Langland was sheltered by London's most notorious courtesan, that she slept in her bed even, Briony's character will be ruined forever."

"Word won't get around," said Ravensworth firmly. "Harriette Wilson is more of a lady than most of the titled females of my acquaintance. She never maligns the innocent."

"You should know, old boy, you should know," was the airy rejoinder. "But what possessed Miss Langland to go for a walk?" Avery cocked an inquisitive eyebrow at Ravensworth. His lordship remained silent. "Good God," exclaimed Avery, "you didn't!"

Ravensworth drank off his brandy in one gulp.

"You were right, Avery, and I was wrong. I made a mull of the whole thing."

"Well, no real harm done," said Avery consolingly. "We got her back in one piece. She'll get over it. Plenty more blossoms on the tree, what?"

"Don't tease yourself, Avery," Ravensworth replied heavily. "I haven't given up on the lady yet."

Avery blinked. "You cannot be serious!"

"Of course I'm serious!" was the savage rejoinder.

"Ravensworth, have you lost your senses? As I've told you before, the girl is too virtuous for what you have in mind. Let her alone. You must accept the fact, my friend, that some women would prefer death to having their virtue compromised. Miss Briony Langland is . . . well . . . too refined for one of your voluptuary tastes."

"That's all you know!" retorted Lord Ravensworth, smiling a little to himself. "Besides, you don't know what I have in mind."

Viscount Avery was lost for words. Presently an unholy gleam came into his eye. "Perhaps she won't have you under any circumstance. It could be, you know, Ravensworth, that the lady finds you not in her style."

Ravensworth was about to respond but changed his mind. "It's been a hard day," he said wearily. "I don't know about you, Avery, but I'm for bed."

They parted on the doorstep, and Ravensworth set off at a brisk pace. Half Moon Street was off Picadilly, a mere five minutes' walk to his rooms in Albany House. The cold air cleared his lordship's head.

He was convinced that the lady's heart was his, but winning her, he allowed, was a different matter. She had these infernal scruples. He knew that Briony thought that he, the heir to a dukedom, was quite beneath her touch. What a novel idea! Ravensworth smiled bleakly. She would expect *him* to reform. Damn it, he didn't *wish* to reform. He was, after all, a man of honor—not some unscrupulous blackguard who merely wished to have his way with her.

Ravensworth slammed into the Albany, muttered an angry salutation to the night porter dozing at his post, and took the stairs two at a time. Denby took one look at his master's black brow and forbore to ask his lordship whether the evening had come up to expectation. With the greatest circumspection, the valet relieved his master of his garments and discreetly withdrew before Ravensworth was aware of his absence.

She would try to cut him, thought Ravensworth as he wrapped a brocade dressing gown around his bone-weary

frame. He wouldn't allow it, of course. Avery was his en-
trée into Half Moon Street and there was nothing that
Briony could do about it. He acknowledged that he had a
serious problem to overcome. How could he offer for her
when he had taken such pains to convince her that, for
one of his rank, marriage to her was out of the question?
She would think him more of a cad than she already did.
He would have to tread carefully. Once she was his and
under his authority, he intended to be tolerant of her tender scruples. Good God, he admired her for them. But he
wouldn't allow anything so paltry to stand in the way of
their happiness.

The business with Harriette Wilson gave him an uneasy mind. Briony must not pursue that acquaintance.
Harriette's "profession," he knew, would not weigh with
Briony. The lady had shown her a kindness and she would
not forget it. But she must be protected from her own innocence. Fortunately, it had been dark when he had
brought her home in the carriage and he had had the
foresight to instruct the coachman to take a long route
home. She would never locate the house and Harriette
had mentioned a projected sojourn in Paris with her latest
protector. It would work out for the best.

What a night she had put him through, the little termagant! He hadn't had a wink's sleep in over twenty-four
hours and the sensations of alarm, anger, anguish, and remorse had consumed him every minute of that time. He
had alternatively wanted to choke the life out of her once
he had found her and hold her small, warm body protectively in his arms. The idea that she might go out of his life
was not to be countenanced. He could not allow her to
thwart him in his determination to make her his wife.

Chapter 8

For the better part of the following week Briony remained in her chamber. Although fully recovered from the accident, she was in no hurry to resume what she perceived to be her ignominious place on the social ladder. Every day Lords Avery and Ravensworth called faithfully at Half Moon Street, but she never received them nor could Harriet persuade her cousin to join them for even a few minutes' conversation. Ravensworth's floral tributes she accepted with something less than grace, but Harriet forbore to remark upon it, believing that the accident had shaken Briony more than they had at first supposed.

The wretchedness of Briony's spirits, however, had little to do with the unfortunate accident. Her confused thoughts were wholly occupied by the slights she had received at the disastrous party. When she recalled the cool, indifferent reception which had been her first taste of life in Society, she groaned in mortification. But when she thought of Ravensworth's offensive, contemptible proposal, she ground her teeth in a passion of fury. These excessive swings of mood, however, were soon spent, and Briony's natural good sense began to reassert itself.

For long hours she sat in her chamber in typical Quaker solitude contemplating her situation. With determined logic she began to sift through everything that

she had ever learned about conduct between the sexes.
At the end of the week, Briony had come to her own
conclusions. The beautiful lady who had nursed her, she
reflected, had known a thing or two. One must abide by
one's own convictions. Formerly she had blindly accepted her mother's Quaker teaching, but Mama, as she
had sadly discovered, was not infallible.

Great Aunt Sophy saw nothing amiss in her niece's
withdrawn manner. The cousins regarded this august
lady as a "dear" who never scolded or became overly inquisitive. She was genuinely delighted to enter into all
the girls' amusements, but as a watchful chaperone,
Aunt Sophy left much to be desired. She would never
grudge her presence at any of the dos and parties which
her nieces might attend, but neither would she pay more
than mild attention to her charges once she had delivered them to their destination. Aunt Sophy pursued her
own pleasures among the dowagers. She was a zealous
gossip and an inveterate gambler who invariably settled
herself in the quieter confines of the card room, where
she spent the better part of the evening doing a brisk
business with other like-minded matrons who enjoyed
what they were pleased to call "a little flutter."

She accepted Briony's explanation of the accident at
face value as she did Ravensworth's smooth description of
the solicitous lady who had sheltered her niece. When she
indicated that she wished to call on this paragon who had
shown Briony such extravagant kindness, Ravensworth's
bland avowal that the lady had since removed from town,
she accepted unhesitatingly. Aunt Sophy, who was related
to Briony only through marriage, was not suspicious by nature. Nor was she as observant as Sir John and Lady Esther
would have wished, for when Briony was finally persuaded
to eat at table, it went unremarked by that grande dame

that her niece had removed every vestige of lace which had formerly concealed the rounded swell of her bosom.

Harriet observed the modification in Briony's gowns but tactfully kept silent. She surmised that Briony's humiliation at the hands of the ton had induced her cousin to abandon her rigid adherence to Quaker ways. She was deeply vexed for Briony's mortifying experience, but her admiration for her cousin's courage and good sense outweighed every other feeling. She wished only that Briony would consent to have her hair cut á la mode. She was sure that with the right garments and hair style, Briony could be quite a taking girl.

Briony's first outing in her aunt's carriage was to a small office in Pimlico to consult with the Langlands' man of business. To a courteous and attentive Mr. Jackson, who had been her father's agent for years beyond remembering, she explained that it was her intention of acquiring a new wardrobe for her first Season. Mr. Jackson was not perturbed. He knew how little the Langland ladies ever expended on such frivolities as baubles and gowns. He affably assured the solemn young Quaker lady that as one of the heirs to the Langland fortune, she had more than sufficient funds for her needs. Had he known the full extent of Briony's ambitions, he might have expressed his sentiments more cautiously. Briony was instructed to purchase whatever she needed and send the accounts to his office. His reassuring words brought the dimples to Briony's wan cheeks.

Harriet had been at first stunned and then ecstatic. It had never occurred to her that the Langland branch of the family was a wealthy one. They had certainly never given any indication in their modest style of living that they were anything but comfortably situated, and Sir John and Lady Esther had never breathed a word. Briony explained how it offended every feeling of delicacy for Quakers to admit to wealth. Many Quakers were, however, as rich as nabobs in spite of giving vast sums of money to works of charity and philanthropy. Quakers were honest, industrious, and trustworthy, virtues which reaped monetary rewards when one was engaged in trade or business, and her father had had diverse investments in various companies besides his extensive estates in Shropshire.

Harriet, quite naturally, imparted the information to her beau, Lord Avery, who gleefully told his friend, Lord Ravensworth, in the strictest confidence. That gentleman mulled the information over in his mind. He perceived that there never had been the slightest hope that Briony would ever have accepted what he now came to regard as his preposterous proposal. Not only was she a lady of virtue but, more to the point, she was a lady of independent means.

Briony's financial status was of not the slightest consequence to him, but he could see how, should the on dit become general, his beloved heiress would inevitably be besieged with unsavory suitors. The thought made him quite viciously unpleasant to his devoted valet. Denby was wondering if it was time to tender his resignation since his master had been, quite uncharacteristically, in a taking in the last week or so, and Denby held that a valet of his particular abilities would have little trouble in finding another situation. He decided to wait it out and see.

With impetuous fingers chafing to get at the contents, Briony speedily undid the wrappings of the large dress box which had that very evening been delivered from Madame Godet, a fashionable mantua maker who had her establishment on Seymour Street. With a small sound of wonderment, she withdrew a gown of gossamer, violet silk tissue shot with silver. She stood shivering with anticipation in her thin cotton chemise as Lady Sophy's abigail eased the diaphanous slip of a dress over her head. The square neckline was low-cut but modest by the standards of the day, and the short puffed sleeves were gathered in the middle with a silver satin ribbon. The abigail painstakingly fastened the row of tiny buttons at her back and Briony swung gently from side to side admiring the fullness of the gored skirt with its high waistline fitting snugly under her breasts. It was, Madame Godet had said, the very latest fashion from Paris.

"Thank you, Alice, that will be all."

"If you wish, I could curl your hair," the abigail offered helpfully.

Briony sat down in front of the mirror. "That won't be necessary!" Alice curtsied and made as if to withdraw.

"Ooo, Miss Briony," she said in accents of wonder, "you will be the grandest lady at the ball in that lovely gown."

Briony's eyes grew round and serious. "I intend to be, Alice, I intend to be," she responded without a trace of humor in her voice.

Briony gazed at the mirror and saw a stranger. Her eyes, she noted with wonder, had darkened to a mysterious violet, but when she moved, the silver sheen of her gown changed their color to gray again. Her hair she had quite deliberately kept in tight braids the whole day long. She undid the pins and unwound the long strands carefully, then she brushed her fair tresses till they were lustrous. Her long, thick hair fell in a torrent of soft waves to below her shoulders. Briony inserted two silver combs studded with amethysts just above each ear, and she carefully positioned matching amethyst drops on her ears. She dipped her fingers into a small porcelain pot on her dressing table and rouged her full lips sparingly. From her pale, luminous face reflected in the mirror, dark, violet-gray eyes gazed gravely back at her—eyes with knowledge as old as Eve.

"You were wrong, Mama," Briony softly told her mirror image. "The Quaker mode of dress is *not* a protection from predators. It is a cowardly camouflage that serves only to incite violence. Believe me, dressed like this, I shall appear as merely another leaf on the tree." After a moment's honest reflection, she was compelled to add "or nearly."

On her bed were the accessories which Alice had thoughtfully laid out for her. She pulled on elbow-length white kid gloves, draped a shawl of silver-blue silk negligently across her shoulders, and picked up a French fan richly decorated with mother of pearl. She wondered if she should tuck her snuffbox into her embroidered satin pochette but decided against it. She must remember to look for one studded with amethysts when next she went shopping. Briony nodded sagely at the stranger in her mirror and tilted her head back a trifle. "And now, fair lady," she said huskily, "lead me to the lions."

Viscount Castlereagh's residence was less than a ten-minute walk away at 18 St. James Square—ten minutes by foot, that is, but a full hour by coach since the narrow streets were thronged with the crested carriages of members of the ton who were considered among the elite. To receive an invitation to one of the grandest balls of the Season was a better recommendation than even a voucher to Almack's and much more enjoyable.

Briony was relieved that Lord Ravensworth was not of their party. Avery explained that he was one of Lady Castlereagh's pre-ball dinner guests, a singular honor, but not unexpected for the heir to one of the most prestigious titles in the realm. Briony sniffed. That she was at that moment seated in Ravensworth's crested carriage nettled her more than she cared to admit. If it had been up to her, she would have refused his offer out of hand, but Aunt Sophy saw it as a splendid solution to her particular problem. James, her own coachman, poor man, hated the long delays at these grand crushes, and she hadn't the heart to inconvenience him.

Harriet's eyes glowed as she took in Briony's appearance. That young lady hadn't an envious bone in her body. In her white muslin gown heavily encrusted with seed pearls, Harriet was as pleasing as any young deb could wish to be, but Briony, with her cascade of platinum hair and eyes luminous with some emotion, held a certain allure that made Harriet catch her breath. Even Lord Avery was affected. He wondered, uneasily, how Ravensworth would react.

Ravensworth idly raised his quizzing glass and surveyed the crowded ballroom with a bored eye. Briony, he reflected, had not yet arrived. His absent glance was arrested by the figure of a handsome woman, an Incomparable, who was surrounded by a bevy of eager swains. Ravensworth's lips curved in appreciation. Her glorious blond hair hanging loosely about her shoulders framed a perfectly oval face. She used her fan, he noted, with devastating effect. No disrespect to Briony, but a man must make his bow to beauty. His lordship sauntered with lithe grace toward his quarry, prepared to smile one of his slow smiles should he chance to catch the Beauty's eye.

Briony looked up and saw her adversary only a few feet away. The smile froze on her lips. Ravensworth, she observed sourly, had not recognized her. He threw her a devastating smile. She curtsied deeply and the babble of the swains surrounding her stilled.

Briony tilted her head a trifle and stared resolutely into his lordship's admiring blue eyes. She noted with amusement the sudden, startled recognition that dawned in his expression. Ravensworth blinked rapidly. Defiance lurked in the depths of her steady gaze, mounting fury in his. She felt the blood rush to her cheeks and after an interminable moment she averted her gaze. She had done nothing wrong, she reasoned. Why should she be the one to blush? The man had no shame!

In one long stride he had crossed the distance between them and he grasped her wrist with bone-crushing strength.

"Pray excuse us," he said affably to the group of curious bucks. "My cousin and I have a family matter to discuss." Amid the groans and protests of her admirers, Ravensworth dragged a stumbling Briony unceremoniously into the hall.

"What the devil do you think you're doing?" he demanded, turning on her furiously. He smiled civilly to a passing acquaintance and turned back to her with a growl. "Who gave you permission to wear your hair in that wanton fashion? What do you think this is? A house of ill repute?"

Briony was stunned. "I—I . . . " she began.

"And what the devil . . . is that rouge on your lips?" Ravensworth extracted his snowy white handkerchief and with one vigorous motion had cleansed the lady's lips of the offending stain. Briony began to whimper. Ravensworth's eye softened. He was about to reach for her when Lord Edgewood swaggered into view.

"Miss Langland, this dance is promised to me, I collect?" He laid a proprietary hand on Briony's arm and returned Lord Ravensworth's baleful glare.

"Do excuse us, my dear chap, but your, er, cousin filled me in on her card." His tone was faintly mocking.

For the first time, Ravensworth observed the card which Briony was clutching convulsively in her hands. He snatched it from her grasp and saw that there were four vacant spots on it. He filled his own name in each one of them without so much as a by-your-leave, knowing quite well that more than two dances would proclaim to the watching world that he had as much as engaged himself to the lady. He thrust it back into her shaking hands and, clicking his heels punctiliously, turned his back on her and her admiring cicisbeo.

Harriet's eyes scanned the dancers, searching for a glimpse of her elusive cousin. It had been, she thought with a sigh of satisfaction, an evening of notable success for Briony. She took vicarious pleasure in her cousin's triumph. Briony been the most-sought-after deb at the ball. The young men were wild for her and had dogged her heels the whole night through. Harriet glanced sideways at her companion. The devotion of this one gentleman who was escorting her round the perimeter of the ballroom would have satisfied her modest ambitions, but Avery had become an enigma to her. He was constant but distant in his attentions. Harriet's eyes roved back to the dance floor.

"I say, Avery," she exclaimed, stopping in her tracks, "isn't that Ravensworth partnering Briony *again?* That's the third time this evening. What is he up to? He will compromise her if he shows her such singular attention," said Harriet thoughtfully. "I must warn Briony."

"You'll do no such thing," commanded Avery firmly. "Three dances with Ravensworth won't ruin the girl." He eyed her quizzically. "I remember a time when the irrepressible Miss Grenfell would have snapped her fingers at such a paltry indiscretion."

Harriet was taken aback. "It is ungentlemanly of you, sir, to throw my former follies in my face. It was *your* wish that I acquire a little dignity." Her eyes snapped dangerously and Avery had the grace to look abashed.

"Well, wasn't it?" Harriet demanded vehemently.

Lord Avery swallowed. When he spoke, he appeared to be laboring under some difficulty. "Harriet, I have been meaning to—to say something to you."

Harriet's pulse quickened. "Yes?" she asked breathlessly. To gain a little time, Lord Avery groped in his coat pocket and withdrew a small, round snuffbox. How could he tell this fiery termagant that he thought she had become too tame of late, that he wished she would show a little more of her former spirit? Avery decided he dare not. With habitual delicacy, he placed a pinch of snuff on the back of his wrist. From the corner of his eye, he observed that Harriet was waiting for him to continue. He cast around in his mind for something to say, and said the first thing that came to his lips. "Would you care to partake?" he asked, proffering his wrist.

Harriet drew back as if she had been scorched. "How dare you, sir!" Her voice shook with anger.

It was precisely at that moment that a glum-faced Lord Ravensworth returned a radiant Briony to her cousin's side. The exaggerated court which the young blades, yes, and some of them not so young, had paid to Briony in the course of the evening had evidently ruffled his lordship's feathers.

"Avery," squealed Briony as she laid her hand on his

arm, "may I?" She made as if to draw his wrist to her nose, but a viselike grip on her arm forced her to relinquish it.

"I forbid it!" Ravensworth hissed in her ear.

Such intimidation provoked Briony's eyes to flash with anger. She turned a rigid back on his lordship and addressed herself to the Viscount. "If you please, Lord Avery?" she coaxed.

"Oh no, Briony," pleaded a distracted Harriet.

Then began a discreet tussle between the grim-faced gentleman and the lady with the flashing eyes. There was never any doubt who would win the contest.

Lord Avery's arm grew weary.

"Oh, damn!" said Harriet. She determined to settle the argument once and for all. She hauled Lord Avery's wrist to her nostrils and inhaled most indelicately. With her nose only an inch from Avery's wrist she stole a glance up at him. His eyes glowed warmly with admiration. Harriet tremulously returned his smile. Then Harriet sneezed.

The snuffbox slipped from Avery's inert fingers and rolled toward the row of dowagers along the wall. It struck the wainscotting with a crack and the lid snapped open, spilling the contents over the floor.

With great presence of mind, Lord Ravensworth grabbed the two ladies by the elbow and escorted them determinedly in the opposite direction.

"What about my snuffbox?" demanded a petulant Avery.

"Not now, man, not now."

The Viscount stood irresolutely for only a moment. A dowager sneezed, and then another. Soon a whole row of formidable matrons were bobbing up and down with their little white caps dancing on their heads like the billowing sails of the British Fleet outward bound on a fair wind for France.

Lord Avery took to his heels.

Chapter 9

In the following weeks, their days fell into a predictable pattern. A stream of fawning admirers descended on Half Moon Street to escort the sought-after cousins on a round of pleasure. The girls changed their partners as often as they changed their gloves, and Briony found it impossible to form more than a passing acquaintance with any of her alternating swains. She soon came to perceive that she and Harriet had attracted a certain notoriety by their forward conduct at the Castlereaghs' ball. The snuff incident had not gone unremarked. To have the reputation of a dasher, a high flyer—words that she heard the bucks admiringly bandy about—brought the fetching dimples flashing to Briony's cheeks. She noted wryly that any gentleman who had the good fortune to be seen in the company of either of the scapegrace cousins achieved a certain cachet among his fellows.

Great Aunt Sophy, not unnaturally, saw nothing out of the way in the current vogue among the younger dandies for her nieces' favors. There was only one cloud on the horizon which troubled that obtuse lady. There had been an inexplicable delay in procuring one of the scarce vouchers for Almack's—a slight inconvenience which she was sure would soon be resolved. Harriet knew better but forbore to enlighten her aunt, thankful that for the present her parents were miles away in Bath.

At first, Briony had been amused by her newfound popularity, but it did not take long for it to pall, and she became increasingly bored with the inanity of the interminable excursions in the park in the up-to-the-crack phaetons and curricles which every young man who aspired to fashion was obliged to sport.

Lord Ravensworth's ardor had evidently cooled. He was never to be found among the other gentlemen who came to wait on the cousins in Aunt Sophy's best, upstairs, company drawing room. Briony told herself firmly that she was glad of it. There could be no future for a girl of her gentle breeding and a man of his questionable morals.

That Ravensworth was now in possession of the knowledge that she was an heiress of a considerable competence was confirmed by his conduct. She had, of course, known perfectly well that Avery would apprise his friend of her circumstances. Ravensworth would know, she consoled herself, that there was nothing a man of his ilk could possibly offer that would entice a lady of her character and fortune to accept him on any terms, not even if he were to lay his dukedom at her feet. Miss Briony Langland was far above his touch. She hoped that his lordship knew it.

The Marquess of Ravensworth was not to be numbered among Briony's admirers; nevertheless, he was frequently encountered riding in the park or on any of the innumerable excursions Briony made into Mayfair. He appeared to be in the best of spirits and would doff his hat to her in the most gallant manner and go so far as to engage her in a few minutes' desultory conversation, and since Briony was always accompanied by one of her attentive cicisbeos and Ravensworth invariably had some doting beauty hanging on his sleeve, Briony was compelled to a civility she deplored.

When his lordship addressed her, however, she never again subjected him to one of her clear-eyed gazes, but slid her eyes away to focus on the points of his collar, or even lower, to the top button of his impeccable waistcoat. Once, when she chanced to meet his insolent stare, the provocative glint which she caught lurking in the depths of his eyes brought the color rushing to her cheeks. Briony did not care to be so discomfitted. She sensed that the Marquess was mocking her, that he was flaunting some kind of power over her, and Briony was incensed.

She took to practicing before her mirror and developed quite a repertoire of stares. No aspiring dandy ever spent more time on perfecting the intricate folds of his fine, starched, linen neckcloths than did Briony in assiduously rehearsing the various glances with which she hoped to wither the proud lord. Her imperious "cool appraisal" sent her eyebrows arching disbelievingly into her hair; her "go to the devil" glare had her lips curl in derision. But of them all, she thought her "stare the world down" scrutiny quite the best invention. With eyebrows arched and cheeks sucked in till her rosy lips formed a sullen pout, she would look down her straight nose with studied insolence.

When she tried it on Ravensworth, however, something went amiss. He had contrived a few minutes' private conversation with her at Lady Besborough's musical evening. He laughed outright and asked her if she was shortsighted. Briony thereupon glared fierily into his eyes. She watched the mocking gleam go out of them. His pupils dilated, darkening the irises to black and his eyes held hers. She tried to look away but she was mesmerized until Ravensworth took it into his head to release her. It left Briony breathless and shaken and determined to avoid his lordship's eyes until she became glare perfect.

One morning, before most members of the ton were up and about, Briony made an excursion to Hatchard's book shop on the other side of Piccadilly from Albany House. By some ill fortune she met Ravensworth as she was leaving the premises with her purchase in her hand. It was her intention to ignore him, but he hailed her in a loud, commanding voice, and Briony turned back reluctantly. She greeted him with the "cool appraisal," being careful to lock her eyes on the imperceptible cleft on Ravensworth's chin. She had never noticed it before. She saw it deepen. "My lord?" Briony inquired coolly.

She heard him chuckle. "Miss Langland, I should like to present you to Lady Adèle St. Clair. Our land marches together in Kent. I believe I mentioned that I have an estate in that county," said the Marquess irrepressibly.

Briony's back grew rigid. She gave the lady with the guinea gold locks one of her steady, clear-eyed gazes. Then Briony curtsied and the lady bowed. When next Briony looked into Lady Adèle's eyes, she was met by a hostile stare. The lady's lips, however, curved in imitation of a smile.

Briony perceived at once that Ravensworth's unfriendly companion took her to be a rival for the gentleman's affections and she felt sorry for her. She was, noted Briony, as she openly regarded the dashing cut of the lady's ensemble, exactly the sort of woman to attract the eye of a rake like Ravensworth. Her figure molded tightly by her scarlet morning dress was nothing less than voluptuous. In contrast to the lady's ornate costume, Briony's plain, graygreen, kerseymere pelisse was a model of understatement. Briony smiled reassuringly at the lady.

"I don't recall—did you two ladies encounter each other at the Grenfells' winter ball?" asked Ravensworth mischievously.

Lady Adèle laughed throatily. "One meets so many new faces, how can I tell?" She clung a little closer to Ravensworth's arm and her tawny eyes raked Briony from head to foot with vulgar curiosity. Then satisfied that the unprepossessing chit of a girl posed no threat that she could not handle, she said dismissively with an edge of contempt in her voice, "I have no recollection of Miss Langland."

Briony did not admire the lady's tact and wondered what she had done to merit such venom. She noted that one of the ostrich plumes on her ladyship's bonnet was beginning to wilt and Briony was not sorry.

"We have not met!" said Briony in quelling accents for Ravensworth's benefit. "If we had, I am certain that I should have remembered the occasion."

From the corner of her eye, she glanced up at Ravensworth and saw that he was glowering.

"Where is your abigail?" he demanded rudely.

Briony was at a loss. "My abigail?" she repeated foolishly.

"Your chaperone, girl, your chaperone!"

Briony laughed. "I need no chaperone, my lord. I have only to cross the street and I am home again. What harm can come to me when I am so close to Half Moon Street?"

"You dare to ask that after—" Ravensworth's voice froze in mid-sentence. Briony knew that he was referring to the night of her accident and she sensed that he was trying to protect her from the natural inquisitiveness of the lady by his side. She so far forgot herself as to look frankly into Ravensworth's eyes. His lordship was bristling like a hedgehog.

"I shall escort you home," he said with finality.

"But Hugh," began Lady Adèle peevishly, "you gave me your word to accompany me to my man of business. We are already late. Surely Miss Langland can see herself home? I need you by my side to explain all the intricacies of the late Earl's estate. Such complexities are beyond me." She turned to him with an expression of appeal in her disarming smile.

"Pray do not think of deserting the lady," Briony said icily. "I am no schoolroom miss, sir. I am well able to take care of my own person."

Ravensworth sneered. "I take leave to doubt that, Miss Langland! Pray say no more on the subject. I insist! It will delay us by only a few minutes. Adèle; if you please."

Briony felt compelled, for the sake of good manners, to comply with Ravensworth's bidding, but she was not well pleased with his high-handed ordering of her life.

On the return to Half Moon Street, it was Lady Adèle who exerted herself to engage her two silent companions in the civilities of polite conversation. "May I ask the title of your book, Miss Langland?"

"Pride and Prejudice," returned Briony. "One of my favorites, by an unknown lady. I left my copy in Richmond and cannot bear to be without it. Do you know it?"

"Pshaw!" interrupted his lordship testily. "Romantic drivel which ladies wallow in. I had thought, Miss Langland, that a woman of your intelligence would be above such mediocrity."

"Pray do not include me in your censure," Lady Adèle quickly interpolated. "I read the book and consigned it to the fire. I hope that my catholic taste is more established than to be taken in by such a ferrago of nonsense."

Briony duly noted the slights on her intelligence. They reached the front door of Aunt Sophy's house and she turned on the bottom step to survey her companions. She gave them her "go to the devil" sneer.

"I collect that you mistake the intention of the author," she said cooly. "The genre is of a more humorous bent than romantic. For some, I collect, it takes two or three readings before their intelligence is sufficiently alert to catch the irony."

Lord Ravensworth looked interested. "Perhaps I should give the book a second reading," he allowed. "Can you give me an example of what you mean, Miss Langland?"

"Certainly," Briony replied. "The very first sentence of the book is the key to the author's style. How does it go? 'It is a truth universally acknowledged, that a single man in possession of a good fortune must be in want of a wife.'"

"And do you consider that humorous?" inquired Lady Adèle derisively.

Briony solmenly acknowledged that she did. "It is hilarious!"

Lord Ravensworth looked at her suspiciously. "The humor escapes my comprehension. Pray enlighten me."

"Perhaps you will see the humor of it if you change the gender of the subject and object," Briony replied demurely.

"A woman in possession of a fortune must be in want of a man," intoned Lady Adèle ponderously.

"A ridiculous notion, don't you agree?" Briony flashed Ravensworth a mischievous grin. By the challenging expression she met in his eyes, she knew that he had received the message.

Lady Adèle was no simpleton. She was well aware of the undercurrents in the conversation which flowed between her companions. As Briony took her leave of the lady, she was subjected to a look of implacable enmity from spiteful amber eyes and she shivered.

When Briony next set eyes on Lord Ravensworth, she was a guest of Lord Avery in his box at the Opera. Since the experience was a new one for her, she was absorbing the spectacle with wide-eyed, unabashed curiosity. It was Harriet who whispered the Marquess's direction in her ear. Briony turned her head and saw that his lordship was in the box twice removed on her right. In his hands were a pair of opera glasses which he had trained insolently on her person. She elected not to give him a set-down with one of her stares from her growing repertoire but deigned to bestow on him the frostiest of curt acknowledgments. The glasses were instantly lowered and the Marquess returned an exaggerated bow. Then he smiled one of his slow smiles. She watched under lowered lashes as he inclined his head to catch something which the lady at his elbow had murmured in his ear. He threw back his head and laughed, and Briony was sure that the jest had been at her expense. She recognized the lady at Ravensworth's elbow. It was Lady Adèle St. Clair. Her gown was cut so low that her ample bosom, a vast expanse of white blubber, thought Briony uncharitably, was almost completely bared. Briony averted her chaste eyes and looked balefully in the opposite direction.

It did not take her long to come to the conclusion that Opera was not to her taste. After what seemed like hours of histrionic caterwauling from the renowned Italian soprano on stage, the first interval was upon them. Briony looked about her, studiously avoiding Ravensworth's box on her right. Her eye was taken by the unmistakable beauty of three ladies who were leaning over the edge of their box on the row above. Briony's gaze was arrested. She recognized them as her three angels. She jumped to her feet and waved her hand to attract their attention.

It was clear that she had been seen but the angels averted their heads as if not wishing to acknowledge her presence. She turned to edge her way between Harriet and Avery, who were engaged in earnest conversation. Aunt Sophy was dozing at the back of the box, a container of half-eaten sugar plums resting on her lap.

Briony's eyes were caught by Ravensworth. He, too, had started up. He shook his head vigorously to warn her off. Harriet became aware of the tension in Briony and caught Ravensworth's motion. He gestured to the box above to convey what Briony was about. Harriet clutched at Briony's skirt.

"Oh Briony, no! You cannot! You must not acknowledge the lady. You don't understand," she ended on a wail. Briony tried to remove her cousin's hand. "Oh Briony, it is Harriette Wilson, the courtesan. Now do you understand?"

Comprehension slowly dawned in Briony's eyes. "Of course! How stupid of me! I should have guessed. But how could I when everyone has treated me like the veriest child?"

Harriet relaxed her grip. Lord Avery appeared to be puzzled. "Will someone enlighten me, please?" he asked politely.

Briony looked toward Ravensworth. He stood poised, watching her intently. She threw him a triumphant smile and turned on her heel to dash out of the box. Ravensworth was after her in a flash.

Harriet looked stunned. "Oh damn!" she cursed, and bolted after her incorrigible cousin.

"What the devil is going on?" demanded Avery to no

one in particular. He got to his feet with a sigh, removed a speck of lint from his impeccable sleeve, and followed the ladies out at a leisurely pace.

A little breathless and warm cheeked from her exertion, Briony reached the forbidden box in a matter of minutes. The pins had fallen out of her hair in her mad rush and the blond waves tumbled around her shoulders. No need to wonder if she had found the right box, she reflected wryly. The crush of gentlemen waiting to gain admittance verified her conjecture. A few of these noble lords of the realm looked askance as she elbowed her way past, but no one attempted to bar her entrance to the hallowed portals. Ravensworth, only a few seconds behind Briony, did not meet with such a mild reception. Nothing would induce his peers to listen to his feeble excuses for being admitted out of turn. He was relegated to last in line, where he remained fuming and cursing at the inexcusable impetuosity of the ingenuous lady.

Briony's reception by the three ladies who were holding court was, to say the least of it, chilly. The Vision, who had been so solicitous as a nurse, forbade her to speak until the box was cleared of her sisters and the frankly curious gentlemen. When the lady turned at last to look upon Briony, her eyes were sparkling with anger. Briony opened her mouth, but the lady held up a forbidding hand. The voice which addressed Briony vibrated with outrage.

"So! You have discovered me, and think to throw away your own reputation by being seen in my company! Perhaps you thought that my sisters and I would be overcome by such condescension? How dare you! If you care so little of your own good name, at least have a care for mine!"

"I don't understand," stuttered Briony.

"What you have done, little lady, is to jeopardize my

position, such as it is, in Society. Do you think I wish it to be said that Harriette Wilson has taken to corrupting the morals of young, innocent girls? I should be ostracized by all my friends, and rightly so."

"I never thought . . . I never meant . . . " began Briony horrified.

"That is obvious. I suppose that you are going to tell me that you meant well?"

Briony nodded miserably.

"'She meant well,'" continued the voice icily. "How much plain spitefulness and busybodying is concealed in that alarming epithet. Did it never occur to you once to consider how others might be affected by your rash impulse? Your behavior has been inexcusable!"

"I have been so stupid." Briony swallowed. "I never thought to embarrass you."

The voice softened. "Perhaps something can be contrived. Where is your escort? Is it Ravensworth?"

Amid the howls of protest of the impatient swains at the door, Ravensworth was finally admitted. Briony stole a glance at him and quickly looked away. His expression was murderous.

"Lord Ravensworth," said Harriette Wilson sternly, "permit me to give you some advice. You will ensure that this young lady is removed from town until such time as the scandal has died down. I take leave to tell you that not only have my sisters and I been deeply embarrassed by her unwarranted conduct, but her friends, if she should have any willing to admit to that name by tomorrow morning, will find themselves in the same pass. Perhaps, in a few months' time, this deplorable indiscretion will be forgiven and forgotten, but until such time, it were better that this young woman be kept out of harm's way."

"Sc—scandal?" Briony asked on a tremulous note.

"Do you think that this latest folly has gone unremarked?" demanded Ravensworth cuttingly. "By this time tomorrow, your name will be on the lips of every low-bred roué and voluptuary in London. These are not men of honor, Briony, believe me! I know them. By your conduct tonight you have indicated that you are available for the taking!" Briony shrank from the savagery in his voice, as much as from the words he was saying. His hand reached out to grasp her wrist. "Look around you!" he said implacably. He pulled her closer to his side. "Look at them gawking!"

Briony cast a fearful glance over the dress circle and orchestra pit. She saw with horror that Ravensworth spoke the truth. A sea of opera glasses in the hands of the more flamboyant dandies and boisterous young bucks was riveted to the box they were occupying.

"Look at you," he went on with a sneer. "Your hair, your conduct, everything about you proclaims you, in their eyes, a woman of easy virtue."

Briony shrank from him.

There was a commotion at the door and Harriet burst breathlessly into the box. She took in Ravensworth and Briony at a glance and her eyes glittered belligerently.

"Let her go, Ravensworth!" she commanded, her voice shaking with anger. His hands dropped to his sides and Briony ran to the safety of Harriet's arms. She began to sob softly.

"Oh no," groaned his lordship in disbelief. "Now there are two of them! I don't believe that this is happening to me. What have I ever done to offend the gods?"

Harriette Wilson laid her hand on Ravensworth's sleeve. "May I suggest that you escort these young ladies home before they cause a riot?" Her eyes sparkled with suppressed amusement.

Ravensworth returned her smile wanly. "I apologize

for the intrusion, ma'am." He held the door open and a weeping Briony clinging to a bellicose Harriet slunk past him.

"A moment, Ravensworth." He turned back to the lady. Her words were for his ears only. "Be kind to the child. I like her."

Chapter 10

It was a chastened Aunt Sophy who sat with shoulders slumped in abject wretchedness as Lord Ravensworth, in high dudgeon, enumerated the besetting sins of her scapegrace nieces. She winced as much from his brutal tone as from the damning words.

Briony listened with only half an ear. She had a strong suspicion that his lordship was relishing his role as moral arbitrator and was by no means displeased to have the opportunity of taking her down a peg or two. She sat stiffly in one corner of a long sofa paying him scant attention. Her mind turned to the details of the ignominious evening, of how Ravensworth had hustled them out of the theater halfway through the performance as if they had been deranged criminals.

She stole a quick glance to the other corner of the sofa, where her cousin sat weeping softly. Lord Avery, who had stationed himself close to Harriet, proffered his handkerchief. Harriet dabbed ineffectually at her watery eyes. Her fit of bravado in the opera box when confronted by the spectacle of an irate Ravensworth menacing her beloved cousin had, by this time, evaporated. Harriet was acutely conscious that in some unspecified way which she could not fathom she had failed Briony and the thought made her inconsolable. For her own place in society, Miss Harriet Grenfell cared not a brass button, but that her cousin should forfeit the good opinion of the ton through ignorance or an ingenuous disregard for propriety was more than she could bear.

It was poor Harriet's sudden collapse which had put some starch into Briony's spine. She would not cower like some poor-spirited creature. To be chastised for embarrassing a lady of Harriette Wilson's gentle disposition would have been just and accepted without demur. But to have her character held up to ridicule for merely inhaling the odd pinch of snuff, imbibing the *very* infrequent glass of wine, and being caught out smoking on only *one* occasion was intolerable meddling on the haughty nobleman's part. Tittletattler, thought Briony sourly, as she glanced forebodingly in his direction.

Briony looked approvingly at Lord Avery as he reassuringly patted Harriet's hand. That nobleman was more truly the gentleman, for his manner had been everything that was solicitous. It had been he who had escorted the ladies home, having been instructed curtly by Ravensworth to await his pleasure in Half Moon Street. Briony conjectured that the impatient Adèle must needs be attended to first. With unmaidenly curiosity, she speculated about the lady's relationship to Ravensworth. No doubt the aristocratic lady would find favor with His Grace, the Duke. I'm sure I wish them happy, thought Briony magnanimously. She sniffed, and the wrinkle on her brow deepened to a frown.

"But Lord Ravensworth," Lady Sophy interjected timidly when his lordship's harangue appeared to be coming to an end, "these are merely high-spirited pranks. Perhaps I have been somewhat remiss in my vigilance as a chaperone, but now that I am apprised of the facts of the case, I shall endeavor to do better." She gave him a tremulous smile.

"Madam," he intoned as though he were lecturing a

backward child, "it is too late to make amends. These 'ladies,' for want of a better word, have become too hot for London to hold! Their ill-considered conduct has put them beyond the pale! This evening's imbroglio was the final straw." His lordship's voice, if anything, became more heated. "They forced, yes, forced their way in, uninvited, to Harriette Wilson's private box. I see by your blushes, ma'am, that you are acquainted with the lady's name. Would to God that these delinquent rapscallions," he said fiercely, riveting the cousins with his piercing blue eyes, "I beg your pardon, would to God that these gently bred females had mastered the maidenly blush!" His voice dripped with sarcasm.

Harriet' shoulders shook even harder, but Briony gritted her teeth and sat up a little straighter in her place.

Aunt Sophy swallowed but went on with dogged persistence, "Does—does this mean, my lord, that the girls have ruined their chances of gaining admittance to Almack's?"

There was a shocked silence, broken only by Harriet's irregular breathing.

"Almack's?" roared Ravensworth, striking his fist forcefully to his head. "Almack's? I beg leave to tell you, madam, that the only place where these 'ladies' will be welcomed is the bed of every licentious libertine in town."

Aunt Sophy's eyes dilated in horror. She emitted a long, sobbing wail and fell back against the cushions in a swoon. "My vinaigrette," she whispered hoarsely, her hand clutching convulsively at her throat. Harriet bounded up and bolted from the room. Avery went after her.

"Now see what you've done!" said Briony, choking with anger as she bent over her aunt to slap her wrists. "Did you have to enact us a Cheltenham tragedy? You have no right, sir, to ring such a peal over poor Aunt Sophy. Nor does your conduct in the past toward me entitle you to pass yourself off as a pattern card of rectitude. You, sir, are a hypocrite!" Briony saw the twinkle in his eyes and turned away primly to give her attention to her swooning aunt. "There, there, Aunt Sophy, do not take on so! Lord Ravensworth exaggerates. Miss Harriette Wilson is a most unexceptionable lady. You would like her!" Aunt Sophy fainted in earnest. Ravensworth sat down holding his head between his hands, but whether in horror or laughter, Briony could not tell.

Harriet returned in a moment and held the vinaigrette under Lady Sophy's nose. The lady came to herself with a shudder. "It is the Grenfell blood," she moaned softly. "I should have known better than to think it had missed a generation. Like father like son, like mother like daughter."

"What Grenfell blood?" asked Ravensworth, thinking the lady's mind had become unhinged.

"The girls are tainted," Lady Sophy lamented as if she had not heard him. "It's in the blood, you see. I warned my niece, your mother dear," she said, turning to Harriet. "I warned her to have nothing to do with John Grenfell. We Woodwards have always been most circumspect in our manners and morals, while the Grenfells never cared a fig for propriety. The duels he fought! The high flyers he had in his keeping! But your dear mother would have him— and see what has come of it!" She looked mournfully at Harriet.

"My father?" asked Harriet, her tears suddenly arrested by Lady Sophy's shocking disclosure. "I don't believe it. Why, he is so straitlaced, so sanctimonious. Do you tell me that Papa was . . . a rake?" She giggled nervously at the thought.

"Well, not latterly, of course, but his reputation, to put it mildly, was not quite the thing before he wed your mother—a long time ago, I grant you. Oh Harriet dear, it's in your blood." She groped for her vinaigrette once more.

"What did I tell you?" said Avery in an amused aside to Ravensworth.

"And Miss Langland's mother?" inquired Ravensworth blandly.

"Oh—even worse! They were known as the Scapegrace Grenfells. There was no tomfoolery that the tear-away Jane Grenfell would not dare! She had a veritable talent for mischief—but how could she help it with that knave of a brother as her guardian? He encouraged her! It pains me to tell you, Briony, but your mother was not received in the best drawing rooms. Not that she cared. She snapped her fingers at the world and went her own way."

Briony was scandalized. "Do you tell me, Aunt Sophy, that my mother was licentious?"

"Not in the way you mean! Of course not! But . . . well . . . how can I put it? She was a headstrong gel inclined to wildness. Why, she got herself compromised and *had* to marry your father!"

"My father?" asked Briony dumbfounded. She looked bleakly at Harriet and the two girls moved closer for comfort.

"Never could understand that," mused Lady Sophy aloud. "Graeme Langland's deportment was always of the first stare. A gentleman in every sense of the word! But he compromised your mother—no getting round it, and her brother, Sir John, compelled him to marry her. Of course, by that time Sir John was married himself and had become quite respectable."

"But—but Mama was always so proper . . . so dignified . . . so ladylike."

"Daresay she was, in later years. But I assure you, she and Sir John were the talk of the town. When they got shackled, everybody called it 'The Taming of the Grenfells.' Matrimony can do that, you know—reform even the worst of characters."

Ravensworth suppressed a chuckle, and glanced at Briony. He caught the cool, speculative look in her eye and raised his brows quizzically. He gave her a sly wink and smiled broadly when she bristled.

"That's the solution!" exclaimed Aunt Sophy in sudden inspiration. All eyes rested on her with expectant interest.

The color came flooding back to her cheeks. When she spoke, her voice became quite animated. "Of course! Don't you see?" She sat up stiffly in her chair. "The girls must marry as soon as possible! Sir John will arrange it. They must leave for Bath at once. Tomorrow! We shall send for your brother, Briony, and have him escort you! I, of course, shall remain in town. I am too old to travel, and I really could not bear to have my sanctimonious nephew ring a peal over me. In some ways," she added apologetically, "I liked him better as a rake."

"A moment, please," interposed Ravensworth smoothly. "No need to send for young Vernon. He is too inexperienced for such a task. Why, these girls would have him twisted round their thumbs before they reached Kensington. May Lord Avery and I offer our services, Lady Sophy? This is a labor for men, if not for Hercules himself." He smiled condescendingly at Briony. "I put my carriage at your disposal. We shall escort the ladies, and with the presence of an abigail, I believe the proprieties shall be observed?"

Briony seethed with resentment. "Marry us off as soon as possible. Be conveyed to Bath like criminals under the escort of guards! I'll not hear of it! We are not your wards, my lord," she said tartly to Ravensworth. "Harriet, tell him."

"Briony, what's the use? The moment you entered

Harriette Wilson's box, I knew what the end would be," Harriet replied, the fight gone out of her.

"Enough!" commanded an austere Lady Sophy. "My mind is resolved! I thank you for your generous offer, Lord Ravensworth, and I accept. Shall we say ten o'clock tomorrow morning?"

"No. Eight o'clock is preferable, I think. By ten, every roué in town will be beating a path to your door." He smiled malevolently. "One valise only, ladies, if you please! Even if it means you must marry your prospective husbands in your shifts." Briony gave him the "cool appraisal." Quite undaunted, his lordship surreptitiously chucked her under the chin.

Briony pushed open the door to Harriet's chamber and entered. "I saw the light," she said with a smile of apology, "and decided to investigate."

Harriet was sitting on the edge of her bed listlessly brushing her golden locks. She put aside the brush at Briony's entrance. "Briony," she said with a catch in her voice, "I promised Mama that I would take care of you. I can't tell you how sorry I am that I have failed so lamentably." She had no more tears to cry, but she sniffed miserably into a damp handkerchief which was crushed tightly in her fist.

Briony quickly crossed the room and gathered the desolate girl into her arms. "Harriet! Harriet! Shame on you, you poor-spirited creature! Don't hang your head so, you wretched girl! Do I look as if I need mothering? You have not failed me, cousin!" She gave her a slight shake. "My dear, you did not really think, did you, that I would conform to the ways of the beau monde?"

Harriet raised her head and looked into her cousin's

reassuring eyes. "But if you are ostracized from society, if people won't receive you, you will be ruined."

"Nonsense!" said Briony brusquely. "I am an heiress to a considerable competence. In one year I reach my majority and may do whatever I like. You don't imagine for a moment that I wish to marry one of the fribbles I have been introduced to and let my fortune pass out of my control?"

Harriet's sniffing ceased abruptly. She looked disbelievingly into her cousin's eyes. She met her steady gaze and after a moment rewarded her with a faint smile. "You truly don't mind?"

"I truly don't mind for myself," amended Briony truthfully. "But it grieves me to think that I may have caused you pain. Harriet, do you want to cut a dash in Society? Tell me frankly if I have ruined your chances of gaining the good opinion of the ton."

Harriet looked incredulous. "The good opinion of the ton? You must know how little I crave such a questionable distinction for myself! I have never given a button for the inscrutable ways of my so-called betters."

"Then why so dismal? Surely not on my behalf? Can't you see that we are of one mind? Why do you wish for me what I, too, despise?"

Harriet's expressive face showed first surprise and then relief. She giggled. "Briony," she breathed on a whisper, "do you think that it is in our blood?"

"It's possible," said Briony, her voice edged with humor, "but I am a scapegrace by conviction, not merely by ties of blood."

Harriet gurgled at some fleeting recollection. "The scapegrace Grenfells," she said with a knowing smile.

"The tear-away twins!"

"The conniving cousins!"

"The mischievous maidens!"

"The lamentable ladies!"

"The wayward women!"

Two pairs of eyes twinkled in wry amusement.

"Harriet," said Briony mischievously, "does this mean that we can share the occasional, very occasional, pinch of snuff in the privacy of our boudoir?"

Without a word, the elder girl retrieved a mother-of-pearl snuffbox from the drawer of a dresser and presented it to her cousin with a flourish.

With the elegant movements of long practice, Briony offered the snuffbox to her bright-eyed cousin. "Would you care to partake?" she drawled. Harriet said that she would be delighted.

The girls went on in this lighthearted vein for the better part of an hour. Briony was deeply grateful to see Harriet regain some of her former sparkle. When the subject of packing their valises for the morrow's journey was broached, however, they became more sober.

"I don't look forward to meeting up with Mama and Papa," said Harriet gloomily.

"What can they do to us?" asked Briony airily. "We have done no wrong. They can't eat us."

"Oh can't they!" replied Harriet, her voice full of foreboding.

Briony shrugged. "No matter, we have each other, and Lord Avery's presence, for you at least, must be of some consolation."

"And what of Lord Ravensworth?" asked Harriet archly, subjecting Briony to a penetrating appraisal.

Briony shook her head. "He must be endured, I suppose. But I have no intention of allowing his lordship to dictate terms to me. We are going to Bath. This is an adventure, Harriet, and I intend to enjoy every minute of it."

Harriet blinked. After a moment's reflection, she

nodded her assent. "You are right, Briony, as usual. We have done nothing to be ashamed of. I won't be cowed by a collection of spiteful gossipmongers. We shall weather this together."

"By the way, Harriet," said Briony in a confidential undertone as she prepared to take her leave, "you will remember to pack your snuffbox, won't you, dear? I haven't had time as yet to acquire a supply of snuff for my own use."

Harriet's eyes grew round with wonder. Startled blue eyes looked into unwavering gray. Briony winked and a slow smile suffused Harriet's face.

"Cousin," said Harriet with perfect comprehension, "you may depend on me."

Chapter 11

It was, his lordship had informed them before going downstairs to bespeak their dinner, the best inn that the town had to offer. If the truth were told, thought Briony dolefully, it was the only inn that the village boasted—if one could call one indifferent row of houses by such a grand name. While other more fortunate travelers rested their weary bones in the comfort of the soft feather beds of The Castle, Ravensworth had seen fit to quarter his party in a picturesque but diminutive hostelry—more like a large cottage—in an insignificant hamlet a good ten miles from the thriving metropolis of Marlborough. He wished, he said, to protect the girls' reputations, such as they were, from the vulgarly curious and there was less likelihood of running into acquaintances in the more out-of-the-way places.

The door to the private parlor was thrown open and Ravensworth strode in. He looked inquiringly around the room. "All alone, Miss Langland? Where are your companions?

Briony, with the proper degree of civility but little warmth in her voice, explained that Lord Avery and Harriet were taking a turn about the yard. "For Lord Avery thought that after the tedious ride in the closed carriage a breath of fresh air might revive Harriet's spirits somewhat."

Ravensworth digested this piece of information in silence for a moment, then crossed to the crackling fire. He extended his hands and rubbed them together. Briony gave her attention to the out-of-date copy of the *Times* on her lap.

"No need to ask if you are suffering from low spirits, Miss Langland," he began affably, turning to warm his back at the blaze. "Nothing, I know, throws you off your stride."

Briony heard the rebuke behind his words and favored him with a slight inclination of the head. "As you say, my lord."

He took the chair facing Briony's and eased himself comfortably back against the cushions. He withdrew an unadorned silver snuffbox from his coat pocket and tapped on the lid absently. A light kindled in Briony's eyes and Ravensworth, on noting it, spoke roughly. "Do not be fool enough to think I shall invite you to join me, my girl. You do not object, I hope, if I enjoy this solitary pleasure?"

Briony signified that he might do whatever he wished, and gave her attention to her paper. After a few moments, Ravensworth again broke the silence between them. "Miss Langland—Briony, satisfy my curiosity, if you would be so kind."

Briony gave him a questioning look and waited.

"I am truly interested in your assessment of what has transpired. Your present situation cannot be a happy one for you. Yet here you are quite unruffled, coolly catching up on yesterday's news as if you hadn't a care in the world. Are you not sorry to have plunged yourself and your cousin into such a deplorable predicament?"

Briony gave him one of her steady gazes. "I see no harm in any of my actions, my lord. If my conscience were troubled, that would be a different matter. In that situation, I would have no peace until I had made amends. But do not think to see me hang my head over a minor transgression of the proprieties. To such absurd flummery I am impervious."

Ravensworth grunted and felt the bile rise in his throat. "Have you no sense, girl, of what is fitting? Your conduct has been sadly lacking in what is becoming in a young woman of taste and propriety. To put it bluntly, Miss Langland, you have brought this disgrace upon yourself."

"Fiddle," interrupted Briony, her temper flaring at the injustice of his remarks. She dashed the newspaper in her hand to the floor. "Disgrace? What wrong have I done? That I have forfeited the good opinion of a class of society that I despise I am willing to concede. Is it wrong to recognize a lady who showed me such singular kindness? I admit that it was unthinking of me to embarrass Miss Wilson at the opera but that was through ignorance not malice." Her voice vibrated with contempt. "This is an upside-down world, my lord, when a Christian lady is condemned out of hand for doing nothing less than her duty but a so-called gentleman of honor is permitted to offer carte blanche to a respectable girl with impunity."

"Have no fears on that head, Miss Langland," said Ravensworth cuttingly. "It has been in my mind long since to withdraw my original offer."

"How dare you, sir!" Briony cried out, starting to her feet. "Do you say that you wish me to renew my offer?" asked Ravensworth in feigned astonishment, looking up at her wrathful face.

She saw that he was mocking her, holding her up to ridicule, and her whole body quivered with suppressed anger. "You know that I do not," she replied in outraged dignity. "I have endeavored, I hope, to make my sentiments perfectly plain on that subject. Your mode of life, your conduct, is completely distasteful to me." Her lip curled unconsciously. "In short, my lord, the man I give myself to will not be one of your ilk."

This last statement brought an angry flush to his lordship's neck. He rose unhurriedly and took a menacing step toward her. Briony retreated until her shaking hands grasped the edge of the high dresser at her back. She steadied herself against it.

He came to her without haste, and with affected negligence leaned one hand on either side of her. His expression was coolly impassive but Briony dimly realized that it masked some deeper emotion. She detected the faint odor of his cologne and averted her head to avoid its unsettling effect. His nearness was intimidating, discomposing, and she could feel her cheeks grow warm. Her breathing became labored and she parted her lips to draw air.

When he spoke, his voice was devoid of all emotion. "Touché, Briony. That last remark was calculated to wound, was it not? And now that you have succeeded in your laudable objective, why so craven? Pray continue. You will not give yourself to a man of my ilk is where, I collect, you left off."

Briony's eyes flickered to the door and she wondered with a feeling compounded of fear and reluctance if she ought at least to try to escape her captor. Ravensworth's voice, deceptively soft close to her ear, warned her against the attempt. "Don't even think it!" His hand caught her chin and turned her face till she was forced to look up at him. "Tell me about a man of my ilk, Briony," he said mildly. "I want to hear."

She would be honest if he killed her for it, she decided. "You are not a man of honor, my lord," she began, trembling at her own audacity. "Nor are you consistent. You chastise me for a trifling want of propriety, yet you thought it proper in me to become your mistress. You cared nothing for my happiness or my family's peace of mind. You thought only of your own selfish gratification. The man I give myself to will be the man I marry. He will be—"

"'The man I give myself to,'" mimicked his lordship derisively. "Listen to me, Miss Briony Langland. The man you give yourself to will be me or you will give yourself to no man." His tone gentled. "Don't you understand anything at all, you foolish girl?" He bent his head to her face, his gaze lingering on every feature, and Briony felt his breath warm against her temple. "Briony?" he murmured hoarsely, as if asking her permission for something.

Although she was not afraid of him, she recognized vaguely that he posed some kind of threat, and that if she allowed him to make love to her, there would be, could be, no turning back. She hesitated. His lips brushed her eyes and Briony's will to resist him weakened. Her pulse quickened and she could feel the familiar tingling sensation as it began its slow spread from the pit of her stomach. Her breath came in ragged, uneven gasps. She noted her symptoms with a peculiar detachment as if she were a doctor observing the onslaught of some illness in a patient.

"Briony?" His voice was gently persuasive and it stirred something deep within her. Her sigh was a curious blend of resignation and anticipation. She turned her face up to invite his kiss. Strong arms pulled her close and his mouth covered hers with tantalizing gentleness. Without thinking, she arched into him, fitting her curves snugly to the planes of his lean frame. Her arms crossed behind his neck. Kissing Hugh Montgomery, thought Briony dizzily, was the most splendid pleasure that she had ever experienced.

He drew away from her with some reluctance and Briony was disappointed.

"Tell me what you are thinking!" he said huskily, his eyes devouring her.

She sighed languidly. "I am thinking that I like kissing you better than anything."

"Better than your passion for snuff?" he asked with a tease in his voice.

She gave him a superior smile. "When I take snuff, only my nose tingles. When you kiss me, the tingling develops into a positive quake."

Her answer seemed to please his lordship immensely. He bent his head to kiss her again and Briony felt the anticipation within her grow to an insatiable longing.

"*Now* tell me what you are thinking," he asked at last.

Her voice was dreamy. "I want more."

"More what?" he murmured provocatively against her hair.

Briony tried to focus her thoughts. She could not say with any certainty what it was that she wanted. But she knew that only he had this strange power to stir her to an intoxicating delirium. "I don't know . . . More of you," she replied, impatiently pulling his head down to hers.

"My darling girl," he said unsteadily before lowering his lips to claim hers. "I want *all* of you."

She could hear his heart beating close to her ribs, racing as erratically as her own. There was a new urgency, a hunger in his mouth as he lowered it to explore the contours of her throat and the soft swell of her breasts. A wild excitement surged through Briony. Ravensworth felt her response and his touch grew more ardent, more possessive, willing her, compelling her to yield to him with unrestrained abandon. Briony became suddenly afraid, confused, and she strained back, searching his face for reassurance. "Tell me what you are thinking," she said breathlessly, trying to read the expression in his half-hooded eyes.

"What I am thinking, my bewitching wench," groaned the unwary gentleman with devastating candor, "is that if I do not bed you soon, I shall become demented."

Briony's lashes fluttered as she assimilated what Ravensworth's words might portend. On feeling her slight withdrawal, his lordship became suddenly aware into what quagmire his unguarded tongue had led him. He tried to retrieve his position.

"Briony, no! You mistake my meaning. I mean you no dishonor. You must know what I intend for your future."

Her cheeks stained scarlet and unshed tears stood brightly in her eyes. She pulled back in an effort to disengage herself from Ravensworth's clasp. "Pray, say no more," she said stiffly. "My wits must have gone a-begging." She essayed a shaky laugh. "I know what manner of man you are. I am at fault for permitting you to take such liberties. This is madness. I am a stranger to myself." She shook her head as if to clear her mind of some derangement. "There can be no place in my life for a man of your character," she went on in a sob. "We are like oil and water." She made a desperate effort to pull away from him. "Turn me loose!" she commanded, the tears spilling over at last.

"Briony, listen to me. I beg your forgiveness. . . "

Sounds of rapid footsteps could be heard on the stairs.

"Hell and damnation!" swore Ravensworth harshly. He released her abruptly and turned back to the fire, striking a casual pose. A flushed Harriet burst into the room. One look at the angry sparkle in the lady's eyes told her companions that the walk with Avery had restored more than her spirits. Avery came racing into the parlor a moment behind her.

With studied composure, Harriet picked up the abandoned *Times* and settled herself in one of the chairs flanking the fireplace. She opened it with a violent rustle and made a pretense of reading it. Avery smiled sheepishly at the others.

Dinner, although far better fare than they had anticipated in such an unpretentiously outfitted establishment, proved to be an embarrassingly silent meal. It was with a sense of relief for all concerned when the ladies finally excused themselves and left the gentlemen to the best brandy the house had to offer.

When the gentlemen were alone, Ravensworth cocked an inquisitive eyebrow. "Well?" he asked.

"Catastrophe!" responded Avery glumly.

"She refused you?"

"Oh no, she accepted me." Lord Avery laughed mirthlessly. "I expect that she will fling my offer in my teeth tomorrow morning."

"Then what went wrong?"

Lord Avery pondered. He sighed. He looked shiftily at Ravensworth. "From something I said, Harriet formed the opinion—a mistaken one, I take leave to tell you—that I blamed her cousin Briony entirely for the pass they are in."

"She is wholly to blame!" Ravensworth growled savagely, drinking back his brandy in one gulp. "You don't offend me by saying so! She has no notion of how to go on in Society! Like mother, like daughter, I don't doubt. Her father should have beaten her more often when she was a child."

"From what I hear, it isn't likely that she was beaten at all."

"That can be soon mended," Ravensworth threatened. He refilled his glass and emptied it almost on the instant.

"D'you still mean to have her?" asked Avery, studiously examining the diamond ring on his finger.

"If I can persuade her, and I shall," responded Ravensworth gloomily as if the thought of winning the lady gave him no pleasure at all.

"You know she will make your life hell."

"I can handle her," said Ravensworth recklessly, the effects of the brandy imbuing him with false confidence. "Should we make our home in the jungles of darkest Africa," he added in an attempt at levity, "I am sure that Briony and Society will rub along together quite tolerably."

Lord Avery smiled. "Harriet wouldn't like that. She dotes on the girl. If you don't mind my saying so, Ravensworth, I don't think Briony is good for Harriet."

"My dear boy," said Ravensworth cordially, "no need to persuade me. Briony isn't good for anybody. She creates murder and mayhem wherever she goes. Look at me. Until I met her, I was a reasonable sort of chap, wouldn't you say?" he asked rhetorically. "Rarely in a foul temper, good company when my friends came to call? I hadn't a care in the world. Yes," he said reflectively as if he were nostalgically remembering the golden days of his youth, "life was uncomplicated then. I enjoyed the occasional dalliance with the bolder beauties of questionable virtue—what man doesn't? My mistake was in letting my eye fall on a virtuous, mild-mannered miss. Be warned by my fall from grace, Avery," he commanded, striving for sobriety. "She's got me so addled," he added on a more ill-humored note, "that I don't know right from wrong anymore. The only time I feel half sensible is when I'm completely insensible in my cups."

"I'll drink to that," replied Avery punctiliously, holding his glass out for Ravensworth to refill from the half-empty bottle.

Two bottles of brandy later, the stupefied gentlemen assisted each other to ascend the staircase, which they swore had become inexplicably steeper. They fell into their respective beds fully clothed, not even remembering to remove their mud-spattered topboots. Denby, thought his lordship hazily, was, thankfully, not present to witness his master's disgrace.

Chapter 12

The next morning dawned gray and threatening, "a day for lying a-bed," the landlord brazenly informed the ladies with a sly wink as he presented them with a note in Ravensworth's bold script. The curt scrawl intimated that their lordships did not expect to join the ladies before noon since both were feeling a trifle under the weather.

The cousins were not deceived. They had been wakened in the night by the unholy revels of Lords Ravensworth and Avery as they had beat an unsteady path to their chambers. That the gentlemen might be suffering the after-effects of the previous evening's gross intemperance brought a grim smile of satisfaction to the cousins' lips, for while Ravensworth and Avery had freely indulged themselves in the port and brandy, they had denied even a drop of anything stronger than ratafia to the girls. Such cavalier treatment was not calculated to please.

"Poetic justice!" remarked Briony to Harriet, quickly scanning the few remaining lines of the short epistle. Ravensworth had added a caveat warning the ladies in the strongest possible terms to remain out of the public eye (and harm's way) in their private parlor until such time as they were ready to continue their journey. Their abigail—underlined heavily several times—was to be in their company at all times to act as their chaperone. It was impossible, however, to comply with this last gratuitous impertinence since Alice had wakened that morning with a raging fever and could not rise from her bed.

When the girls had finished their meager breakfast of toast and hot chocolate, leaving the congealing kippers, ham, and scrambled eggs for the gentlemen to consume at their leisure, they repaired to their chamber, where Alice lay tossing and turning on the small trestle bed which had been set up to observe the proprieties in the bedroom the ladies shared. As was to be expected, Lords Ravensworth and Avery had the luxury of their own private chambers.

Briony saw at a glance how severely the poor girl was suffering and insisted that she be moved at once to her own larger, more comfortable bed. Harriet was left to look after this office while Briony went in search of the landlord to solicit a bowl of thin gruel and a cup of hot tea for the invalid. That she had to disregard Ravensworth's injunction to remain out of the public rooms troubled her a little, but she reasoned that it would be positively heathenish not to do all that she could to alleviate the poor girl's distress.

For most of the morning, the ladies took turns ministering to their hapless maid. The threatening storm broke over them and the rain came down in torrents so that Harriet and Briony could not relieve the monotony of their vigil, even if they had wished to, by taking a turn in the yard, notwithstanding Ravensworth's instructions. When Alice fell into a deep slumber, however, Briony passed the time in washing the dust of their journey from her hair and she left it to dry loosely around her shoulders. For some reason, Ravensworth strongly objected to Briony's unbound tresses and she had taken pains while under his lordship's escort to dress it modestly in a smooth coil at the nape of her neck. With Ravensworth indisposed and keeping to his bed, however, Briony grew bold.

By late afternoon, and still no sign of the gentlemen, it became evident that Alice's condition had worsened and a doctor must needs be summoned. This was not as simple a matter as would have been the case under normal circumstances since the storm, which gave no sign of letting up, had made the dirt roads well-nigh impassable and the inn had been filling up with travelers bent on finding a place to rack up for the night before they were stranded in some deserted stretch of road. Briony was deputized in the absence of their lordships to go in search of their coachman and instruct him to find a physician.

She stood irresolutely on the half landing listening to the hilarity that issued from the public dining room. From the ribald phrases that came to her ears, it was evident that a party of young bucks had taken over the ground floor of the establishment and were intent on making a night of it. Not a lackey was in sight to do her bidding. It was too bad of Ravensworth, she thought, her ire rising, to leave them in such straits.

She made her way to his chamber and rattled on the door. "Ravensworth!" she called as loudly as she dared. "Ravensworth! Get up, I tell you!" Nothing happened. She tried the door. Finding it unlocked, she opened it a crack. "Ravensworth!" she hissed irately. "Ravensworth, will you get up? We need a doctor for Alice. If you don't get up, I myself shall go and fetch him."

Ravensworth stirred. He opened one eye and groaned with the exertion of it. "Go away!" he said weakly. "I can't help you. Can't you see I am near death? Do as you see fit."

Briony's anger came to a hot boil. She slammed the

door shut and for good measure shook the loose door handle till it rattled. When she heard Ravensworth's weak moans, her lips pursed with malevolent pleasure. In high dudgeon, she marched boldly down the stairs, her hair flying in all directions, and went in search of the elusive landlord. When she found him in the kitchen, she told him tartly to find his lordship's coachman and send him to his lordship's private parlor forthwith. The startled host did not recognize the lady and gaped disbelievingly at the vision with the golden cascade of hair, the sparkling eyes, and the heaving bosom, and wondered to which fortunate gentleman the stunning bit of muslin might belong.

Briony retraced her steps with dignity, beginning to believe that Ravensworth's fears for the safety of an unchaperoned lady in a public place were unfounded. Her progress, she believed, had gone quite unremarked. In this, Briony was mistaken.

When she reached the first landing, her way was barred by a foppish gentleman of an age with Ravensworth. He was leaning nonchalantly against the doorjamb rearranging the folds of his cravat. Briony hesitated, but when she saw that the gentleman's interest was not fixed on her person, she attempted to pass him with her eyes demurely downcast. "I beg your pardon," she said, waiting patiently for the gentleman to remove himself.

He straightened slowly and gave her a measuring look. "Miss Langland?" he asked in a slow drawl. "Miss Briony Langland, is it not?"

Briony looked questioningly into his eyes but what she read there made her cheeks flame uncomfortably. "I do not know you, sir," she replied, her voice as cool as ice.

"I should be happy to rectify that omission," responded the gentleman smoothly. "We have a mutual acquaintance, I collect."

"Yes?" asked Briony, a trifle out of breath.

The gentleman gave her a knowing smile. "Miss Harriette Wilson. I was in her box the other night when you graced it with your presence. Harriette did not introduce us—a regrettable oversight. I am Reginald Overton, Earl of Grafton, your devoted servant, ma'am." His voice caressed her.

"Miss Wilson has done me a great service, sir," said Briony stiffly as she tried to edge her way past. There was something unsavory, something overly bold in the way his eyes swept her figure. Briony cringed.

The gentleman drew nearer and Briony could feel his hateful breath on her cheek. "Damn, but you're a taking little thing," he said huskily, reaching out to stroke her hair. Briony recoiled, but he caught her shoulders and drew her inexorably into his arms.

For a moment she was too surprised, too frightened to resist, but when his hot lips covered hers in a smothering embrace, she threw her head back with a sob. He laughed softly and would have drawn her through the door into what she now recognized as a bedchamber—*his* bedchamber. Sheer panic gave Briony the strength to fight him off. He bent to kiss her again and she bit down hard on his lip. Grafton yelped, but before he had time to recover, Briony brought a high-heeled shoe viciously down on his foot and pushed against his chest with all her might. The gentleman staggered back with an oath and Briony kicked off her shoes and took off up the next short flight of stairs.

She did not hesitate for an instant. She knew instinctively where safety lay and she made for it like a homing pigeon. She passed the door to her own bedchamber and to Avery's room and made straight for Ravensworth. Grafton was hard on her heels. Gasping for breath, she flung Ravensworth's door open and threw herself sobbing with relief into his lordship's arms.

Ravensworth, to say the least of it, was dumbfounded. After Briony had left, her words had slowly penetrated his consciousness and he had been instantly restored to sobriety. He had poured a pitcher of cold water over his head into a basin and was frantically buttoning his shirt when Briony rushed in. His arms clasped the frightened girl firmly to his side. When he looked to the open door, he recognized the Earl framed against it. Grafton took a step into the room, and Briony clung closer to Ravensworth's protecting arms.

The Marquess's eyes narrowed as he took in the blood dripping on Grafton's chin and the blood-spattered neckcloth. The Earl dabbed at the tear on his lip with his handkerchief and did not mark the dangerous glint in Ravensworth's eyes.

"You did not tell me, Miss Langland," said the Earl in a note of aggrievement, "that you were with Ravensworth. We might have come to some arrangement. We might still, with Ravensworth's consent, of course."

Briony was at a loss to understand the Earl's words, but the Marquess understood their sinister meaning perfectly. He stood a reluctant Briony away from him over her protests and advanced on the unwary lord. Briony heard the crack but never saw what happened. Ravensworth, breathing hard, was bending over a prostrate and dazed Lord Grafton.

"If you touch the lady again," said Ravensworth in the gentlest tone Briony had ever heard in him, "I shall kill you. If you wish satisfaction, name your weapons, name your seconds."

The sullen Earl threw a look of suppressed fury at his attacker. He sat nursing his jaw. "How was I to know," he asked peevishly, "that the lady was under your protection?"

"Ravensworth," said Briony, a glimmer of under-standing beginning to penetrate her brain. "Lord Grafton saw me in company of Harriette Wilson. If we explain everything to him . . ."

"Hush, Briony!" replied Ravensworth testily.

The unsteady Earl got to his knees, then to his feet.

"You owe the lady an apology, Grafton," said Ravensworth with a concealed threat in his voice.

Briony spoke again. "Ravensworth," she said severely, "explain our situation to Lord Grafton."

"Explain what, my love?" asked Ravensworth, looking at her with a curiously blank expression.

Briony frowned at the endearment but chose to ignore it. "Tell him, sir, that my abigail travels with us, that we are chaperoned, and that there is no impropriety in our conduct."

"You heard the lady," responded Ravensworth dutifully. Grafton's sneer was ill concealed. "I apologize, Miss Langland, for my impetuous conduct. I had entirely mistaken the situation." He retreated cautiously to the door. "I beg you will excuse my intrusion, Ravensworth? A natural error in judgment, I think you will agree?"

Ravensworth said nothing. Briony was exasperated at the innuendoes in the conversation. She took a step forward. "Lord Grafton, I beg you will listen to me. We do not travel alone. My companions are—"

"Enough, I said, Briony," roared Ravensworth. Briony was shocked into silence.

When Grafton had gone, Ravensworth shut the door firmly behind him. "Well, madam," he began in a voice of studied gentleness. "I know that you have an excellent reason at hand to explain this last escapade?"

For the first time, Briony became conscious that his lordship was dressed in only his breeches and shirt, and *that* was open to the waist, revealing a thick mat of dark hair curling on his chest. She felt an irresistible urge to reach out and touch it. Briony suppressed the impulse ruthlessly. She was alone with a man in his chamber. She ought to have been terrified out of her wits as she had been with Grafton. Her eyes searched Ravensworth's darkening gaze and she looked down at her hands in agitation, hoping that he had not read what was in her mind. She heard him cough and when she looked up he was donning his black coat, his eyes shuttered.

"He kissed you and you bit him," remarked Ravensworth noncommittally.

"He molested me!" retorted Briony. "It was revolting."

Ravensworth arched an eyebrow. "What? No tingling?" he asked affably as he continued to dress.

Briony shook her head. "Nausea!" she said, shuddering in disgust, remembering the hot mouth glued to hers.

"Now I wonder what that signifies?" asked Ravensworth quizzically as he tied his neckcloth in the knot named for him.

"What?" asked Briony, regarding him with frank curiosity.

Ravensworth's mouth turned down. "Briony, sometimes you are not a very bright girl. Now tell me how it came about."

Briony told him. She waited for his anger to break over her but he only chuckled. "Let that be a lesson to you," he finally said as if he did not mind in the least that she had been subjected to a harrowing experience. "A woman needs to be under the protection of a man who knows how to look after her. If the world knew that you belonged to me, none of this would have happened."

Briony was disappointed in him. Perhaps he still harbored the hope that she would be tempted to accept his odious offer. That pretension she would depress once and for all.

She stood a little straighter. "Then I shall marry," she told him with an edge of acid in her voice. "I shall find some Quaker boy—a man of my own background who will respect my principles and cherish my happiness. Yes, a Quaker husband would suit me very well. I should enjoy a freedom that is denied to most women."

"It won't answer," said Ravensworth dampeningly, his brows knit together. "There isn't the man living—I don't care if he is a Quaker, a Hindu, or a saint from heaven—who will allow a woman under his care to thwart his authority."

Briony was irritated by his air of masculine superiority. "You don't know Quakers," she said with an air of condescension.

"And you don't know men," retorted Ravensworth bitingly. "Besides, I have told you what your destiny is. Better get used to it." He gave her a wicked grin.

Briony's lips clamped together. Ravensworth seemed not to notice. He drew her hand through his arm.

"Shall we join the others?" He opened the door for her and Briony stamped past him.

On the other side of the door they met a startled Avery and Harriet coming from opposite directions. They could not fail to notice that their respective friends had been closeted in Ravensworth's bedchamber. Avery looked away, but Harriet's mouth gaped open. She stammered an incoherent greeting.

Briony made haste to correct her cousin's mistaken impression. "Harriet," she began nervously, "a most odious gentleman was after me. He mistook me for . . . for an intimate friend of Harriette Wilson." Her voice became even more breathless in the telling of the complex tale. "I ran into Ravensworth's room for safety. He kissed me and tried to drag me into his chamber, but I bit him."

"Not me, you understand," said Ravensworth with an unholy gleam of appreciation in his eye, "but the other gentleman. She forced her way into my chamber uninvited."

"Of course," said Briony, annoyed at Ravensworth's levity. "I went to you for protection."

"That explains everything," said an unrepentant Ravensworth. "Now, shall we take care of the matter which precipitated the whole adventure in the first place? Something to do with Alice, I collect?"

The conviction grew in Briony's mind that Ravensworth was enjoying her predicament. A few well-chosen words on his part would have exonerated her odd behavior, but every sentence that he uttered appeared to give the impression that Briony had invented the mythical gentleman who had pursued her so hotly. She soon gave up the attempt to explain away her presence in Ravensworth's room, for indeed she knew herself to be sadly in the wrong in having remained with him once the threat to her person had been removed.

Harriet had informed her in frigid accents that she and Avery had been looking for her for a good five minutes and had passed Ravensworth's *closed* door on more than one occasion in their fruitless search. Briony looked to Ravensworth for assistance, but that odious gentleman merely smiled and said nothing, leaving her to bear the burden of the explanations. She dismissed the whole episode as unworthy of comment, and for the rest of the day retreated behind her copy of *Pride and Prejudice,* but her jaundiced eye noted sourly that for some unfathomable reason, his lordship was in high good humor.

Alice's fever was such that the doctor advised against

moving her for another day. Briony quaked to hear what Ravensworth might have to say on the further delay, but it seemed that nothing could shake his lordship from his amiable temper. Thus it was that a journey which would have taken two days to complete in normal circumstances was extended to four.

Chapter 13

Despite the girls' brave words that they would regard their sojourn in Bath as a high adventure, their nearer proximity to that pleasant city and, more particularly, to the forbidding presence of their parent and guardian, gave them increasing pause for thought. As the carriage horses began their slow descent of the steep slopes to the town center, conversation between the two female occupants faltered to a halt. The gentlemen, who had acted as outriders for a good part of the journey, were fully occupied in helping the coachman control the nervous lead animals, for, so Ravensworth had tersely told them through the open carriage window, "The fair city of Bath is a walker's dream but a nightmare for even the most accomplished driver."

And it *was* a fair city, thought Briony readily, but the forthcoming interview with Sir John, which the girls expected would be a stormy one, robbed them of half the pleasure they might otherwise have enjoyed in the serenely classical beauty of the Georgian town. Despite their feelings of foreboding, however, they could not fail to be impressed by the dazzling splendor of the long-windowed buildings of sparkling Bath stone flanking the broad streets.

Harriet's sister, Fanny, and her husband, the Reverend

Edward Darnell, had their dwelling in Laura Place just across the Pulteney Bridge in the newer part of town. The coach came to a halt before a terrace of tall, imposing residences which gave way onto Pulteney Street, the main access to the Sydney Gardens. Briony shaded her eyes against the sun and looked toward the famed gardens where, she had heard, picnics, concerts, ridottos, and displays of fireworks were held almost every other day of the week for the entertainment of Bath's mostly temporary residents. Before Briony had time to collect her thoughts, the front door was opened and a fierce-faced Sir John descended the steps toward them. His first words were ominous.

"We have been expecting you these two days past."

Briony and Harriet glanced uneasily in each other's direction. This was bad news indeed, for they had no way of knowing who had intimated the tidings of their projected arrival. Certainly not Aunt Sophy.

"Leave everything for the servants, that's what they're paid for," expostulated Sir John, as if the girls were making a deliberate attempt to delay the fate he had in store for them. "Ravensworth," said Sir John, riveting his lordship with a penetrating stare, "I particularly want a word in *your* ear."

Ravensworth smiled blandly at the irate gentleman. "I don't doubt it, Sir John, as I wish in yours. However, you will not object if Lord Avery and I set about finding a place to rack up for the night before we get down to business? The York on George Street, as I remember, is a most comfortable establishment but quite like to be the first to let all its rooms."

"There's a perfectly good hotel at the end of Pulteney Street," retorted Sir John. "You'll find a room there soon enough *after* you hear what I have to say to you."

Briony looked askance at her uncle. It really seemed

unjust in him to vent his spleen on Lord Ravensworth when that gentleman had gone out of his way to convey them all the way from London.

"But Uncle John—" she began rashly.

"Silence, miss!" He glowered her down and Briony swallowed.

A flicker of annoyance creased Ravensworth's brow. "I collect you are thinking of the Sydney Hotel, sir," he said levelly. "I don't doubt there are rooms there that go begging. The Sydney Gardens are too close for comfort, for my taste." His words were civil, but his bearing was every inch the aristocrat as he faced the elder man. Sir John's steady gaze never wavered from his face. After a moment, he seemed to come to a decision, and spoke in a more modulated tone.

"I beg your pardon. No offense meant. I would deem it an honor if you would dine with us this evening."

The tension seemed to go out of Lord Ravensworth and Briony realized she had been holding her breath. She let it out on a soft sigh.

"Delighted," replied his lordship on a warmer note. "It would be foolish to embark on long explanations until all parties concerned have rid themselves of the dirt and tedium of their journey, don't you agree?"

The two gentlemen exchanged a measuring stare and Briony looked from one to the other sensing that a hidden message had passed between them. She glanced at Harriet for confirmation of her suspicions, but her cousin was intent on pushing a pebble on the ground with her toe. Lord Avery had not even taken the trouble to dismount but looked uneasily away as if he did not wish to be drawn into the conversation. It was borne in on Briony that she was the only person present not party to the little drama being enacted out by Ravensworth and her uncle. She felt vaguely troubled.

* * *

Briony's sense of dread grew as the afternoon progressed. She had resigned herself to accept the inevitable tongue-lashing which she was sure her uncle and her aunt felt duty bound to accord her. It never materialized. Although their manner toward her was stiff and formal to an excessive degree, not one word of censure passed their tightly compressed lips. She became conscious that when Harriet and Lady Esther spoke to her, they evaded looking directly into her eyes. Only Edmund's and Fanny's manner seemed natural, but Briony thought that she caught a look of pity in some of their exchanged glances and she felt bewildered. Nanny she met briefly on the stairs for only a moment. Her eyes were red-rimmed with crying copious tears. She hugged Briony to her with a strangled, "Oh ma wee lamb," before pushing past to attend to her duties in the nursery on the floor above. Briony gloomily deduced that the punishment which was about to fall on her must be a fearful one indeed.

The dinner hour did nothing to lessen her grave misgivings, for when she was called to the drawing room, Ravensworth was the only guest. She stopped on the threshold, her heart hammering wildly against her breast.

"Where's Avery?" she asked without preamble.

Ravensworth's smile was meant to be reassuring. "He sends his regrets. He had a previous engagement."

"It's not possible!" she returned without thinking.

"If you say so," said Ravensworth politely, turning away to take up his conversation with Fanny where it had left off.

To Briony's overwrought sensibilities the atmosphere at the dinner table that evening was positively charged with electricity. She could feel the hair at the nape of her neck rising. When the thunderbolt fell, she was certain that it would strike her first. She began to fantasize about the fate which her uncle might be contemplating for her, but short of sending her to the colonies, nothing really fearsome came to mind. She told herself resolutely that she was being foolish and made a valiant effort to lay her unreasonable fears to rest. Nevertheless, hardly a bite of food passed her lips and as dinner progressed she fell altogether silent. She was dimly aware that of everyone present only Ravensworth never seemed to lag for conversation and his appetite was as hearty as she had ever seen it.

When the covers were removed and the port brought for the gentlemen, Fanny rose gracefully to signal that the ladies should retire. Ravensworth moved to exchange a few whispered words with Sir John.

"Briony, be so kind as to give me a few moments of your time." Sir John's voice brooked no denial. Ravensworth came to her side and gently guided her by the elbow to the seat next to his. Edmund smiled encouragingly and followed the ladies out. Only the three of them remained.

Ravensworth poured some port in a glass and handed it to Briony. "Drink it!" he told Briony. "You look half scared to death."

"I am," she breathed, and gulped down a draught.

Sir John looked thoughtfully at the Marquess. "Shall you begin or shall I?" he asked at last.

"Oh you, sir," responded Ravensworth airily. "I know pretty well what you are going to say, but I am certain that Briony hasn't an inkling. I am depending on you to talk some sense into her."

Briony reached for her glass and drew deeply on the port. More and more sinister, she thought darkly.

"Very well then," Sir John replied thin lipped, looking

for all the world like some sanctimonious parson. Briony suddenly recalled Aunt Sophy's disclosure that in his youth, Sir John had been a rakeshame devil and she giggled involuntarily. She reached for her glass of port but Ravensworth's strong clasp stayed her hand.

"Slowly, my girl!" he admonished. Briony meekly obeyed.

"Where shall I begin?" mused Sir John softly to himself. "Oh yes—on Tuesday I learned in the Pump Room from that busybody gossipmonger, Lady Hamington, that my daughter and my ward had been causing tongues to wag in London by their high-spirited antics—something to do with snuff, I recall."

"I can explain that," Briony hastily interposed.

"Don't put yourself to the trouble," said Sir John in acid accents. "That folly I am quite prepared to overlook. Now where was I? Oh yes. On Thursday at the Assembly Rooms, Lady Harrington had further tidings to convey. My daughter and my ward, so I was given to understand, had been presented to the infamous Harriette Wilson at the Opera by none other than the Most Honorable, the Marquess of Ravensworth."

"I can explain that," said Briony in a small, tentative voice. Ravensworth suppressed a chortle.

"Don't trouble," said her uncle with a freezing look. "At first, I could not, would not entertain such a notion," he went on, his voice ringing with rising anger. "I was so enraged at the old she-goat that I warned her if she had been a man, I would have called her out. But when she introduced me to three young gentlemen, one of whom was her nephew but *all* of whom collaborated her unlikely tale, I was ready to die of mortification." At this point, Sir John made heavy inroads into his glass of port and poured himself another.

"Is that all, sir?" asked Ravensworth encouragingly.

Briony's hand surreptitiously snaked out to retrieve her glass while Ravensworth's attention was diverted. She drained it and felt a warm glow spread through her shaking limbs. She liked the sensation better than the cold fear which had held her in its grip. The decanter was at her uncle's elbow, too far away for her to reach.

"Would you like more port, my lord?" she asked Ravensworth ingenuously. An unsuspecting Sir John passed the port to his lordship. Briony watched in fascinated interest as Ravensworth refilled his glass.

"That is by no means all," Sir John finally responded with a piercing look. "Yesterday evening at a concert in the Sydney Gardens, when I had made up my mind to return to London forthwith, whom do you think I chanced to encounter?"

"Lady Harrington?" asked Briony helpfully, one hand resting absently on the port decanter.

Sir John gave a sinister smile at no one in particular. "I was accosted by that jackanapes, the Earl of Grafton."

"Really?" asked Ravensworth, his eyes twinkling. "Now the story gets interesting, I collect."

He turned to glance at Briony but when he noted the full glass of port in her hand he examined the decanter suspiciously and removed it from her reach.

"A charming gentleman," responded a slightly befuddled Briony, nodding to her uncle. "We met him on the road."

"You don't say!" Sir John's voice was coolly impassive. "The tidbit that *that* 'charming gentleman' was pleased to divulge was that my niece, Miss Briony Langland, had become the *mistress* of the Marquess of Ravensworth."

There was a shocked silence and Sir John settled back in his chair with a self-satisfied smirk on his lips.

"I wonder what gave him that idea?" Ravensworth inquired innocently.

"A trifling matter of Briony being in your chamber, in your arms in fact, when you were naked."

"I can explain that," said Briony in a strangled squeak.

"My dear girl, it's too late now for explanations! I don't doubt that you and Ravensworth have done nothing excessively wrong. As I once told your father, *explanations* of his questionable conduct toward your mother would signify nothing in the eyes of the ton. It's actions that count."

Ravensworth looked interested. "I should have liked to have met the gentleman."

"Papa *was* a gentleman," said Briony with a hint of menace. "He would never have taken advantage of Mama. He loved her."

"He was a man of honor," intoned Sir John in a threatening manner, "and he knew his duty."

"Ah yes," Ravensworth purred. "Briony, put your port down and pay close attention. Your uncle is about to give you a lesson in the ways of the wicked world."

Sir John frowned. "I don't like your tone, sir."

"Perhaps not," Ravensworth responded with a disarming smile, "but let me put your mind at rest, Sir John. I am a man of honor. Try explaining that to Briony." He refilled his glass from the decanter and, with a rakish grin, topped up Briony's glass.

Sir John did not mince words. He addressed himself primarily to Briony. "It is imperative that Ravensworth wed you without delay, before the gossip about your delinquent conduct becomes universal knowledge. Your reputation may be a tad tarnished, but with the strong hand of a husband to restrain your wilder impulses and with your family behind you, I see no reason why you should be ostracized by Society."

Briony's mouth gaped open. "Marry Ravensworth? Don't be ridic—redic . . . " She felt her voice slurring and ended on a lame note, ". . . foolish."

"There's no getting around it. You must marry me," said his lordship with melancholy conviction. "You have hopelessly compromised me, you see." He scrupulously avoided Briony's gaze.

"I? Compromised you?" she asked, shocked to the core.

His lordship's eyebrows rose in a supercilious arc. "Who forced her way into my chamber? Who delayed our journey by two extra days? Who involved me in a duel with Grafton—almost? If you don't marry me, I shall be ruined. No one will receive me. No *decent* woman will wish to marry me. Why, I won't even be able to beget a *legitimate* heir to please my dear papa! Surely, as a woman of conscience, you must see your duty?"

Sir John looked as if he were about to say something. Ravensworth silenced him with a speaking look. "I think you can safely leave it to me now, sir." Sir John shut his lips firmly, shuffled to his feet, and strode from the room.

Briony blinked at Ravensworth. "This is worse than the colonies," she told him with a stricken look. "You know we cannot marry."

"How so, Briony?" he asked, clasping her free hand in one of his strong ones. She sipped at her port as she tried to unravel the puzzle.

"Ravensworth," she began diffidently, "I am so sorry. I did not mean to ruin you."

At the tremulous words, a look of guilt fleetingly passed over his lordship's face, but he shrugged it off. "You don't hear me complaining, do you? You know that I always intended to have you, one way or another. Can't we just make the best of it, my dear?"

"But what of your father?" she asked, gazing up at him round-eyed with fright. "He will not countenance such a match."

Ravensworth hesitated, choosing his words with care.

"He has no choice now. He would not wish to see me an outcast."

Briony shook her head. "I don't understand, at all. When you asked me to be your mistress, *that* wasn't about to ruin you, was it? But now, if I don't marry you, that *will* ruin you? You would be well advised, sir, to pursue your earlier suit," she finished with an absurdly wicked look.

The wine, Ravensworth noted drily, was having a deleterious effect on his beloved. He brought the full force of his powerful logic to persuade the reluctant lady to his will. "But when I asked you to share my life without benefit of matrimony," he began cautiously, "I did not know that you were an heiress."

"Does that make a difference?"

"Well, of course!"

"In what way?"

"Briony, I wished to protect you, cherish you, lift you out of poverty. The world would have commended me for my noble intention."

"Then the world is more of an ass than I suspected!" retorted the reckless lady in her plain style.

It took great effort of will, but Ravensworth controlled the retort that sprang to his lips. "But now that the world knows who you are and that you could very easily make a creditable match," he went on smoothly, "I shall be blamed for ruining your chances, even though it was you who compromised me."

"You don't say!" said Briony, by now well on the way to being half foxed. "What an idio—idio—stupid notion. I don't care what the world says, do you, Ravensh—Ravensh—Ravensh—Hugh?"

His lordship smiled wanly. "For myself, no. But think of my poor father. Is it right for me, for *us*, to deprive him of the heir he so desperately desires? I am an only son," he finished wistfully.

"Some girl of your own station will be glad to marry you," Briony consoled, clutching at his arm. For some reason, the thought dismayed her dreadfully, and she gave a pathetic sniff.

"Why not you, Briony?" asked his lordship softly, prizing the empty glass out of her fingers. He lifted her bodily from her chair to lie across his lap. "Why not you?"

Her response to his touch was immediate. Briony was no novice to a man's embrace. Ravensworth, after all, had kissed her on three separate occasions. He had barely covered her mouth with his lips when one hand coiled round his neck and pulled his head down with sufficient force to deepen his tentative embrace. Ravensworth groaned and in desperation held her away at arm's length. Briony's fingers began to undo the buttons of his lordship's shirt. He slapped her wrists. "Madam, behave yourself," he said sternly. Briony pouted.

"Kiss me, Hugh," she pleaded softly. "You know how much I like it."

Ravensworth was sorely tempted but he ruthlessly crushed his burgeoning desire. "No more kisses until we wed." After a moment he amended, "Or at least till we are properly betrothed. You are just taking advantage of me again."

"I know. I am sorry," replied Briony, hanging her head. "But it only happens when you touch me."

A shaken Ravensworth deposited her firmly back in her own place. "Then it is settled?" he asked her, his voice husky with controlled desire.

"Yes," she sighed through a happy, intoxicating haze, but whether it was induced by the effects of the wine or

Hugh Montgomery's discomposing presence, Briony
could not say. And even although she had promised to be
his wife, Ravensworth could not be persuaded to permit
her to take advantage of him again. Briony was bitterly
disappointed.

Chapter 14

In the days preceding their nuptials, the Marquess and his bride came to points on a matter of no small consequence. Ravensworth was somewhat taken aback to discover that Briony intended to be party to the negotiations respecting their marriage contract—a most unusual arrangement in his opinion. Further aggravation awaited his lordship. The lady displayed an aptitude for business and came to the negotiating table with a certain stipulation on which she would not budge, namely, that the income from her fortune be credited in its entirety to her account. Ravensworth protested, for such a handsome sum, he soon perceived, would ensure that his wife to all intents and purposes would remain independent of her husband's management.

"Precisely," Briony had replied in dulcet accents. Ravensworth appealed to Sir John, who did his best to dissuade Briony from such an unwarranted course of action, but Briony remained adamant. Her fortune, at her demise, would be equally divided amongst her heirs, but until such time, the income from it would be hers to administer as she saw fit. Ravensworth would have been happy to see the interest held in trust for their children, but no argument of his could persuade his recalcitrant bride, not even when Sir John disclosed the amount of the handsome settlement that Ravensworth was prepared to make. Briony pointed out, quite reasonably, that to an heiress such a competence was quite irrelevant. Ravensworth ground his teeth in rage—to no avail. Miss Briony Langland would not trust herself completely to the protection of any male.

For a disquieting hour or two, it looked to Sir John that the wedding might be called off. Ravensworth, he knew, was insulted by Briony's provocative persistence. He contrived a few minutes' private conversation with his lordship and finally convinced him that a *married* Briony, although she might technically be a woman of independent means, in reality would be powerless to thwart a husband's will. Ravensworth considered and finally relented, but Sir John could see that he was not well pleased that his future wife had questioned his integrity. Briony protested that his logic was glaringly abroad since she proposed to leave the management of her fortune to her husband's discretion. She trusted him implicitly, so she said.

Ravensworth had no way of knowing that Briony's determination to retain a modicum of independence in her marriage did not emanate from a distrust of him in particular, but from the teaching and practice of her mother and other Quaker ladies of her acquaintance. Ladies of the Quaker persuasion were accorded a deference and independence by their menfolk which would have shaken his lordship had he but known of it. They were esteemed for their qualities of resourcefulness and leadership and encouraged to participate as equals in the management of whatever interest and aptitude had fitted them for.

Ravensworth knew nothing of Briony's background, nor was he interested. Whatever else she was, she was the one woman in the world who had the power to utterly confuse him. His volatile emotions swung from one extreme to the other. At times he was swept by a fierce desire to cherish and protect her while at others the impulse to throttle the life out of her had to be severely restrained. His longing for Briony had long since surpassed the mere physical desire to satiate his lust. He could not live without her. He wanted her to share his life. It was as simple as that.

He had played his cards well, so he congratulated himself, and was not about to throw in his hand over this last piece of feminine resistance. The slight twinge of remorse which afflicted him when he thought of the gross deception he had practiced to ensure Briony's compliance in falling in with his wishes, he easily suppressed by reminding himself that the lady returned his affections. He would not permit her to sacrifice their happiness on the altar of her misguided scruples.

His vanity, however, smarted from the wounds inflicted by Briony and he was determined to demonstrate his mastery from the moment he had his ring securely on her finger. For the few days before their marriage he gave himself up to daydreaming of a chastened Briony who would be compelled to do her lord and master's bidding without demur.

The marriage was celebrated a week after their arrival in Bath in the front parlor of the house on Laura Place with the Reverend Edmund Darnell officiating. Ravensworth had readily agreed that Briony might have a Quaker wedding if she so desired, but on discovering that Quakers were in the habit of exchanging their vows without benefit of clergy, he had been shocked into hastily revoking his promise. Briony was somewhat mollified when the Marquess pointed out that it was unthinkable that in future years aspersions might be cast on the legitimacy of their progeny. They would be, when all was said and done, heirs to the dukedom of Dalbreck, and their claims must be unassailable. On this contentious issue, Briony gracefully gave way.

She had found Ravensworth rather cool and distant in the days leading up to the wedding and believed that he was blaming her for the embarrassing circumstances which had forced their marriage. His withdrawal depressed her spirits, for she could not but see what a comedown marriage to her must seem to one of his consequence. That his lordship was not a suitable mate for a Quaker girl she never doubted for a moment, but Briony, honest enough to admit to herself that she had developed an aching tendre for the profligate lord, was beginning to harbor hopes that she might reform him.

The first gala evening of the Season to be held in Sydney Gardens chanced to occur on the very day that Briony and Ravensworth were married. There was to be a musical concert in the earlier part of the evening and a display of fireworks when dusk fell. Ravensworth proposed that, prior to the planned entertainment, a small family party including the Grenfells, the Darnells, and of course, Lord Avery, should repair to the Sydney Hotel to enjoy a champagne supper in one of the booths overlooking the courtyard. It promised to be an agreeable evening.

Briony sipped her champagne slowly under the watchful eye of her groom and surveyed with interest the continuous flow of stylish promenaders who streamed into the Gardens. All of Bath, so it appeared, was intent on making a night of it. When she heard her uncle ask Ravensworth what his immediate plans were, she turned back to give her attention to her table companions.

"I haven't really decided," said his lordship carelessly,

dabbing his lips fastidiously with his table napkin. "I thought we might stay on for a bit in Bath and have half a mind to take lodgings for us in The Circus. On the other hand, my estate in Kent promises good riding and fishing at this time of year. I daresay a little rustication in the country after recent events wouldn't do any harm," he concluded with a meaningful look at his bride.

Briony bristled. It was bad enough that Ravensworth had not solicited her opinion, but to cast her past misdemeanors in her teeth before witnesses was inexcusable. "You have not consulted my wishes in the matter, my lord," she said in a voice clipped with irritation.

Ravensworth's dark brows drew together, and the hand holding his glass of wine froze halfway to his lips. He replaced it on the table and regarded Briony impassively. "Did I not, my love?" His tone was mild but Briony could see by his expression that she had angered him. "Then permit me to correct the omission." He scraped back his chair and offered her his arm. "A turn in the Gardens is in order, madam wife, I think."

Briony's eyes flew to her cousin's in mute appeal and on seeing it, Harriet started to her feet. "A capital idea," she said in a rush, and reached for her shawl. "Why don't we all go? I've heard that the illuminations are quite extraordinary at night." Avery shook his head in silent warning, but Sir John was before him.

"Sit down, miss," he said bluntly, grasping Harriet by the wrist. "Can't you tell when you're not wanted? I know that you and Briony have been as thick as thieves since you first met up with each other, but I take leave to tell you that you're wide of the mark if you think that Ravensworth and I will permit that unwholesome relationship to continue as before." When he saw Harriet open her mouth to protest, his expression hardened.

"Did you hear me, miss? I said sit down." He yanked on Harriet's arm and she fell back into her seat.

There was an uncomfortable silence for a moment or two, then Lady Esther, with customary aplomb, set herself to ease the tension of what gave every indication of becoming an ugly contretemps. She addressed herself to Ravensworth. "Run along with your bride, sir. On this occasion only, we shall permit you to monopolize Briony's society." Her words were lightly spoken and her smile arch. "In future, try to remember, Ravensworth, that it is not good ton for married couples to behave like lovelorn halflings. I shall send Avery and Harriet to look for you in half an hour."

Ravensworth bowed gracefully in acknowledgment. "Your servant, ma'am," he responded with a returning smile, "and I shall try to compress all my lover-like sentiments in the scant time I have been granted." The look bestowed on Briony, however, in that young lady's estimation, was far from lover-like.

She walked reluctantly at Ravensworth's side, not in the least deceived by the last convivial exchange between her aunt and her husband. She had observed that Ravensworth's temper had been on a tight rein for some time and the conviction was growing that he intended to unleash the full force of his fury against her at any moment. The thought goaded her into taking the offensive.

"How dare you treat me like some brainless child and in front of my relations?" she demanded in a voice tight with anger. "Who gave you the absolute right to decide where we are to reside in the future? It would have been civil in you, my lord, if you had consulted my wishes. Your manners are deplorable."

"Tch, tch," Ravensworth responded, not at all displeased with Briony's show of resistance. "The lady is only a bride of hours and so soon she wishes to usurp the authority of her husband! It would be better for you, madam wife," he went on with an edge of quiet menace in his voice, "if you learned to resign yourself to your fate. You may have tricked me into this precipitous marriage," he added with relish, "but don't think to find me a complacent husband. As my mistress, my dear, you would have been in a much better position to dictate terms. As my wife, you have forfeited every claim except to that of my name and my bed." There was a malicious light in his eyes.

Briony was speechless, but only for a moment. Her bosom rose and fell in her agitation. "You . . . unscrupulous, insufferable, ungentlemanly brute," she hissed at him through clenched teeth. "Is this all the gratitude I am to receive for the sacrifice I have made to save your miserable skin? You know as well as I do that this marriage of convenience is as little to my liking as it is to yours."

"Don't put yourself to the trouble of denying that events have fallen out just as you wished," went on his lordship blandly with a sideways glance at his seething companion. "You succeeded where other females failed because you caught me off guard. I never expected such duplicity in a Quaker lady," he added to fuel her fires.

They had come to a secluded part of the walk and Ravensworth halted and turned Briony to face him. She was magnificent when she was angry, he thought as his hands cupped her face. He itched to take the pins from her coiled hair and let his fingers run through the swath of soft blond silk. The thought of the tempestuous night ahead of him as he tamed this wayward girl made his breath choke in his throat. The longing to possess ker and make her his own in every respect was a raw ache inside of him. His blue eyes darkening to slate absorbed everything about her. "Deny it on peril of your immortal soul, Lady Ravensworth," he dared her, "that you cherish a tendre for me in your breast."

It was so unfair in him to use one of her few virtues to gain mastery over her. How could she answer him? "Don't count on it, Ravensworth," she whispered as his lips moved over her face. "A very small flame is easily extinguished."

His hands moved to her back, molding her to his length. "But I shall take such pains to fan it," he responded, capturing her pouting lips with his own.

Footsteps were heard approaching and Ravensworth reluctantly released Briony. His eyes continued to drink her in as though he could absorb her, and Briony could not bear to tear her gaze away.

"Ravensworth, you sly dog!" a husky, feminine voice intoned. Briony recognized it instantly and inwardly flinched. She turned to acknowledge the presence of Lady Adèle St. Clair and noticed with a start that her escort was the Earl of Grafton, quite recovered, so it seemed, from the wound she had inflicted on his lip. The lady's eyes were sparkling with some emotion that Briony could not read. Ravensworth, at her side, seemed completely at his ease.

"Adèle!" said Ravensworth with a show of pleasure. "What a delightful surprise. The last time I was in your company you gave no indication that you intended to come to this godforsaken town. I would have thought that the diversions which this magnet for dowagers and graybeards boasts too tame by half for one of your discriminating tastes." His bow to the man who had attempted to rape her, Briony observed darkly, was everything that was civil.

"My dear," the beauty at Ravensworth's elbow said in a throaty voice, "when you told me about your little errand here"—she swept Briony with a patronizing look and smiled knowingly at Ravensworth—"I thought that it might relieve the tedium for you if I should join you, but you have completely overset my good intentions. How could I know that you would fall prey to the wiles of some ingenuous wench? Let that be a lesson to you, Hugh." Then rounding on Briony, the fair lady said, "You are to be congratulated! You have captured the most eligible bachelor in England." Her eyes narrowed with malice. "Grafton told me how you accomplished it, but I shan't hold it against you. All is fair in love and war, is it not?" The challenge to Briony was unmistakable. Ravensworth appeared to be flattered, but Briony was completely taken aback.

"Permit me to offer my felicitations," said a bemused Grafton quietly in Briony's ear. She gave him one of her clear-eyed gazes, but was not reassured by the measuring expression which she caught in his eyes. There was something about the Earl that Briony deeply distrusted.

"Thank you," she answered stiffly. He proffered his arm. Briony looked to Ravensworth for guidance but that capricious gentleman had already forgotten her presence and was leading the way with the flirtatious Countess. She fell silently into step with the Earl, watching the couple ahead of her closely as they became engrossed in animated conversation, blond and black heads bent intimately together. Briony felt abandoned.

"I owe you an apology, my lady," she heard her companion say. She felt uneasy. The distance between herself and Ravensworth was growing. Grafton seemed to be careless of keeping pace with their companions and Ravensworth never once looked over his shoulder to ascertain that his wife was following. Briony's anger at her husband for such cavalier treatment on their wedding night, of all nights, began to simmer to a slow boil.

"I don't wish to be reminded of your insulting behavior when we first met," Briony finally responded in as cool a voice as she could command. "I prefer to forget the circumstances of that encounter."

Grafton's smile was enigmatic. "Oh, you mistake if you think I mean to apologize for my former conduct toward you. Any red-blooded male would have acted as I. How could I help it?" His admiring look held a hint of insolence. "Your appearance, on that occasion, as I recollect, was far different from the restrained lady whom I am now privileged to partner."

Briony was puzzled. "What then?" she asked, ignoring the blatant provocation in his words.

"I wish to apologize for escorting Adèle here to plague you. If I had known that you were to be in attendance this evening, please believe me, nothing would have persuaded me to bring the lady."

"Why, what can you mean, sir?" asked Briony perplexed. "Lady St. Clair has every right to enjoy herself as much as I."

"With your husband?" he asked dryly.

Briony froze. "What are you saying, sir? Speak plainly, if you please."

"Forgive me if I have spoken out of turn. I thought you knew."

"What should I know? Tell me at once if you have something to say."

Grafton shrugged his shoulders nonchalantly. "Ravensworth's long-standing liaison with Adèle is universally known. The lady had ambitions, I collect, to become the next Marchioness."

It took a moment or two for his meaning to penetrate. Briony's eyes widened in disbelief. "Are you suggesting, my lord, that Adèle is his mistress?"

Grafton looked pained. "I have said too much already," he replied in a regretful tone. "This loose tongue of mine will be the death of me. Please forget that I ever mentioned it."

Briony's mind went numb. As she looked along the walk, she could see that Ravensworth and his inamorata had turned to wait for them. The distance between them gave her a little time to compose herself. She gave a convincing laugh which she hoped was carried to the ears of the shameless couple up ahead. "Do not refine too much upon it, Lord Grafton," she said with a proud lift of her head. "You must know that this marriage is one of convenience only. I am sorry that I have robbed the lady of her rightful place. I take leave to tell you that it was not my intention."

They were on a level with the Marquess, and Briony was sufficiently recovered to face the bewitching creature who had pressed herself close to Ravensworth's side. Briony masked the aching pain in her breast and looked defiantly into Ravensworth's questioning gaze.

Ravensworth's eyes flickered to Grafton then returned to Briony. He saw the fragility behind her false air of bravado and knew intuitively what had transpired. In some perverse way, he was glad that she knew about Adèle—glad that it had the power to give her pain. In some small way it made up for all the slights which he had suffered at her hands since the first moment of their acquaintance. He had always intended to explain about Adèle when the right opportunity presented itself, since she moved in the same circles as he and he wanted to protect Briony from the barbs of malicious tongues. Grafton had got to her first, though, and the damage was done. He cursed himself silently for having delayed in confessing his involvement with the worldly widow. But Briony's confounded scruples had made him more dishonest than he wished to be. She was the worst kind of idealist imaginable. Well, tonight she had had a brush with reality and she didn't care for it. What had she expected from him, he thought in exasperation. He wasn't a bloodless monk, after all, and it was months since he had given Adele her congó. Briony surely couldn't believe that he had arranged for the notorious lady's removal to Bath. That notion was idiotish, and he dismissed it instantly from his mind. He would make it up to her, he thought impatiently, his eyes eloquently expressing his silent apology for all he knew she must be suffering.

Briony's eyes flashed daggers at him. "Ravensworth," she said in a voice brittle with emotion, "Lord Grafton has been amusing me with the latest on dit from London, and I can barely wait to share it with Harriet. She will be as highly diverted as I." Ravensworth's eyes narrowed. "It would appear," she went on with false gaiety, forcing her lips into a smile, "that a gentleman of our acquaintance who has expressed himself quite severely on *my* want of conduct is not the pattern card of propriety which he pretends to the world." She noticed the imperceptible tensing of his shoulders and felt fiercely glad. "I should like to return to my cousin," said Briony, giving Ravensworth her indifferent "cool appraisal" stare. "Harriet, like myself, finds the practiced deceptions of hypocrites too droll for words."

"All in good time, my dear," responded Ravensworth, his eyes growing cold. "What do you think? Adèle has got up a number of people for a house party at her estate in Kent. They leave tomorrow and we have been invited to join them.

"I had told you, as I recall, that we are near neighbors? The idea has much to recommend it. London is out of the question for the present. Your scrapes there will not be forgotten for some time to come. Bath has neither the allure of the big city nor the rural attractions of the true countryside. For the present, I collect that Kent will suit us very well."

He had been on the point of refusing Adèle's invitation, but Briony's cutting words and smoldering expression of hostility had goaded him into retaliation.

The angle of Briony's chin elevated a trifle, and she regarded Ravensworth with that cool disdain which he found so irritating. "I like Bath, and wish to remain with my cousin. Her company is all that I require."

Ravensworth's jaw hardened. "Tch, tch, my lady wife," he returned smoothly. "I think you have done enough damage to the frail reputation of poor Harriet. I collect her parents will be happy to see her removed from your influence for a month or two. We go to Kent and there is an end of it." He turned his back on her and gave his attention to Adèle, a gesture calculated to wound his intractable wife.

Briony's hands flew to her mouth. He had injured her where she was most vulnerable. It was too much. She gave a stifled cry and turned on her heel to run back the way she had come. She heard Ravensworth call her name but ignored it. Lady Adèle's startled laugh hung on the air at her back. To marry such a rakeshame bounder had been the worst mistake of her life, but she would correct it. She would sue for an annulment, she thought wildly.

She met no one she knew as she made her exit from the Gardens and quickened her footsteps along Pulteney Street to Laura Place. As she reached the front door, she was momentarily startled by the sudden explosion of fireworks as they arced overhead. "Paltry squibs!" she muttered brokenly as the door opened to admit her, and she ran convulsed for breath upstairs to her room. She locked the door with unsteady fingers and leaned against it. Ravensworth had been assigned a room along the corridor, but there was no connecting door to their chambers. He would have to break down the door to get to her. I hope he enjoys his wedding night, she thought bitterly and, throwing herself upon the bed, cried her heart out.

Chapter 15

His lordship could have gladly choked the life out of Briony when he came home after a fruitless search of Sydney Gardens to find her safely locked in her chamber. He had stormed and thundered outside her door but Briony could not be induced to turn the key to permit him to enter. Her muffled threats of seeking an annulment of their marriage, hurled defiantly at him through the protection of the stout door, had him in a paroxysm of anger. When he saw that he was getting nowhere and was moreover attracting the servants' curiosity, he flung into his own room in a flaming temper and threw himself into a chair.

How dare she thwart him like this, he asked himself over and over again. He had it in his power to crush her, to cut her off from Society, to send her to oblivion if he had a mind to. What did it take to convince the unruly, hot-at-hand damsel that it was in her best interests to show a more tractable disposition to her lord? She had cheated him of what he had intended to be a glorious night of love. Damn the woman! She ought to be, at this minute, in his arms surrendering to his possession. That she had the barefaced effrontery to threaten him with an annulment of their unconsummated marriage was more than he would countenance. His pride was outraged. His Marchioness would find that she was sadly mistaken, he thought fiercely to himself, if she entertained the notion that she would prevail in this clash of wills. He would bring her to heel or his name wasn't Hugh Montgomery.

"Who is it?" asked Briony in a timid voice when the rap on her door came for the second time.

"It's Alice, miss, with your morning chocolate."

Briony let out a shuddering sigh of relief and threw back the covers of her bed. She carelessly draped her dressing gown over her shoulders and crossed the cold, uncarpeted floor to unlock the door. Ravensworth, his features set in implacable lines, brushed by her and threw her a malevolent glare. Briony cautiously eased away.

Alice set down the tray with the cup of hot chocolate, her eyes openly examining the couple who held themselves stiffly to attention. "That will be all, thank you, Alice," said Ravensworth, taking her firmly by the elbow and propelling her out of the room. He shut the door on the curious maid and turned the key in the lock.

Briony meantime had thrust her arms roughly into her dressing gown and belted it tightly around her. She pulled herself up to all of her sixty-four inches and faced Ravensworth with a show of confidence she was far from feeling. With the greatest effort, she controlled the tremor in her voice when she addressed him. "I meant what I said last night, Ravensworth," she told him before he could begin to berate her. "I shall ask my uncle to procure an annulment of the marriage." A note of rancor crept into her voice. "I have no wish to deprive Lady Adèle of her just reward for services rendered."

Ravensworth's eyes hardened as he looked steadily at her. "I am not going to apologize for past history,

Briony," he said tersely. "Adèle never meant anything to me. Her place in my life, if one could call it a place, was negligible. You are my wife and I am here to discuss your future."

The sight of the crumpled bedclothes and Briony's disheveled appearance were beginning to have an effect on him. He stifled the sudden desire to take her in his arms. He had decided that his bride needed a firm hand, and he was determined not to waver.

"You will observe that we are alone in a locked room," he went on with a menacing expression. Briony licked her dry lips and Ravensworth smiled grimly to see it. His voice dropped to a whisper. "One more ill-advised word from you about an annulment, madam wife, and I shall proceed to consummate our marriage in such a manner that you will wish you had never thwarted my claims upon you. Do you take my meaning?"

Briony did and retreated with as much dignity as she could muster to the other side of the bed, watching him warily.

"Good, I see that you do." His voice was like silk. "I want your word, Briony, that there will be no more foolish talk of an annulment. You know the alternative."

Briony was silent but thinking furiously. It was not the time or place, she thought, suppressing her rising resentment, to come to points with a Ravensworth who looked as if he would do murder at the slightest provocation.

"Do I have your word?" he asked in a voice edged with steel. He took a step toward her and Briony quickly nodded in dumb assent.

When he took her chin in his hand, she schooled her gaze to an expression of indifference, but when his thumb traced the outline of her lips in a slow, sensual gesture, she slid her eyes away to hide the unsettling effect his touch had on her.

He released her abruptly and moved away to stare out of the window. "Briony," he tried in a more conciliatory note. "Don't try my patience too far, and don't argue with me. For once in your life, just listen and say nothing. We leave for Kent in one hour. I shall send Alice to you to help you pack." He seemed to hesitate then went on firmly. "My decision had nothing to do with Adèle's house party. It is based solely on self-interest." When he finally turned to look at her, Briony was sure that she saw a softening in his expression. "Perhaps I rushed you into marriage before you had time to accustom yourself to the idea. We need a period of grace away from everybody, some peace and quiet where we can come to know each other." He waited for Briony to make some overture but she stood passively, her crystal-clear eyes regarding him with a somber expression. "Dammit Briony, can't you come halfway to meet me?" he demanded, his voice vibrant with emotion.

"Adèle?" she questioned softly, trying to keep the reproach out of her voice, wanting to believe the words he was telling her. "If we go to Kent, will it not be necessary to receive her and—"

"Of course I can't cut her," Ravensworth interrupted with rising exasperation. "Why should I? She has done nothing to offend me and we are neighbors. It would create an impossible situation. People will be watching us. I have no intention of giving them something to gloat over. There's nothing better they would like than to see my wife and my—Adèle," he amended quickly, "come to points like dogs haggling over some bone. Can't you see that it is your indifference, your handling of the situation, which will take the wind out of their sails? Anything less will set their vicious tongues wagging, and I have no desire to become a laughingstock, the butt of every tasteless jest of lay-about fribbles who have nothing better to do with their time."

Briony's spine straightened as she faced him. She had caught his quick correction and knew that he had been on the point of saying "mistress." "You ask too much, sir," she replied with quiet dignity. Their eyes held, gray eyes flashing with indomitable resistance and blue freezing to ice with unyielding resolve. An angry flush darkened Ravensworth's saturnine features.

"Nevertheless, in this you *will* obey me, Briony." He turned on his heel and strode to the door. She heard the rattle of the key as he unlocked it. "If you are not ready in one hour," he flung over his shoulder, "I shall personally see to your dressing and carry you off as you are." She waited a moment or two until she heard his footsteps retreating down the landing, but when she went to lock the door behind him, she found that he had taken the key.

One hour later saw them embark on their journey in the same coach that had brought them from London to Bath. It was a strained farewell, although Briony's relatives had no way of knowing what had taken place the previous evening. That something was amiss, they could tell by Ravensworth's dark looks at his bride. Briony, however, conducted herself as naturally as possible under the circumstances, courteously inviting them all to visit when they had concluded their stay in Bath. When it came time for the cousins to take leave of each other, Harriet hugged Briony fiercely to her. Briony managed a few whispered, breathless words in Harriet's ear which she was careful to conceal from the assembled company. "Find a way to come to Kent as soon as ever you can."

Harriet held Briony at arm's length and by the briefest inclination of her head showed that the message had been received and understood. All that remained was for Briony to entrust a letter for her brother to her uncle, for Vernon must be apprised of what had so recently transpired. That she had also urgently invited Vernon in rather hysterical terms to present himself in Kent at the earliest opportunity, she forbore to mention to her stern-faced husband.

Her eyes flickered to his impassive face as he handed her into the carriage. She had been forced to marry Ravensworth as a matter of conscience. She had never pretended to be other than she was. If he thought he could change her into some passive, prettily behaved, mindless creature, he would soon learn his error.

The day after Ravensworth had spirited away his bride to his estate in Kent saw a decorous and somewhat dispirited Miss Grenfell taking a turn with Lord Avery in the splendor of Sydney Gardens. To a casual observer, the couple gave every evidence of being in perfect charity with each other, but to the more discriminating it would have been remarked that Harriet and Avery spoke only in commonplaces when they spoke at all. His lordship's manner was gravely courteous, but his companion, usually so outgoing and vivacious, was very much on her dignity. When his lordship requested the lady to seat herself on a bench overlooking one of the fountains, she consented with a show of formal civility.

Avery removed his curly-brimmed beaver and ran a nervous hand through his neatly brushed locks. The resulting disarray of brown hair shot through with gold gave the gentleman a decidedly raffish air. Harriet quickly averted her eyes, which had been drinking in Avery's boyish good looks. Fortunately, at that moment, the gentleman was unsmiling, for Avery's habitual, self-deprecating grin was, in Harriet's opinion, irresistible and Harriet had every intention of resisting his lordship.

Avery turned to regard the silent lady through the veil of his thick lashes. The air of injured innocence which Harriet assumed whenever she became aware that his eyes were on her, which was frequently, she wore like an encompassing cloak to conceal her person from his prying eyes. He had suffered her to keep him at arm's length by this ruse on more occasions than he cared to remember. Lord Avery's patience was wearing thin. He summoned up the remnants of his courage and put his fate to the touch.

"Harriet, I don't wish for a long betrothal," began Avery in his usual, soft-spoken manner.

"What betrothal?" asked his companion in what his lordship thought was a rather churlish tone of voice for one who looked so devastatingly pretty. He regarded her calmly for a moment or two as if considering how best to manage such a temperamental filly.

"I have taken the precaution of procuring a special license," Avery went on as if Harriet had not spoken. "Long engagements are not to my liking and it is almost a twelve-month since I first offered for you."

"*That* engagement was broken within weeks of its making," said Harriet with a disdainful shrug of her lovely shoulders.

"Yes," responded Avery in a thoughtful tone. 'That is precisely my meaning. Our betrothals last on average scarce a month. If we marry by special license within the week, we shall break this deplorable habit you seem to have acquired of returning my ring with irritating regularity." Avery smiled in a self-conscious, deprecating way and Harriet's bones melted.

"I cannot return what I do not have, my lord," she replied in what she hoped were depressing accents. "I can scarce remember what your betrothal ring looks like. It has been in your possession more often than it has been in mine.

Lord Avery smiled wryly. "Only for safekeeping, my love. As soon as we are wed, I shall give it back to you. But I have no desire to become engaged to you again. There has been enough ill talk of our on–off-again betrothal to last me a lifetime. You have made me a laughingstock." As soon as the words were out, Avery realized his mistake and hastened to forestall the angry retort which he knew was hovering on Harriet's parted lips. He threw up his hands. "It's no use, Harriet! I capitulate! Total surrender! What more can I say?" He laughed weakly and captured her hand. "Life is unbearably flat without you, my dear. I was a fool to try to change you—to erase those very qualities which endeared you to me in the first place. Harriet," he went on in desperate earnest, "I no longer wish to tame you. I admire you just the way you are. It was a dashing out-and-outer who captured my jaded heart. If you consent to marry me, I promise not to make you over into a conformable wife."

Harriet gazed up at him, a frown of perplexity wrinkling her brow. "Do you mean to say that if I marry you, you will permit me to take snuff and smoke cigars and drink wine and so on?"

"Mmm," said Avery, drawing her closer by the simple expedient of slipping his arm round her shoulders and tightening his grip. "Within limits, my love," he said a trifle hoarsely. "I may even go so far as to permit you to kiss me in public."

Harriet's lips parted in mute incredulity as Avery's head bent to capture her unresisting lips. When he drew away, Harriet's mouth formed a round O. The Viscount searched her face anxiously. It was the first time he had ever dared take such liberties with her.

"Avery," Harriet managed on a tremulous breath, "did you feel it?"

Neither of them paid the slightest attention to the occasional strollers who were casting curious and outraged glances in their direction.

"What did you feel, my love?" asked Avery, a light leaping into his eyes. Harriet, he observed with the deepest gratification, lay softly panting in his arms. Without waiting for her answer, he pressed her closer and kissed her again. When he drew away, Harriet's eyes were round with wonder.

"Oh Avery," she sighed when she had recovered her breath, "you should have kissed me long since. I never knew, my dear." When he would have kissed her again, she protested and struggled free of his arms. "You are every bit as bad as my cousin Briony," she expostulated with a smile in her eyes. "It is impossible for me to go against convention when I have to keep you two originals in line. Somebody has to have a sense of what is fitting in this family." She laughed ruefully and reached a finger up to touch his lips in a playful gesture. Avery's hand closed over her wrist.

"Harriet, let's get married right away. Here in Bath, if you like, or in London, or at my mother's place in Kent. All these misunderstandings which have plagued us from the beginning of our courtship would soon be resolved if I could only take you into my arms. I am wearied of being your escort, or your dancing partner, or even your friend. Oh my darling girl," he went on more passionately, "I would be so much more to you, if you will let me."

Harriet gave a shaky laugh as she tried to school her emotions into a semblance of composure. This impetuous, amorous Avery was a new experience for her, and his ardent words and gestures were upsetting her equilibrium, sending shivers of anticipation along her spine. She had always admired him, loved him even, in a controlled sort of way. But his kisses had unleashed a strange longing that left her half afraid. "Please marry me soon, Avery," she said with affecting simplicity.

After a moment of stunned silence, Avery threw back his head and hooted with laughter. It had been that simple! Gudgeon that he was not to have taken advantage of her sooner! Damn propriety and the insane assumption that a gently bred girl would be revolted by a show of passion! At last he had awakened her. Now, when he caught her eye, she would know what he was thinking. When at last he came to himself, he caught her in his arms and said gaily, "Tell me where and when and it will be accomplished, my adorable Harriet."

"Would next week be too soon?" she asked, looking shyly into his shining eyes.

Avery chortled. "Not soon enough for my part, my love, and I daresay I can talk your father round."

A thought suddenly occurred to Harriet. "Avery," she began in a wheedling voice which his lordship deeply mistrusted, "what of your mother? She rarely leaves your estate in Kent. Oughtn't we to pay her a bridal visit? I don't mean right away," she went on in a rush when she saw Avery's brow pucker in a frown. "But in a week or two. To do anything less would be shockingly uncivil!"

"Ah yes. And it just so happens that Ravensworth's estate is in the same county. No doubt you will wish to spend a day or two in Briony's company?"

"Could we, Avery?" she asked persuasively. "I know that Briony is not altogether happy. If I could just see her and speak to her, it would set my mind at rest. She particularly asked me to come, and I can't just turn my back on her. We have been too close for that."

Lord Avery shuddered to think what Ravensworth's reaction would be if the two cousins should meet up again so soon after parting. He would not welcome meddling in his dealings with Briony, of that Avery was certain.

"Harriet, my love," Avery coaxed, "don't you think a visit to Briony is ill advised at the present moment? In a month or two, I would not hesitate to endorse your suggestion." He chose his next words with care. "The two of you are very close, I know, closer even than sisters. But when a woman becomes a wife, that sort of intimacy belongs more properly to her husband." He lifted her chin with the back of his hand and looked deeply into her eyes. "I confess that I have found myself many times jealous of Briony and the exclusiveness of your relationship. When we marry, Harriet," he went on a little wistfully, "I would wish to be the object of your devotion and your loyalty."

"You shall be, I promise," Harriet answered with feeling. "But don't you see, I gave Briony my word? I must see her, just once more. I don't understand the nature of this alliance with Ravensworth, but I know that Briony desperately needs a friend. Trust me in this, Avery. I swear I won't come between them, if that is what troubles you." She waited anxiously for his reply.

"What can I say?" he asked with a resigned smile. "I daresay it would be unfriendly in us not to visit when we are in the neighborhood. And they ought to be among the first to know of our nuptials. But Harriet, will you be advised by me if I deem it expedient to withdraw? Ravensworth has the devil's own temper, and if he should venture to unleash it against you, I am afraid that our longstanding friendship would be broken forever. And I would miss him," he added ruefully.

Harriet promised solemnly to abide by her betrothed's decisions in all matters relating to their projected visit. Avery should have been reassured, but he was left with the melancholy conviction that their presence at Ravensworth's estate was courting disaster.

Chapter 16

Toward evening of the second day of their journey into Kent, Ravensworth's carriage rolled into a deep rut in the road and the wheel on the right front side wobbled precariously. At that moment, his lordship was reclining against the squabs, cushioning a sleeping Briony against his shoulder. The carriage shuddered to a sudden standstill and lurched dangerously, tipping the occupants from their comfortable perch. Briony was jolted awake and Ravensworth, immediately alert to their perilous position, threw open the coach door and jumped down onto the roadway, dragging his protesting bride with him. He set Briony away from him with a few brusque words and went to inspect the damage, shouting curt orders to the irresolute outriders and coachmen. Briony stood in some confusion, endeavoring to gather her reeling wits.

The frantic grooms were attempting to unhitch the horses when the black clouds overhead were illuminated by a shaft of lightning which streaked across the sky. The vibrations of the ensuing roll of thunder shook the ground beneath them. Briony started violently and cowered closer to the tottering carriage.

The skies opened and the sudden deluge of driving rain lashed man and beast mercilessly. Briony was half conscious of Ravensworth hurling some command at her as he tended to the horses but a second flash of lightning and the almost simultaneous crack of thunder muffled his words. Panic engulfed her. She knew that her reaction was beyond all reason but she was helpless to control it. She could taste the same dry terror in her mouth as she had experienced when she had watched her parents drown. She felt as if she were reliving the old nightmare of impending doom. With shaking fingers, she covered her ears to stifle the terrifying noise of the storm, heedless that her cloak had slipped from her shoulders to lie at her feet in a sodden heap.

It was the third peal of thunder which had her running. As the ground trembled beneath her, a thin scream was forced from her lips and she bolted in blind panic, stumbling and falling her length as she tried to conceal herself in the thick underbrush at the side of the road. Wicked thorns tore at her hands and face but Briony disregarded them, scarcely aware of them. She wanted only to find some sanctuary from her unreasoning fears.

She was caught from behind and lifted, clawing and lashing out in her terror, to lie against the breadth of Ravensworth's chest. She felt the warmth of his body against her and clung to him with desperate strength, brokenly murmuring his name against his throat. In one easy movement, he enveloped her in the voluminous folds of his traveling cloak, protecting them both from the relentless rain. His soothing words washed over her, crooning words of comfort as if he were speaking to a frightened child. Her dry, wracking sobs gave way to tears as some of the hysteria left her. The intelligence that they must make for the inn ahead where their rooms were bespoken registered vaguely in her frozen mind. But when Ravensworth gave her into the arms of his waiting groom till he should mount one of the horses, Briony moaned her protest and struggled to keep hold of him. She was lifted before him into the saddle and turned her face into his shoulder, her arms firmly encircling his waist.

By the time they reached the coaching inn, the storm had spent itself and Briony lay impassive in Ravensworth's arms. When he tried to set her down, however, she clutched at him with renewed tenacity and had to be prized free of his arms. Then he lifted her high against his chest and carried her to their chamber. Once the door was shut against intruders, Ravensworth stripped Briony's dripping garments from her back and toweled her dry before a blazing fire. That Briony made not the slightest protest to such liberties from a husband who had as yet to exercise his rights over her troubled Ravensworth more than he cared to admit. He found a nightdress in her valise and drew it gently over her head and finally draped the coverlet from the bed around her shoulders. Then he settled himself in a chair flanking the fireplace, cradling the trembling girl in his arms.

As he gently stroked her hair, he could feel her begin to relax against him. He spoke soft, reassuring words of comfort against her eyes. It was this and the sense of deliverance from some dread catastrophe which unleashed a flood of therapeutic tears. Coaxed by his softly spoken questioning, Briony, in slow, halting sentences, began to stammer out the tragic sequence of events which she had witnessed on that never-to-be-forgotten day when her parents had been swept to their watery grave in the turbulent waters of Lake Windermere. Ravensworth listened silently as she described her feelings of helplessness as she had been forced to watch, powerless to lift a finger to save the two people she had loved best in the world. When she came to the end of her story, Briony felt strangely comforted. The steady beat of Ravensworth's heart at her breast was like a drug dulling the raw endings of her overstrung nerves. Ravensworth's low baritone continued its soothing effect as he stroked her hair, and after a few shuddering sighs, Briony succumbed to sleep in the shield of his sheltering arms.

For a long time afterward, Ravensworth remained motionless, a frown of concentration puckering his dark brows as he gazed at the softly breathing girl. She stirred and his arms tightened protectively around her. His expression hardened as his eyes continued to drink her in. How could he have thought to coerce this defenseless child into becoming his reluctant bride?

The girl who had clung to him so tenaciously at the height of the storm and who had melted into his arms with such touching confidence, submitting herself to his protection, was almost a stranger to him. When he had first made Briony's acquaintance, he had been captured by her demeanor of quiet self-possession, and by her air of tranquility which was leavened by a wry, engaging wit. In a perverse way he had admired her adherence to her scruples, which had brought them both into such open conflict. Briony had never lacked courage in her attempts to thwart him at every turn. It had been these qualities and his awareness of the latent sensuality which he had awakened in her which had determined him to possess her in every way.

But the defenseless child-woman who had trusted him to such a degree that she permitted him to strip her naked and who had submitted wordlessly to attentions of the most personal nature awakened in his breast feelings that he had never before experienced. The knowledge that he loved Briony he had grasped early in their acquaintance. That was no novelty. But the sense of utter unworthiness which now settled heavily around his heart was an emotion that felt strange and unwelcome to Lord Ravensworth. No matter how he cut it, he knew that he did not deserve the love of a woman like Briony

Langland. She was far too good for him, too innocent for one of his unsavory past, too idealistic, too honest, too virtuous, too deserving of a much better man than he. Not that his lordship entertained the idea for an instant of permitting Briony to go to anyone else. He was willing to concede that the lady was above his touch, but Briony Langland belonged to him and his she would remain as long as he had breath in his body.

The twinges of conscience which he had formerly felt when he considered how he had outflanked Briony paled into insignificance beside the wave of remorse which now engulfed him. In pursuit of his driving need to possess her, he had used the most underhanded duplicity to bend the lady to his will, totally indifferent to Briony's sentiments. This egotistical streak was natural to him. Hugh Montgomery had always been in the habit of taking what he wanted by one means or another. But what Hugh Montgomery wanted now could not be taken by force, or by bribery or by begging. He wanted Briony's esteem. He wanted Briony to turn to him with the same show of defenseless, confiding trust as she had displayed when she was near hysterical with fear. Hugh Montgomery, Marquess of Ravensworth, would not be content with an esteem that was based on a sham. He wanted to earn Briony's respect, to be worthy of it. In short, Ravensworth resolved to win the lady by demonstrating that he had reformed. Such humility of spirit sat oddly upon him, but he determined to put his new resolve immediately into effect.

He shut his eyes against the delectable picture of a scantily clad Briony softly nestled against his chest and lifted her effortlessly in his arms to deposit her on the inviting bed. It was with a look of lingering regret that the repentant Lord Ravensworth turned aside from the one woman in the world he wanted to make love to and covered her soft contours with the feather coverlet. With a sigh of resignation he turned deliberately on his heel and made for the door, vigorously suppressing the graphic images which had haunted his waking and sleeping hours since the ingenuous Briony had come into his life. He wondered idly how long it would be before Briony would succumb to the courting of the new Ravensworth and fervently hoped that it would be accomplished within the sennight. Cold baths, thought his lordship with an involuntary shiver as he closed the door firmly behind him, were not to his liking.

When Briony awoke the next morning, Ravensworth was nowhere to be seen, nor was there any evidence that he had ever been in the room. Briony conjectured, quite correctly, that his lordship had bespoken a private chamber for himself. She let the thought revolve in her mind for some few moments as she dressed with the help of the landlord's daughter, who had been pressed into serving temporarily as her abigail. That he had not seized such a perfect opportunity to consummate the marriage, she regarded as highly significant. She wondered darkly if it had anything to do with the ravishing Adèle. This depressing thought she pushed resolutely from her mind.

Briony's recollection of the details of what had transpired after the onslaught of the storm was far from clear, but the feelings which Ravensworth had evoked by his show of selfless chivalry were vividly etched in her mind. She had never thought to find such solace, such devotion, such consideration for the foibles of others in a man of Ravensworth's stamp. That he would have behaved to the veriest stranger in like vein she did not doubt for a moment. Scrupulous honesty compelled her to confess that there was more to Ravensworth's character than she had been willing to admit. The man was something of an enigma. His conduct toward her was so inconsistent as to be deemed almost eccentric. Nevertheless, on more than one occasion she had cause to be grateful for his timely rescue, and if he had berated her rather harshly for what he considered her want of propriety, she was willing to concede that, by his lights, he had a point. Briony was not adverse to admitting that no Quaker lady of her acquaintance had ever won the dubious notoriety which she had achieved, and she was sensible of the fact that she must conduct herself in future with greater circumspection. That much a wife owed her husband.

It was with feelings of anticipation that she looked forward to taking her place as mistress of Oakdale Court, Ravensworth's estate in Kent. The life of indolence which she had been forced to endure as a young lady of quality could not come too soon to an end for one of her simple tastes. As she flung a paisley shawl negligently around her shoulders prior to descending to the private parlor where she had been informed his lordship was breakfasting, she reflected on how essential her mother's role had been in promoting the welfare of all her dependents on her father's estate. Briony's dearest wish was to follow in Mama's footsteps and be a fitting helpmate to a husband who shared her love for country life and her deep-felt concern to be of service to others. How she had had the misfortune to fall in love with a frippery fellow like Ravensworth, Briony could not conceive. But then, he had shown her a glimpse of a different Ravensworth. She could not believe that a man who could give such comfort to a woman in the throes of hysteria could be all bad.

Briony found the reformed Ravensworth's exaggerated solicitude cold and depressing and she wondered if he had taken her in disgust for her craven conduct of the night before. When she would have thanked him for the consolation of his unselfish ministrations in her chamber, she noted the dull flush of color beneath his skin, Ravensworth's habitual aspect whenever he was moved to anger.

Briony was forced to the conclusion that he had found her conduct distasteful and had been put out of countenance by her hysterical insistence that only he be allowed to assist her undress. The final insult, in Briony's eyes, was when Ravensworth elected to act as outrider and she was left to her own devices as the carriage began the last, short lap of their journey to Oakdale Court. Briony was far more subdued by Ravensworth's show of civility than ever she would have been if he had taken her to task for her childish fears. It did not take long for Briony's wounded pride to kindle a martial light in the lady's eye. So much for thinking that Ravensworth concealed some of the softer qualities in his character.

Chapter 17

Oakdale Court was everything that Briony could have wished it to be—rundown, neglected, and sadly in need of repairs and refurbishing. The gardens were completely choked with weeds and the outhouses in a dangerous state of disrepair. Nothing could have been more suited to the purposes of the new mistress. Her eyes glowed with a queer, zealous light as she contemplated the task that lay ahead of her. The management of manor and estate was something with which Briony Langland was entirely familiar. Henry VIII could not have viewed the magnificence of his Hampton Court with more admiring eyes than Ravensworth's Marchioness viewed the derelict pile of bricks which was to be her future home.

Lord Ravensworth acted as tour guide throughout and seemed rather abashed at the squalor of the place. The stench of decay which hung in the air was an offense to his nostrils and a pungent reminder that he had never thought to spend a groat on the upkeep of the house since he had graced the old heap of stones only infrequently and mostly in company of his more rackety familiars and the notorious "ladies" of the demimonde. The thought of the former debauchery which had transpired within the crumbling walls brought a guilty flush to Ravensworth's neck. Perhaps it had been a mistake to bring Briony, reflected his lordship.

He watched Briony with a guarded expression as he led her through the public rooms on the ground floor. The lady was unusually quiet—not that he blamed her. "What do you think?" he asked doubtfully as Briony got down on her knees to inspect the filthy relic of what had once been a rug.

"Aubusson," she replied on a note of regret, "but quite irredeemable, more's the pity. Moth, I think."

"Not the rug. I mean about the house. Perhaps it was a mistake to come. Better pack it in and return to town, d'you think?"

Briony was taken aback. "And leave the place to go to rack and ruin? You surely don't mean it, Ravensworth?" She could not bear it now if he were to throw an obstacle in the path of the ambitions she had begun to cherish. She bent an accusing look at him.

His lordship was conscious that he had unwittingly ruffled her feathers and spoke reassuringly. "No, no! It shall be just as you wish, my dear. If you don't object to the inconvenience of what has been up till now a bachelor establishment. Now that I am in the way of becoming a family man, naturally I shall set about making a few changes."

"Naturally," she concurred rather dryly as she moved to examine the cavernous fireplace which was heaped to the gunnels with what looked to be years of burnt offerings. "Better get the skivvy on to clearing these ashes. I'll need them for my garden. By the way, Ravensworth, where *are* the servants?" Her delicate brows lifted in inquiry.

His lordship looked shiftily at his Marchioness. "There are a couple of caretakers on the place somewhere," he said stiffly, "and Denby, my valet, will be here from London directly with the rest of our baggage."

"Your valet? He'll be a big help, I'm sure."

Ravensworth's jaw hardened. "If I had had the least

notion that the house was so uninhabitable, I would never have suggested that we remove from Bath."

"Oh, you never *suggested* it," said Briony in what his lordship thought was a deliberate attempt to provoke him to anger. He ignored the interruption.

"Naturally I shall set about engaging extra staff, as many as you deem necessary to put the place to rights."

"Perhaps we could enlist Wellington's army?" suggested Briony with a touch of asperity, now scrutinizing the solid oak Jacobean furniture which was coated with years of accumulated soot and dust. She extended her index finger and inscribed "please clean me" along the top of a particularly filthy library table. When she became aware of an unnaturally silent Ravensworth observing her wrathfully, she knew that she was goading him beyond endurance.

"Well now," said Briony, flashing Ravensworth a conciliatory smile, "it's really not so bad. The first thing to do is to get hold of our estate manager and tell him exactly what we have in mind."

His lordship cleared his throat nervously and was hard put to look squarely into her ladyship's eyes. "I collect that he, um, resigned some months ago. The fact had entirely slipped my mind until the present moment."

"That doesn't surprise me!" Briony snapped, almost oversetting a vase of indeterminate make which she had been on the point of picking up to examine. "You obviously had far more important things to occupy your thoughts." There came fleetingly to her mind the recollection of those frivolous diversions which had so captured the interest of her brother, Vernon, and the young bucks who had hung out with him in Richmond and which had caused her no little distress at the time. She looked at Ravensworth with something like a reproachful sneer. "No, my lord, it does not surprise me to learn that you have neglected your obligations to your dependents. A man-about-town must ever be occupied with more pressing matters—such as the fold of his neck cloth or whether his next coat should come from Weston or what's-his-name. How should he spare a thought for the livelihood of others when he possesses a fortune to squander on such vices as cockfighting, those vulgar mills at Jackson's boxing saloon, gambling at the obligatory clubs for gentlemen or, even worse, gaming hells for all I know, not to mention drinking to excess at the least provocation, and, it goes without saying—womanizing."

Until that moment, Ravensworth had given every evidence of being thoroughly chastened. As he heard Briony out, however, his emotions underwent a change from shock at the violence of her diatribe to out-and-out indignation. It was not what Briony said which overset his temper, but that she should call him to account for what every man in England, more or less, indulged in was an iniquitous injustice. He allowed that there were some episodes in his past that were best forgotten but nothing that warranted such a trimming. The trouble with Briony was that she was such an innocent. Most women in her position would have the grace to turn a blind eye to a husband's former indiscretions. Damnation, he thought, how can I convince her that I mean to change—have changed, in fact, since she first thrust herself uninvited into my carefree existence?

"Briony," he said at last when he had mastered his temper, "I wish you would refrain from stirring up the embers of my lamentable past. It has nothing to say to the present. I may have raised a few eyebrows in my time but my conduct was never, well, scandalous." He favored her with a knowing smile. "Even you, madam wife, have sailed close to the wind on the odd occasion. Furthermore, I take great exception to being called a 'womanizer.' Acquit me of that charge at least." Here his lordship hesitated and chose his next words with care. "I have never yet had a woman in my keeping. I see that surprises you—but it is the truth, I swear it, Briony. You were the only woman for whom I ever cared enough to offer—well, that part of our courtship is best forgotten. I made a cake of myself, and I beg your forgiveness. I wish to be completely honest with you, you see. I admit that I have sown a few wild oats in my time, but no more than other men. What I lacked was discretion." Briony's silence and impassive stance goaded him to a more passionate declaration. "Good God, Briony, the fact that I have chosen to bind myself to one woman irrevocably should prove *something* to you!"

Her eyes registered surprise. "This marriage, as I recall, was thrust upon us. You never had any intention of making me your wife. The facts of the case are that I inadvertently compromised you, for which I am truly sorry, Ravensworth. It is I who should be begging your pardon."

Ravensworth's conscience troubled him greatly. "Briony . . . my dear . . ." he began haltingly, "I have been meaning to talk to you about the circumstances of our marriage." He chanced to look deeply into his wife's clear-eyed expression and his good intentions evaporated. How could he tell this innocent girl that he had deliberately engineered their marriage? Honesty was the supreme virtue in her eyes. She would despise him for it. He would confess his duplicity when a more propitious moment presented itself, Ravensworth silently promised himself.

"You were saying?" encouraged Briony. "Something about the circumstances of our marriage?"

Ravensworth recovered himself quickly. "I only meant that, whatever the circumstances of our marriage, I am not sorry to find myself married to you." He captured her grimy hand and spoke in earnest entreaty. "Briony, all I ask is a chance to prove that I can be a husband worthy of your confidence. Can't we call a truce and begin afresh? I will never give you cause to regret that you married me—and that's a promise, word of honor."

This impassioned speech had Briony, quite uncharacteristically, at a loss for words. She was scarcely aware that she nodded her assent. Ravensworth was not slow to take advantage of her hesitation. He tucked her hand confidently into the crook of his arm and escorted her through the remainder of the house, and although she saw a good deal with which she might have reproached him, Briony kept her own counsel. For some reason which was beyond her power to fathom, she was happier than she had ever been in her life.

Oakdale Court was a red-bricked Jacobean edifice of approximately sixty spacious apartments and extensive outbuildings including a magnificent stable which lay empty except for the eight nags and the one coach which had conveyed them from Bath. Briony's taste in architecture and furnishings could not have been more gratified with the solid simplicity of the massive Jacobean fireplaces and the open-beamed ceilings. The new mistress of Oakdale Court esteemed simplicity and comfort above all things.

Simplicity of style, notwithstanding the size of the house, she had in good measure. Briony was not immune to the beauty of the pseudo-classical Palladian architecture of Bath and other grand houses around Richmond which she had visited, but there was something more honest, in her opinion, in the unadorned lines of Oakdale Court. It was so thoroughly, unpretentiously English and brought to mind an earlier era of stolid yeoman stock which had made England prosperous and a power to be reckoned with in the world.

Comfort, however, was sadly lacking, and Briony set herself to providing it in abundant measure. Within twenty-four hours of her first tour of the dilapidated house, her small staff of six grooms and two old caretakers, whose days of active service had long since passed, was augmented by an army of retainers whom Ravensworth had miraculously procured. For a moment Briony half believed that Ravensworth had taken her literally and commandeered the British army. Some judicious inquiry, however, set her mind at rest. Every able-bodied man and woman on the estate who was free from other duties had been enticed into service on the promise of a handsome bonus from his lordship if the old mausoleum of a place could be set to rights within the month. Poverty is a compelling master. Briony, as Ravensworth had promised, was given her army of minions to do her bidding, and under her able direction, years of neglect along with moldering carpets and draperies, were swept away. She was an astute and hard taskmaster, turning away immediately anyone whom she suspected of malingering. In this she merely copied her father's methods of management. There were a few complaints, but those whom the mistress dismissed invariably found employment with the master. That gentleman was found to have a more forgiving disposition.

Night after night during their first week of residence, Briony fell into an exhausted slumber immediately her head touched the pillow of her massive four-poster bed in her solitary chamber. His lordship was not so fortunate, although no less exhausted. He, too, had been doing his part to bring the estate into shape. Briony's efforts were confined to the house. Ravensworth had over a thousand acres to oversee and a new agent to break in besides. He had authorized the spending of considerable sums of money in repairs and new machines for the next harvest. As he threw himself into the task of bringing order from the sad neglect which was everywhere in evidence, he was surprised to discover that he had never been happier in his life. A man who had every intention of siring a quiverful of strapping sons and one or two girls in the image of their beautiful mama had need of a settled domicile to anchor his life. That Briony was bone weary and too tired to say more than two syllables over dinner every evening was a major obstacle to the fulfillment of his lordship's desires. His patience, never one of his strongest virtues, was beginning to wear thin. As he tossed and turned nightly in his lonely couch, he demanded of himself how much longer he could endure to forgo the pleasures of Briony's bed. It would be unjust in her, and therefore quite out of character, to keep him at bay when he had taken such pains to demonstrate that he was serious in his intention of pursuing a more regular, settled way of living. In all conscience, and Briony prided herself on conscience, she must come to see that he had earned his reward.

As was to be expected, their neighbor, Lady Adèle, put in an appearance before many days had passed and at the most inopportune moment. Briony, dressed in an old kerseymere smock and a straw bonnet that had seen better days, had set to work with a vengeance, clearing the herb garden of the encroaching weeds. As she hacked, pulled, and dug, heedless of the dabs of mud which clung to her skirts and which somehow had become smeared on her face, she had been delighted to discover that beneath the jungle of rampant foliage a few herbs were flourishing. She had just crushed a sprig of lemon balm in her hands and was inhaling the sweet scent when a group of riders rounded the corner of the house and came toward her. In the lead was her husband, looking, as was his wont, like a tailor's mannequin. Briony eyed him enviously. Such were the benefits of keeping in one's employ a valet whose sole occupation was to ensure that his master was properly turned out. Her abigail was the new cook's helper, a raw-boned, ham-fisted woman who was pressed into service only when desperately needed. Briony rarely required her services.

As Ravensworth took in his wife's disreputable appearance, he cantered ahead of his companions and came to a halt a few feet away. Briony straightened and put a hand to her aching back.

"You look like a damned scarecrow," said Ravensworth in a wrathful undertone. "Where are the gardeners? I'll turn them off for dereliction of duty. This is not an occupation fitting for a lady."

"Why did you bring them here?" parried Briony in some irritation, deeply embarrassed to be discovered in such a predicament and by a troop of impeccable fashion plates who looked as if they had just stepped out of a picture by Lawrence. She caught a glimpse of Adèle in a black-and-tan riding habit in the high kick of fashion and Briony hastened to conceal her own dowdy weeds behind Ravensworth's mount. "Take them to the house. I'll join you directly in the drawing room," she flung at him.

Ravensworth wheeled his mount to do her bidding but the redoubtable Adèle was before him. "How do you do, Lady Ravensworth?" she cooed, her omniscient glance sweeping Briony. "Hugh has been quite literally singing your praises. My, my, but you have been a busy little chatelaine since you arrived. Your resourcefulness is most commendable but then I collect I already mentioned that fact to you at Bath?"

"You flatter me, Lady St. Clair," said Briony with as much good humor as she could muster under the circumstances.

"Do I? I don't mean to," said the lady, bending a quizzical look at Ravensworth, who sat impassively upon his mount.

As a Quaker, Briony had been taught to address herself to the good, the divine spark in each individual, but as she looked with dislike at the unlovely beauty who was holding her up to ridicule, she came to see the sense in Nanny's Puritan dogma, that man is a worm with no good in him. Her lips parted in preparation of administering a freezing set-down to the overconfident lady, but a quick glance at Ravensworth's troubled expression stayed the words on her lips. She remembered that he had said the world would be eagerly watching her reaction to his former paramour and Briony had no wish to discomfit him before strangers. That pleasure she would reserve for a more private encounter. She stripped her gardening gloves from her fingers and strove for a welcoming expression as she addressed the company in general.

"I bid you welcome. As you see, the new mistress of Oakdale is an avid gardener." She flashed a deprecating smile and moved among them with what she hoped was regal grace as if she had been outfitted in the latest fashion from Paris. "Ravensworth will do the honors while I set myself to rights. I'll arrange for sherry and biscuits to be served in the drawing room. Ah, Lord Grafton, how do you do?" she intoned as she spotted the Earl. Briony had been making her way unobtrusively to the kitchen entrance and with a last, forced smile, disappeared through the door. Once inside, her expression changed to an unbecoming scowl. She ran up the servants' staircase calling for Nell to come and assist her at once. In a matter of minutes she had made herself presentable and changed into a simple gray frock which suited her admirably but was too demure by half to compete with the strikingly handsome ensemble of her rival. Briony had one weapon which she used only rarely, since Ravensworth objected. But this was one occasion, she told herself, which required all her resources. She shook out her hair till it cascaded in waves around her shoulders. The change in her appearance was dramatic. With a last, reassuring glance at the looking glass, she made her way to the drawing room with a becoming smile turning up her lips.

Chapter 18

One quick look at Ravensworth's darkening expression informed Briony instantly that her loose tresses did not find favor in his eyes, but since the Countess had cornered him in a private tête-à-tête on a sofa, Briony felt assured of a short respite from her husband's censure. It was left to Grafton to make the introductions to the other members of the party, and Briony noted with some surprise and no little pleasure that they were, with the notable odd exception, all of the first respectability.

The visit lasted only half an hour, as was customary, and as their guests rose to take their leave, Briony directed a few commonplaces to her husband, addressing him by his title as was her habit. The Countess immediately drew the attention of all present to the unexpected formality in Briony's address.

"What's this, Hugh?" she asked pertly. "Are you encouraging your little wife to treat you with the deference of a servant? If you call him 'Ravensworth,' my dear," she said to Briony with the appearance of innocence, "you will be the only woman in London who is not on familiar terms with the disreputable rogue."

The comment demanded some kind of response and Briony was highly conscious of the embarrassed glances of not a few of her departing guests. Ravensworth looked as if he had taken root where he stood. She could not very well blurt out the truth and disclose that she still felt very much of a stranger with her new husband and he had never so much as intimated to her that he wished to be addressed by his Christian name. She hung her head and gave Ravensworth a sideways, coquettish grin.

"Oh, I have a pet name for my husband which I use only in private. I scarce like to mention it without his permission." She gave him a challenging smile.

"Be my guest," Ravensworth responded with commendable confidence.

"If you say so, Monty, my dear," uttered Briony at her most ingenuous.

Ravensworth's nostrils flared, but he preserved his calm countenance admirably. His arm snaked around Briony's waist and he pulled her hard against his side. "Short for Montgomery," said the Marquess with well-bred affability.

Briony turned her mouth to his ear. "Or mountebank," she whispered softly, but loud enough for the Countess to hear. Briony was not above flaunting her position as Ravensworth's wife. Her deliberately flirtatious manner was meant to convey the message that she was on the most intimate terms with her husband. The Countess's back grew rigid, and Briony was not displeased.

"Monty is not his favorite soubriquet," Briony went on airily. "There are a few other names I call him, but not in general to his face." The viselike grip on her waist tightened and Briony sobered.

With an arm firmly encircling Briony's waist, thus effectively foiling the quick escape he was sure she was contemplating, Ravensworth saw their guests off the premises, promising that he and Briony would look in on them later for an informal evening of dinner and cards.

Once inside the foyer again, he turned to face her and Briony, studiously avoiding his eyes, mumbled that there were a million things that required her immediate attention. She was pulled roughly into Ravensworth's arms. "What a woman you are, Briony Langland," said Ravensworth, his eyes warm with admiration. "What grace, what dash, what a pleasure to see you in action."

"And what quick thinking," snorted Briony.

"Monty indeed!" He tipped her head back. "Is it too much to ask that you use my Christian name?"

"Would you make a liar of me?" she countered. "You'll get used to it, Monty. Besides, when you hear that soubriquet, you'll know that the lady who wants you is your wife. See that you come to heel when I call," she said with a bold look.

"I intend to, my love, my own sweet briar patch."

"Briar patch?"

"My pet name for you. You remind me of the untamed gardens you seem to admire so much. I give you leave to do what you will on the estate. But for this particular untamed patch of weeds," he went on, giving her a playful shake, "there will be only one gardener—myself. I'll cultivate my briar patch with jealous care."

"Cultivate?"

"Like this." He cupped her face in his hands and looked deeply into her luminous eyes as if trying to gauge the effect of his impulsive gesture. Briony looked steadily up at him and read the uncertainty in his usually confident expression. She knew instinctively that she had some terrible power over him and could shatter his self-confidence with one look or a word. She smiled a slow smile (â la Ravensworth) and was abruptly swept into an embrace that threatened to suffocate her.

Months of deprivation with vivid images of a receptive Briony nestled in his arms to torment him had his senses on fire from the moment he felt her warm lips respond beneath his. He groaned his pleasure at the heat of her soft body melting against his. Her receptivity to his embrace inflamed him. His hands traveled the length of her body, wanting to possess all of her. He could not get close enough to her. He kissed the rounded swell of her breasts, and the soft, whimpering sounds deep in her throat had him in a fever of passion. He raised his head, and his lips curved in an exultant smile at the desire he saw mirrored in Briony's smokey gray eyes.

"I can't let you go now. Take pity on me, Briony," he coaxed. "You know that there is some unfinished business between us that needs to be urgently settled." His lips moved tantalizingly against her throat. "Come to bed with me now. You won't regret it."

Briony strove to retain some of her composure. "It's not possible," she finally managed, regaining her breath. His head jerked back and Briony found herself looking into a pair of stormy blue eyes.

"Briony!" he growled. "Don't try my patience too far."

"We can't," she said apologetically, biting down on her lip. "This is Tuesday and the floors of all the usptairs bedrooms are to be sanded. The servants will be there now."

"Well, the library will suffice," Ravensworth went on in a mode of quiet desperation.

Briony was shocked to the core. "There are no drapes," she responded, her voice rising.

"The attic?" he suggested on a note of forlorn hope.

"Be reasonable, Hugh," said Briony placatingly, rearranging the folds of his lordship's disarranged neckcloth. "Come to me tonight."

The simple invitation took Ravensworth's breath away. "Oh my dear," he said softly as he stroked her hair, "how I have longed to hear those words." He bent to kiss her again, but the unexpected appearance of two of the upstairs maids had Ravensworth and Briony draw apart in a guilty start. Briony slipped out of his arms and with a saucy gait moved to ascend the staircase. She threw him a flirtatious glance over her shoulder. Ravensworth stood watching her retreating back with a gleam of anticipation in his eye. As Dolly and Polly, or was it Polly and Dolly, moved to pass him demurely, he gave a sudden high kick in the air almost startling the housemaids out of their wits.

Ravensworth's admiring eyes held Briony's momentarily before he turned back to give his attention to his table companion. He was in a fever of impatience to have this obligatory evening with Adèle over and done with so that he could at last be alone with his wife in a house which, he sincerely hoped, was devoid of Briony's overzealous lackeys. A small smile at some private reflection curved his lips as he strove to give the semblance of an intelligent reply to the query of the lady on his left. He watched Briony covertly and noted with approval her easy grace as she conversed with the shy young man who seemed to gain confidence under her approving smile—a younger son destined for holy orders, if he remembered correctly. He wondered idly what topic of conversation could have so engrossed the young man's attention.

Ravensworth was not the only one who was watching Briony with covert interest. Lady Adèle St. Clair, although resigned to the fact that her former lover was lost to her forever and indeed had attached Grafton to herself to stave off boredom and loneliness, was not averse to baiting the younger woman. To have lost the Marquess to a chit of a girl with so little to recommend her, she took to be in the nature of a personal insult. What could a man of his appetites see in the prim and proper miss with her modest frock and old-maidish chignon?

Lady Adèle was not to know that Briony's demure appearance that evening was far from expressing Briony's preference. It was Ravensworth who had insisted that his wife coil her wayward locks and clothe herself like what he was pleased to call "a virtuous lady." What he was willing to permit in the boudoir for his eyes only was one thing, but to allow his wife to flaunt her charms before lecherous men was a thing he would not countenance. He viewed with distaste the open invitation to every man in Adèle's provocative glances. That she had dampened her petticoats to make her gown of lavender silk cling like a second skin went without saying. It amazed him to think that he had once found her overblown beauty enticing. Briony had changed his taste in women irrevocably. When he had daughters of his own, he would give them a few pointers from the benefit of his experience, thought his lordship, allowing his warm gaze to settle on his wife's person. When he found himself mentally undressing her, he forced himself to initiate a conversation with the Honorable Miss Brown on the unexceptionable topic of the vagaries of the unseasonably warm weather.

"Did I hear the word 'Newgate'?" asked Lady Adèle of Briony and her table companion Mr. Guy Sommerville. Briony looked up and was dismayed to see that the whole company was looking in her direction.

"By Jove, yes," said the young Mr. Sommerville, his eyes warm with admiration for Briony. "Lady Ravensworth is acquainted with Mrs. Elizabeth Fry, a Quaker lady who has taken up penal reform."

"Never heard of her," drawled Grafton.

"You will," responded Briony succinctly.

"Lady Ravensworth has paid a visit to Newgate in person," interjected Mr. Sommerville, drawing a murmur of surprise from quite a few of the guests. Briony stole a quick look at Ravensworth and was relieved to note that his expression held more interest than displeasure.

"Is this true, Briony?"

"Yes. Mrs. Fry was a friend of Mama. Naturally, when I came to town, I renewed the acquaintance. When she invited me to examine in person the inhuman conditions which prevail for the women of Newgate, not to mention their innocent children, I felt duty bound to accept. Mama would have done no less, and many Quaker ladies have since taken up the work."

"Hardly a fitting occupation for a lady of refinement," said Lady Adèle dismissively.

Briony's eyes were as cool as ice as she looked at her hostess. "Do you know, that is the second time today that someone has said something like that to me? Fortunately, I do not aspire to be a lady of refinement, so my sensibilities remain untouched."

"Well, I think Lady Ravensworth is top o' the trees," interposed Sommerville in an attitude of belligerence.

"What I think," said Lady Adèle, her temper rising at the implied rebuke, "is that they should lock them up and throw away the keys. They've broken the law and must be taught a lesson."

Briony was thoroughly roused and refused to heed her husband's warning look.

"Laws!" she said scathingly, her voice shaking. "What laws are there to protect the disadvantaged? These women steal to feed their hungry children and we brand them as criminals."

"Let their husbands and fathers feed them, if they have any," a masculine voice farther down the table mumbled.

Briony threw down her knife and fork in a gesture of impatience. "Now there, sir, your erudition quite overwhelms me, for you have wittingly or unwittingly, as the case may be, uncovered the heart of the matter. If these husbands and fathers would simply desert the British Army, the problem would be less pressing. They should be home where they belong looking after their families."

"Desert the Army?" Even Mr. Sommerville was stunned. Ravensworth bent a withering look at Briony. "Lady Ravensworth is but jesting," he broke into the astonished silence. "Tell them, my dear!"

Briony did. "War is a most ridiculous method of solving our problems. Take poor Napoleon, for example!" She ignored the shocked gasps around the table. "Think of all the good he has done for France—fairer taxes, more equitable laws, schools and university education for the masses. Even our cousins in America admire him. I don't mean to say that the man's a paragon of virtue, but he is not as bad as we have been led to believe. The man has heart. We should have made a friend of him, not confined him to Elba like a common criminal."

"Madam, you forget yourself," said Ravensworth tersely, wishing that he could wring her neck.

"Oh forget it, Ravensworth," Lord Grafton broke in. "We are all friends here. Even Lord Byron expresses himself in much the same terms. I find myself in agreement with Briony, especially about the Americans. I've never understood the nature of our quarrel with them. They're British the same as you and I. Damned inconvenience if you ask me. Some of my cousins are American."

Lord Grafton's words fueled the flames of Ravensworth's anger. "May I remind you, sir, and everyone present, that in some quarters such remarks would be regarded as treasonable? As a peer of the realm and a loyal subject of His Majesty, I know where my duty lies. We are at war with the United States of America. It behooves us to speak and act with discretion. At this very moment, the far-flung British Army might well be under attack by American forces. If we lose this war, would that please you? Do you wish the Americans to annex Canada?"

Lord Grafton shrugged his indifference, but Briony was by no means finished. "Of course I shouldn't wish any harm to come to Canada. But who provoked this stupid quarrel in the first place? The House of Hanover—"

"Briony," roared his lordship at his wits' end, "will you be silent on this subject!" It was a command, not a question, and Briony, observing the dangerous glitter in Ravensworth's eyes, yielded to the ferocity of his expression.

When the covers had been removed, Ravensworth cornered her before the ladies withdrew to leave the gentlemen to their port. "For pity's sake, Briony, mind your tongue. If you don't take thought for yourself, think of my position. Any question of my loyalty to the Crown would ruin me." He squeezed her arm to convey that his anger had been more for public display than personal rebuke. "Now be a good girl and talk to the ladies about babies or weddings or some indifferent subject."

Conversation among the ladies in the drawing room was rather boring and desultory until Briony found a Miss Brown who shared her interest in herb gardening. The lady, a native of Yorkshire who had been out for three Seasons, had an extensive knowledge of medicinal herbs. Briony was enthralled as she compared notes with a fellow devotee. Lady Adèle came to stand beside them for a moment or two but, perceiving that the conversation held no interest for her, stifled a yawn and moved to another group. With no males in attendance, Lady Adèle took little pains to conceal her boredom and made not the least push to entertain her female guests.

"You will be a daughter-in-law after the Duke's heart," said Miss Brown conversationally to Briony. "Your father-in-law has a thing about herbs, I collect. His gardens at Dalbreck Hall are famous in Yorkshire. But your husband will have told you about his father's passion for gardening."

Briony's ears pricked up. "I know nothing at all about the Duke except that he is rather forbidding."

"Forbidding? The Duke of Dalbreck? What gammon! Someone has been hoaxing you, my dear. He's as gentle as a lamb. Ask Lord Ravensworth."

"Do you know him?"

"Not well. He does not come into company since his wife died. He can't bear to tear himself away from his seat in Yorkshire. I'm told that he is often mistaken for the gardener. Like you and I, he likes nothing better than to don old togs and putter about the herbary."

"No, really?" asked Briony, mentally revising her picture of His Grace. "But still, a man of his consequence must be disappointed that his son has not looked higher for a wife." She realized, too late, that she had spoken her thoughts aloud.

"Not a bit of it," said Miss Brown, genuinely shocked. "He dotes on his son. Why, Ravensworth's mother was the daughter of a country squire. It was a love match and a great shock to the old Duke, who *was* conscious to a degree of his own consequence. The present Duke isn't a bit like that. He is much freer and easier than, well, even Lord Ravensworth. He doesn't stand on ceremony. I am certain you will get along famously together."

"Shall we?" asked Briony thoughtfully. Miss Brown's description of her father-in-law was not at all what Ravensworth had led her to believe. She tried to recall the circumstances of when she had first heard the Duke's name mentioned. Yes, the weeks leading up to the night that Ravensworth had tried to make her his mistress. He had said then that he could not make her an offer of marriage because—What was it?—his father, the Duke, expected him to marry someone of his own station. Dawning comprehension had Briony's cheeks flushing a becoming pink. The unmitigated impertinence of the despicable liar! It had been his excuse for not offering her marriage—a sham to manipulate her.

She was brought out of her reverie by a question from Lady Adèle. "I beg your pardon? I am afraid I was woolgathering. What was it you wished to know?" asked Briony politely.

"Merely your opinion, my dear. We are discussing whether it is ethical for a lady to use any means at her disposal to catch the attention of a gentleman for whom she has developed a tendre?"

"Honesty is always the best policy," replied Briony rather primly.

This brought a howl of protests from the ladies, and a flood of personal anecdotes on how to bring a reluctant gentleman up to scratch. Briony listened to their good-natured banter with an indulgent smile.

"It seems that we are willing to go to almost any lengths in quest of our quarry," said Miss Brown gaily, "broken-down carriages, books or gloves dropped at the opportune moment, fainting spells or sprained ankles when the right pair of strong arms is there to catch us. What a bunch of hussies we are, to be sure."

"Don't you believe it," said Lady Susan, a red-haired, freckled girl who was known to have five brothers. "Men are worse. They will stop at nothing to achieve their ends. Our tactics are child's play compared to theirs. I've heard my brothers discuss their flirts and worse—those ladies whom we gently bred girls are supposed to know nothing about. The more unattainable the object of their desire, the more desperate their attempts to gain it."

"What is the worst they can possibly do?" asked Briony, her interest caught.

"Well, I heard once of a lady who was abducted, but gentlemen don't generally go to *that* extreme. However, I believe that compromising a lady is a ploy that is quite common. Of course, a woman's reputation is easily ruined but a gentleman's honor in such situations is never seriously damaged whether or not he offers marriage."

"How can that be?" asked Briony in some perplexity. "I don't think I quite understand what you infer."

"Simple," said another lady, breaking into the conversation for the first time. "If a man does tarnish his reputation a little, who cares even? He gets the name of being a bit of a rake, but he is not cut or ostracized by Society. It even enhances his reputation among the ladies, clods that we are."

"But a woman caught in the same position is utterly ruined if the gentleman refuses to marry her," said Lady Susan. "So any gentleman who is determined to have a particular lady needs only to arrange things to suit himself. Of course, heiresses are the worst target. Some pretend to be paupers to escape the toils of unscrupulous fortune hunters!"

"So it behooves all young ladies to be properly chaperoned at all times!" said one of the matrons in a reproving tone. "Then your reputations will be above reproach. But you girls never pay the least heed to what we chaperones say," she ended on a note of resignation.

"I see," said Briony, lapsing into one of her meditative silences. Her thoughts were in a turmoil. She had no clear idea of what her new knowledge signified. Only one thing was perfectly obvious. Ravensworth was an inveterate liar. He had lied to her to inveigle her into becoming his mistress and he had lied to her when he had persuaded her to marry him to save him from ruin. The man had as smooth a tongue as the Devil. The bright sparkle in the lady's eyes and the rosy bloom suffusing her normally pallid complexion gave her an animation which she seldom achieved.

As he entered the drawing room with the rest of the gentlemen, his lordship feasted his eyes on Briony and thought her as pretty a picture as he had ever beheld.

Chapter 19

It did not take long for Ravensworth to perceive that Briony was in high dudgeon. Her eyes refused to meet his, and every attempt on his part to engage her interest was met with dogged rebuff. He soon gave it up, for he had no wish to impart the intelligence to the other members of the house party that he had come to cuffs with his wife. Briony's cool demeanor was not calculated to placate her husband's acknowledged mercurial temper, and by the time they had climbed into their carriage for the homeward drive, hostilities on both sides were on the point of being resumed. It was his lordship who fired the opening salvo.

"Better cover that cold shoulder," he said, adjusting Briony's wrap. "We wouldn't want you catching a chill. Did you notice how the temperature suddenly plummeted? Very unseasonable weather for this time of year."

As the evening could safely be said to be balmy, there was no mistaking the sarcasm behind Ravensworth's words. Briony, very much on her dignity, was not slow to join battle. "It is my perception," she began in a brittle voice, "that the temperature in this carriage will soon be so hot that you will be wishing yourself at Hades."

Ravensworth threw back his head and laughed. "Have I landed in the briars again, my sweet Briony?" he asked, chucking her under the chin. "No, don't glare at me.

How can I defend myself if I don't know what my offense is? You are surely not going to give me a scold simply because I silenced you at the dinner table? I take leave to tell you," he went on in a more serious vein, "that you gave me a few unquiet moments with your traitorous talk, but I think I convinced everyone that you would be loyal to your husband whatever your sentiments." He flicked her nose playfully but Briony was not to be deflected from her purpose.

"Sir, you are a liar," she said without preamble. "You lied to me when you said that your father would be averse to our match. You tried to make me your mistress by pretending that it was impossible for you to offer me marriage. But that was not the truth, was it, Ravensworth?"

Ravensworth's heart missed a beat. That particular deception had completely slipped his mind. It was evident that one of the ladies had put Briony wise to him. She would have discovered it sooner or later. He should have confessed the whole to her while he had the chance. "Briony, my dear, that is an episode that is best forgotten. I am not the man I was then. I was selfish, arrogant, if you like. I don't deny it. But I have changed. Why won't you believe me?"

"Oh?" said Briony with feigned sweetness. "And when did this change come about?"

Ravensworth drew her hands into his and answered with perfect sincerity. "Almost immediately after I made that preposterous offer. When you ran away and I had no knowledge of where you were or what had happened to you. Let me tell you, I went through hell. For the first time in my life, I realized that I cared for someone more than I cared for myself."

Briony firmly withdrew her hands from his clasp and smiled faintly. "Was that before or after you discovered that marrige to me would bring you a fortune?"

"What fortune?" asked Ravensworth baffled.

"Come, come, Ravensworth. You can do better than that. You are no novice dissembler. On the contrary, you are the most accomplished liar it has ever been my misfortune to encounter. 'What fortune?'" she mimicked scathingly.

Ravensworth was thunderstruck. "Are you saying that I am a fortune hunter?" he demanded, his anger rising to match hers.

"Did you or did you not deliberately set out to compromise me to force me to marry you?" she countered.

Ravensworth's jaw clenched. "Not exactly."

"What does that mean? Tell me the truth for once in your life." Briony's cool exterior cracked.

"It means that events turned out just as I wished. It was my intention to offer for you, but I wasn't sure that you would accept me on my own merits."

"What merits?" Briony howled. "I knew you for a libertine—a man of questionable morals. The first time I clapped eyes on you, you were attempting to have your way with that flaxen-haired doxy, a lady, so I thought at the time. Not long afterward, you had the effrontery to try to make me your mistress. You played on my regard for you, thinking I would set aside my scruples because it was impossible for you to offer me marriage. You cad! And you engineered our marriage in the most underhand way, pretending that it was my duty to marry you to save your reputation. You unscrupulous devil!"

Ravensworth kept his temper on a tight rein. "Calm yourself, Briony. I don't deny that there is some justification in what you say. Haven't I admitted my faults already? If I was not completely honest with you, it was not without reason. The end justified the means. I knew you to be overscrupulous to a degree. If I concealed my true intentions from you, it was simply to secure our happiness.

You would have refused my suit for the most frivolous of reasons. I knew that you had taken me in aversion simply because I was fool enough to offer you carte blanche. Your pride was wounded, nothing more. I have tried to make amends, to no avail. Perhaps it was high-handed in me to secure your consent to our marriage by pretending that I would be ruined if you refused, but I did it with the best will in the world—to save *you* from ruin."

"Did you so?" she asked crushingly. "Well, I take leave to tell you my lord, that the road to hell is paved with good intentions."

There seemed to be no suitable reply to this, and Ravensworth and Briony lapsed into an angry silence until the carriage rolled up to the main entrance of Oakdale. As he helped Briony alight, he made one last, futile attempt to breach her defenses. "Does this mean, my love, that you would rather not share my bed tonight?"

Briony stumbled and Ravensworth's strong arms caught her before she fell. The spate of invective which issued from those innocent lips would have daunted the most ardent admirer. Ravensworth, only slightly shaken, tweaked her ear and said teasingly, "I esteem a woman of passion. That you admit to hating me shows that you are weakening. It is only indifference that a lover fears."

As she stalked into the house with as much dignity as she could muster, the last thing she heard was Ravensworth's laughter mocking at her back.

The first of their visitors arrived the next morning. Ravensworth returned home to find Briony in the library pouring tea for two young gentlemen. Her brother, Vernon, he recognized almost instantly, but his companion was a stranger to him. Their conversation, he noted idly, was conducted in undertones. Ravensworth made his presence known and the startled glances of brother and sister gave him the distinct impression that he had disturbed them in the plotting of some nefarious scheme. His eyes flicked to Briony, and her shuttered expression and stammered introductions roused his suspicions even further.

"R-Ravensworth, are you here? May I present my c-cousin, Mr. John Caldwell, who is on a visit from C-Canada."

Vernon's companion had risen to make his bows. He was a well-set-up young man of about five and twenty with nothing of the gentleman of fashion about him. His plain but well-fitting black coat and beige leather breeches, unrelieved by any ostentation, won from Ravensworth a silent approval.

"Are you of the Grenfell or the Langland branch of the family?" asked Ravensworth conversationally, accepting a cup of tea from Briony. He noticed a slight tremor in her hand and his brows knit together.

"The Langland," said brother and sister in swift unison. "The Langland branch," repeated Mr. Caldwell in a soft, colonial drawl. "Our connection is very tenuous. Cousins—two or three times removed, I collect."

This vague response did nothing to satisfy Ravensworth's curiosity. By dint of persistent questioning he tried to pin down the precise particulars of Mr. Caldwell's parentage, domicile, and purpose in coming to England. At the end of fifteen minutes or so, he found himself hardly the wiser. Just when he was closing in on his quarry, Briony would interrupt with a non sequitur and the conversation would be directed into other channels. In other circumstances, Ravensworth would have forced the issue, but given Briony's penchant for absolute honesty, he dismissed from his mind the notion that something of moment was being concealed from him.

"Do you remain long in England?" inquired Ravensworth politely.

"Not long now. There is some trifling business of a personal nature which needs to be settled before I take passage for home. I reckon I have one more week at my disposal. I hope I do not inconvenience you with my presence here?"

"Not at all," Briony interposed swiftly. "Families must stick together. We are delighted to be of service."

"Quite so!" seconded Ravensworth, silently wondering what sort of service Briony referred to. It dawned on him that Vernon and Caldwell had perhaps landed in some spot of bother peculiar to gentlemen of that age and had deemed it prudent to spend a week or two rusticating in the country. The thought that Briony's male relations were far from being the pattern cards of rectitude which she supposed them, he found quite cheering. Obviously he had disturbed them as they had been making the facts of the case known to Briony. From his own experience, he conjectured that they were escaping the clutches of some scheming wench, a jealous husband bent on revenge, or the strong-armed men of the notorious three percenters. Briony was probably wishing him at Jericho this minute so that she could ring a peal over the young bounders. No, that supposition would not do for Mr. Caldwell. He looked to be a young man who knew how to handle himself. His every move exuded a quiet confidence. Ravensworth's gaze shifted to Vernon. Now that lad was very ill at ease. Very well then. Caldwell had seen fit to rescue Vernon from some imbroglio in town and had brought him to the bosom of the family for protection. That must be it—or something close to it. Ravensworth smiled indulgently at his young brother-in-law, and on seeing it, Vernon began to quake in his shoes. The Marquess rose leisurely and made his excuses, saying that he looked forward to furthering Mr. Caldwell's acquaintance at dinner. As he passed Vernon's chair, he clapped the boy on the shoulder. "Don't take your sister too much to heart, my boy. I'll stand bail for you if you need a friend."

When the door closed behind him, the three occupants turned back to stare at each other. Only Caldwell's eyes held a spark of amusement. "His lordship has jumped to the wrong conclusion."

"What conclusion?" asked Briony tremulously.

"That Vernon has been up to some devilry and needs rescuing. Not an unusual circumstance for a callow youth separated from his family. Your husband's logic, in this instance, is far out."

"I *lied* to him," said Briony, her voice breaking.

"What possessed you?" asked Vernon, starting to his feet and beginning to pace. "There was no need for it. I would never have brought John here if I had not *known* that Ravensworth had some sympathy for the Americans."

"No, no! You are mistaken, Vernon. Ravensworth is loyal to the Crown, right or wrong. He told me as much himself a few nights ago. Indeed, he took me to task for expressing my disgust for the futility of war. I could not reveal the fact that you are an American, Mr. Caldwell. He would have handed you over to the authorities without hesitation. To him, you are an enemy, you see."

"Nevertheless," began Caldwell seriously, "I still think we ought to apprise Ravensworth of the truth. I am no threat to England. It is because the war in Canada is going badly for the British that I have suddenly become persona non grata here. We Quakers are held in the deepest suspicion by both sides because we refuse to take up arms. Your husband seems to be a man of reason. Let me tell him the truth. And if he does choose to hand me over to the authorities, I stand in no real danger. His Majesty's

Government will simply confine me in a comfortable cell for the duration of the war."

"Tell Ravensworth that I lied to him?" asked Briony, her whole demeanor expressing her horror. "He would never forgive me. He would kill me! Say no more on that score, Mr. Caldwell. I would never be able to face him again." She looked at him with mute appeal.

"Nor I," said Vernon gloomily. "Ravensworth is generous to a fault. He's bailed me out of a scrape or two in my time—nothing that you need worry your head about, Sis. Besides, he's bailed you out of a few scrapes too, as I hear. He's top o' the trees, Mr. Caldwell, but damnably proud. Thing is, I should hate to lose his good opinion, and if he finds out that I've been party to a lie, I think I should."

Mr. Caldwell took only a moment to come to a decision. "Very well then. Although I cannot like it, it shall be as you say. The less you know of my plans, the better. Suffice it to say that I shall be leaving for the coast under cover of darkness within the week. Vernon will accompany me, then make for London. Since Ravensworth takes us for a couple of young bloods hot on the scent of—well, never mind, he won't be in the least surprised at our hasty departure, quite the reverse I should think."

"How did you come to meet Mr. Caldwell?" Briony asked Vernon.

"Through some mutual acquaintances who knew of our Quaker sympathies. They were looking for a safe house near the coast where John could lie low until there was a boat to take him off. When I got your letter practically begging me to present myself at Oakdale, it seemed like the perfect solution, especially as I personally have heard Ravensworth say that successive governments have mishandled the American question for decades. I was sure he would be sympathetic."

"You must be mistaken," said Briony earnestly. "As a peer of the realm, he would be regarded as a traitor should he afford aid to an enemy of the Crown. He told me so himself. Trust me in this."

Mr. Caldwell looked closely at Briony. "Set your mind at rest, my lady. Ravensworth shall not hear the truth from me. I shall call you Cousin Briony, if I may, and of course, you must call me John. If we are to proceed with this deception, then let it be with a modicum of caution. Now what is our relationship precisely? Is there some Langland relative who emigrated to Canada whom I might claim as my antecedent?"

"Not to my knowledge," said Briony deep in thought. "As a matter of fact, we have no Langland relatives except an elderly spinster aunt in Shropshire. That is why Vernon and I became wards of our uncle, Sir John Grenfell. No matter, every family has some black sheep in its past who has emigrated to the colonies at some time or other, even if they are in ignorance of it."

Mr. Caldwell's lips quivered at this unconscious slight on his parentage.

"We must invent a relative," Briony went on, unmindful of her companion's suppressed mirth. "Let us say that my father had an uncle, a certain John Langland who emigrated to Canada under some cloud or other. His daughter married your father. That should do it. What do you think, Mr. Caldwell?"

"Cousin John," he corrected with a twinkle in his eye. "To quote the Bard, Cousin Briony, 'O what a tangled web we weave when first we practice to deceive.' Let that be our story then, but pray do not work it out too precisely. I doubt if we will be called on to do more than acknowledge a distant connection. Fortunately, I shall soon be gone and there is no one at Oakdale who can disprove our relationship. Your husband will never learn of your deception unless you choose to tell him."

On that note, the three conspirators withdrew to their respective chambers to dress for dinner. Briony took comfort from Mr. Caldwell's intelligence that there was no one at Oakdale to disprove the deception which she had seen fit to perpetrate on Ravensworth. How he would despise her if he knew of it. She had set herself up as a paragon of virtue. He trusted her implicitly and she had betrayed him. She could not bear to think of Ravensworth's disgust should he ever find out. He would never believe that her motives were pure. She had been faced with two choices—to tell Ravensworth the truth and so have Mr. Caldwell thrown in jail, perhaps for years, or to lie to Ravensworth and help Mr. Caldwell escape. She had chosen the lesser of two evils, but Ravensworth would never understand that. Why should he? She had vilified him at every opportunity, denigrating his Code of Honor, subjecting him to the severest censure. She would not, could not, face him with her lie. To do so would be to lose his regard forever, and that was not to be borne. If she must deceive him, she must do it convincingly.

Chapter 20

It was fortunate for Briony that Nanny was not in residence at Oakdale Court, for that shrewd retainer of long standing would have immediately tumbled to the fact that her "nurseling" was suffering from a Surfeit of Conscience, and Nanny would have given her young mistress no peace until she had wormed out of her the reason for the hint of tragedy which lurked in the depths of her troubled gray eyes. Ravensworth, on the other hand, never before having been in the position of catching Briony out in any sort of wickedness, put quite a different complexion on his beloved's soulful expression and he visibly bristled at the patent reproach he read in her mournful gaze.

It was evident to him that his former less-than-exemplary conduct had put him beyond the pale and that he was no nearer attaining those privileges of a husband which he so earnestly desired. To add insult to injury, in his opinion, Briony was devoting the hours at her disposal in catering to the whims and fancies of her long-lost cousin and had taken to reserving her smiles (and dimples), not to mention her clear-eyed gazes, for that unexceptionable young gentleman while with her lord and master she was reticent to a degree and would hardly deign to look in his direction. Ravensworth took it into his head that Briony was paying off old scores by setting up a mild flirtation with her cousin. In other circumstances, the Marquess would have taken to the natural, inoffensive manners of Mr. Caldwell, but a rival for his wife's affections was something that was not to be borne.

Smarting under Briony's blatant neglect, Ravensworth took to dropping in on his neighbor, Lady Adèle, and found her mode of extravagant but harmless flattery very soothing to his wounded ego. In some situations, his lordship was willing to concede, a woman's lack of originality in conversation was not necessarily a detriment to whiling away a very pleasant hour or two. Adèle might not be an intellectual giant—some might even call her bird-witted—but when it came to making a gentleman feel cosseted, the Countess had few equals among her sex. In this accomplishment, his Marchioness was sadly lacking.

That Briony made no objection to his frequent absences from her board, however, did nothing to allay the suspicions which her distant manner had engendered—quite the reverse. Indeed, Ravensworth's keen eye perceived that, far from incurring Briony's displeasure, his truancy seemed to meet with tacit approval. Her indifference left him more shaken than he cared to admit. And when next he entered the breakfast room and the spate of Briony's uninhibited laughter to a smiling Caldwell froze in mid-stream, Ravensworth's hackles began to rise.

"By the by," he threw at her carelessly when he chanced to encounter her later that morning quite alone as they passed on the oak-paneled staircase, "don't hold dinner for me this evening, my pet. I am promised to Adèle—didn't I tell you? She has asked me to put her in the way of a team for her town carriage. Haldane's cattle are to be auctioned off today, and with any luck, she should manage to pick up something suitable without having pockets to let after the transaction. No saying how long the business may take, though."

Briony shot a penetrating glance at him. "Adèle? When did you see her?" she asked sharply.

Ravensworth smoothed an invisible wrinkle from his sleeve. "As a matter of common courtesy, my dear, I have paid my respects at Beechwood whenever I have been in the vicinity—every other day, I collect."

Ravensworth had the satisfaction of seeing the shock register on Briony's face at this bold statement. In a moment, she had recovered herself sufficiently, however, to go on with a semblance of her usual calm.

"How—thoughtful of you, my lord. And do you take it upon yourself to be on such terms of—civility with all our neighbors?"

He smiled indulgently. "Certainly not. Adèle's place is within easy distance of Oakdale. Besides, I have known Adèle this age. Since the Earl's demise, she has depended on my counsel. Nothing would give me greater pleasure than to have you by my side but, unfortunately, my curricle holds only two comfortably. You don't object, I hope, that I have undertaken this small office for the lady?"

The raging sense of injustice which these provocative words evoked was the perfect antidote to the burden of guilt which had cowed her spirits since she had first told the Awful Lie. "Why should I object?" Briony asked, averting her eyes to conceal their sudden flash of hostility. "As you say, your intimacy—I beg your pardon—your friendship with the lady is of long standing. Indeed, the first time I set eyes on her—no, now I think on it, that would have been in the library of Broomhill, but that scene of depravity is best forgotten, is it not, my lord?" she asked tightly, and felt that she had won a small victory when the bland smile was wiped clean from Ravensworth's face.

"The second time I set eyes on her, when you kindly introduced us outside Hatchard's, you were even then acting in the capacity of the lady's man of business—something to do with her late husband's estate, as I recall. Obviously, Adèle has never been in the way of administering her own affairs." This veiled reference to Briony's sole management of the income from her considerable fortune had Ravensworth's brow as black as thunder, but Briony was in full spate and nothing could dam her now.

"No doubt the experience of being looked up to is a very gratifying one for you," she went on, her voice dripping with condescension, for all the world as if such a thing was so extraordinary as to be almost unthinkable. "Pray, do not concern yourself about my feelings in the matter, for I have none. In your absence," she went on smoothly, not above throwing in a malicious jibe of her own, "I daresay I shall continue to amuse myself tolerably well with only my cousin for company since Vernon has some errand which necessitates a trip to town."

"Indeed? Then I bid you good day, madam," Ravensworth replied as stiff as a board, and jamming his curly-brimmed beaver smartly on his head, descended the staircase calling for his curricle to be made ready at the double.

Briony's temper was at full boil as she watched him stalk out through the foyer and slam the door violently in his wake. An hour before in the breakfast room and laboring under the crushing weight of her guilty conscience had seen her tongue-tied in Ravensworth's presence. Such a circumstance was not to be wondered at. She had been raised to prize honesty as a supreme virtue, eschewing even those little white lies which Society deemed indispensable for social intercourse. She knew that she had done wrong. But his iniquitous conduct in paying court to a lady of dubious reputation, even though Briony dismissed the notion that Adèle was a serious rival for her husband's affections, had overset her equilibrium completely. Her sense of inner serenity before Ravensworth had come into her life had been a constant, as safe and dependable as the Bank of England. She had been a passive sort of a girl then, as far as she could remember. Now look at her! She had quite deliberately fanned his smoldering anger to a white heat, nor was she sorry to have given him what, in vulgar terms, was called a "leveler." He deserved it.

She caught up her skirts and went racing up the stairs to her room. Within minutes, she was donning her best olive green bombazine riding habit in a gesture of defiance calculated to make her feel as dashing as the flamboyant Adèle. Ravensworth would not be there to appreciate it, but she had promised to conduct Caldwell on a tour of the estate and was determined that at least one gentleman would be made aware that Briony Langland was not some negligible quizz who could be ignored with impunity.

It was a gentleman of Caldwell's ilk and background that she had once taunted Ravensworth with as being most suitable as a parti for a Quaker girl. He was everything that was pleasing. He understood her scruples and misgivings. He shared her outlook and opinions. He was a man of Conscience. How strange, then, that she should find him rather too tame and colorless to excite even a mild interest in her breast. Ravensworth, unpredictable, spoiled, overbearing, hot-tempered, and unscrupulous as he might be, had completely captured her reluctant heart. Love was an emotion which was incomprehensible and illogical, she told herself morosely, and she wanted nothing to do with it.

* * *

Vernon's errand to the port of Folkstone was in the nature of a reconnoitering expedition. He had used all his powers of persuasion—with good reason as it turned out—to convince the doubting American not to venture abroad at such a critical moment. Caldwell had finally given way, not without some reluctance, and had given Vernon the direction of his Quaker contacts with instructions to ascertain whether all was in readiness for his departure on the morrow as had long since been arranged. It was Caldwell's intention to board ship in the middle of the English Channel (with a captain who had been well bribed for his assistance) and to pass himself off as one of the crew. When the ship docked in Halifax some weeks later, he hoped to make his way by easy stages to his home in Rhode Island, confident that on the way he would find shelter and assistance with any Canadian or American who claimed to be of the Quaker persuasion notwithstanding the present state of hostilties which existed between the two countries. Caldwell knew that to Quakers such a circumstance would weigh little or nothing.

He had deemed it prudent to keep his hosts ignorant of the exact day of his departure since he had no wish to have Ravensworth, out of a sense of obligation, accompany him on any part of his journey. He did not think that the sudden decampment of two young bucks of fashion for greener pastures would discommode their host in the least and he wished to protect Briony should Ravensworth take it into his head to question her closely about the movements of her guests.

Vernon returned late in the afternoon with some disquieting news. As he rode toward the stables at breakneck speed, he caught sight of his sister and friend taking a turn in the herbary. Ravensworth, he noted with some relief, was nowhere to be seen. Without loss of motion, he wheeled his steed and bore down upon them, a cloud of dust kicking up at his heels. He reined in sharply, and at the unexpected pressure on its mouth, his mount reared and stamped to a sudden halt. Vernon was on his feet in an instant, running to close the short gap between himself and Caldwell.

"There's no time to lose," he began, his breath labored from his exertion. "We must leave at once. The constable is on his way. He means to speak to Ravensworth about some poor devil of an American who has escaped detention." He stood with shoulders heaving, fighting to regain his breath.

For a moment Caldwell looked at the younger man in some bewilderment. Then his friend's sense of urgency seemed to transmit itself to him. "The constable is on his way, you say?"

"I rode like the devil to warn you. He cannot be more than half an hour behind me. All foreigners have to show their papers, so you see, you cannot pass yourself off as a Canadian."

Caldwell stood irresolute for a moment as he assimilated Vernon's words. "What about the Heriots?" he asked at last. "When do they expect me?"

Vernon made a show of impatience as his friend gave no sign that he understood the urgency of the situation. "They charged me to tell you to stay out of sight until nightfall. It is unsafe at present to travel while it is still light."

"But where will you go?" asked Briony in a stricken voice.

"It doesn't signify. We'll hide in the woods if we must! For God's sake, hurry!" Vernon exclaimed, and turned on his heel without waiting for a response.

"Hold! I'd like a few words with your sister. See to my horse, will you, Vernon?"

Vernon vaulted into the saddle and flung impatiently

over his shoulder, "Be quick about it. I'd liefer run into the constable than my good-brother."

Caldwell seized Briony by the elbow and propelled her toward the stables. "I must take my leave of you at once. It wouldn't do if you were discovered sheltering me. You would be taken as an accessory, you see."

Briony had been thinking furiously while listening to the exchange between her companions. "Never mind that now," she said, putting her free hand on Caldwell's arm in a compelling manner. "I know the perfect hiding place. There is a broken-down cottage on the estate behind the mill pond—it's used as a store by the groundsmen. You must remember it. We rode past it this morning."

"I know it," he said curtly, taking her roughly by the elbow once more to hasten her along. "Now listen to me. You must remove every evidence of our presence at Oakdale. Do you understand? It must not look as if we've bolted. Tell anyone who asks that Vernon and I heard of a mill—that is, a boxing match—which is taking place in Henley and on the spur of the moment we decided to make for it. Young gentleman of fashion are known to be unpredictable. No one will think us the worse for it. Have you got that, Briony?"

"What about your things? What do you wish me to do with them?"

Caldwell shrugged. "Vernon can come back in a day or two and dispose of them. I shall have to beg, borrow, or steal other garments for the present. It's of no consequence. But in the meantime, hide them or destroy them as you will."

They reached the stable yard just as Vernon led out two fresh mounts saddled and ready.

"Don't look so worried," said Caldwell with a wry smile, and then he swung himself smoothly into the saddle. "By this time tomorrow I shall be safely on the high seas." He raised his hand in salute.

Briony gazed anxiously into the animated faces of the two young men and had the strangest feeling that they were in the throes of some peculiar exhilaration from which she was excluded. "Wait!" she called out as they wheeled their horses in the direction of the gravel drive which led deeper into the estate. "I'll come to you tonight as soon as may be. I'll bring some food and a change of clothes. Wait for me at the cottage."

Caldwell looked doubtful, but Briony had already turned to run back to the house. "Be careful," he shouted after her, then dug in his heels, urging his horse forward in pursuit of Vernon.

Briony had barely finished throwing the last of Vernon's things into his portmanteau when she heard movement and voices below. After a careful check to ensure that the coast was clear, she lost no time in hauling her cumbersome burden to her own chamber, where she deposited it beside Caldwell's small grip. Even in her agitation, she was able to smile ruefully at the discrepancy in the garments which the respective gentlemen favored. Brother Vernon's wardrobe gave every indication that its owner aspired to be a very pink of the ton. Mr. Caldwell's taste in clothes, on the other hand, as was to be expected, was more conservative and proclaimed him to be a follower of the incontestable arbitrar of taste, Mr. George Brummel. For a Quaker, even this was beyond what was deemed acceptable, and Briony inferred that her "cousin" belonged to the fraternity of "gay" Quakers who eschewed the plain ways of the majority of Friends.

With much pushing and pulling, she finally contrived to conceal the incriminating evidence under her bed. She had barely time to smooth the crumpled coverlet when a gentle knocking sounded on her door.

"Your ladyship," came the soft, countrified accents of her maid, "the county constable is below and begs a few minutes of your time."

Briony felt her heart race uncomfortably against her ribs. "Tell him I'll be down directly," she said through the closed door. She must get a grip on herself, she thought, as she tried to steady her breathing. It was not only Caldwell whom she had to protect now, but Ravensworth as well. His loyalty to the Crown must never be in question. He would be ruined if the authorities discovered that he had harbored an enemy of the state under his roof. There was no way he could prove his innocence. Briony shuddered. What a pass she had brought them to. Well, she would get them out of it. In for a penny, in for a pound. And on that encouraging note, the Quaker maid squared her thin shoulders and went resolutely to contend with no less a foe than His Majesty's representative, the Chief Constable of the county of Kent.

Half an hour later, as she saw the King's law ride briskly away, Briony was in high alt. It had never occurred to her that she would have passed muster so easily. How facile a liar she had become with a little practice! The constable had accepted the sudden departure of the young men as a matter of course, just as Caldwell had predicted he would, and had seemed ill at ease in having to subject a lady of Briony's consequence to interrogation. He had made it evident from the outset that his presence at Oakdale was in the nature of a formality and had conducted himself with the utmost civility and deference. His visit lasted barely long enough to consume the glass of sherry which Briony had pressed upon him. So readily did the affable gentleman accept every word that proceeded out the mouth of the devious lady, that the faint hope was born in her that the dreaded in-

terview with Ravensworth might pass off more easily
than she deserved.

As it happened, however, his lordship did not deign to
put in an appearance until well on in the evening, by
which time Briony had gained the comparative security
of her bedchamber. Nor was she sorry that her carefully
rehearsed speech would be delayed until morning when
Caldwell should be safely out of Ravensworth's long
reach. Furthermore, she was grateful for the extra hours
at her disposal which Ravensworth's absence (however
much she might deplore the reason for it) had offered
in which to make her preparations for the coming or-
deal. Once Caldwell was gone, she promised herself, she
would be as honest as the day, but tonight she needed all
her wits about her if she was to successfully pull the wool
over Ravensworth's sharp eyes.

Chapter 21

It was a glorious night. The moon bathed every hill and hollow, every tree and rock in its luminous halo and the stars glittered like diamonds in the velvet black vault of the heavens. The night was alive with sounds. Briony cocked her head to listen and the warm breath of the rising breeze, like some invisible lover, caressed her cheek, and long forgotten childish fancies of naiads and sprites came rushing back to haunt her mind.

It was a night for enchantment, a night for fairies to dance in their magic rings and for nymphs to emerge from the watery depths of stream and lake to bewitch unwary mortals. It was a night for romance.

The mare whinnied softly beneath her and Briony stroked it with a reassuring hand. "Hush, Bessie. No demon stallion will practice his sorcery on you." She sat motionless, alert and wary, drinking in every sight and sound of the world about her made unfamiliar in its strange and awesome moonlit splendor. Bessie's ears twitched restively and Briony crouched in the saddle to murmur, "'Tis not fairy folk we need fear, Bessie. They are but a figment of our imagination though Nanny would cross her superstitious fingers to hear me say so. But Ravensworth! He is a flesh-and-blood creature and more to be feared than any warlock who stalks abroad at the witching hour."

She flicked the ribbons and the mare set off at a sedate trot along the gravel drive. Twenty minutes later saw Briony dismount and tether the nervous beast outside what looked to be a deserted cottage.

"John? Vernon? Where are you?" she called softly.

The door opened and a shaft of light fell on the ground at her feet. With a sense of overwhelming relief, Briony pushed open the door and entered. Caldwell, holding a lantern aloft in his hands, was the only occupant of the room. "Where's Vernon?" she asked at once.

"He's gone ahead to prepare my friends for my advent." Caldwell set the lantern on the stone floor. "I don't want him found with me. Nor do I want you to remain here longer than necessary. If anyone were to find us together . . ." He let his voice trail off and Briony shivered at the implication in his words.

"No one will. I've been careful," she said with a confidence she was far from feeling. Then, recollecting the purpose of her visit, she added, "Here, you must be hungry. I've brought you something to eat."

The window was covered with an old blanket to conceal the faint light of the lantern. Caldwell had found a ramshackle table and a couple of serviceable chairs and had set them in the middle of the room. He held one out indicating that she was to be seated. Briony deposited her bundle on the table. She undid a table cloth and produced a bottle of wine, some thick slices of gammon, half a chicken, a loaf of bread, and a generous slice of pork pie.

"No crockery or cutlery, I'm afraid," she said with a thin smile.

"Don't give it a thought," replied Caldwell, pulling the cork from the opened bottle of wine, which Briony had stolen from the kitchen. "I am not above eating picnic style."

He ate with gusto, and Briony watched him in silence as the mountain of food gradually disappeared. When they spoke, it was in commonplaces. The night had lost its magic. It all seemed so mundane, so anticlimactic, and Briony began to wonder if she had been carried along on a vulgar proclivity for the melodramatic. She sighed and caught the glint of amusement in Caldwell's dark eyes. She looked at him questioningly.

"Not very romantic, I'm afraid," he observed astutely, then fell upon the chicken as if he had not eaten for a week.

Briony's self-mocking laugh acknowledged a hit. "What are your immediate plans?" she asked at last.

"Everything is taken care of, as I explained to you," he said patiently. "I take passage tomorrow. For your own protection, it is better if you know as little as possible."

He finished the last morsel of food and leaned back in his chair with a sigh of satisfaction. "A feast fit for a king. I'm much obliged to you." He drank the wine straight from the bottle and offered some to Briony.

She held it gingerly. "Why not?" she asked rhetorically. "I don't see any harm in it." Then she tipped back her head and drank deeply. The next instant, she was seized with a fit of coughing and the wine dribbled down the front of her habit. She dabbed at it abstractedly with the edge of the tablecloth. Caldwell watched her for a moment or two then seemed to come to a decision.

"Briony, you won't take it amiss, I hope, if I speak to you plainly?"

Briony's eyebrows went up at the serious tone of his voice. "A Quaker scold, Mr. Caldwell?" she asked archly.

"Hardly that! Merely a few words of counsel from a departing friend whom you will most likely never see again."

Briony was discouragingly silent.

"No matter!" He stood as if to go and Briony rose to

follow. He gave her a long, searching look. "Be kind to Ravensworth," he said simply.

They heard the faint sounds of a horse's whinnying. "Bessie was never a patient beast. I should go," Briony observed. "I brought some of your things. They're in my saddlebags."

He drew her hands into his. "Don't fret about me. I shall send word to you somehow when I reach Canada. Thank you for all that you have done for me." He raised her hands to his lips in an uncharacteristic gesture of gallantry and Briony smiled at his awkwardness.

It was at that moment that the door burst open and a dark and menacing figure stood filling the small doorway. A thonged riding crop beat a tattoo against the leather of his mired boots and an aura of bridled energy hung on every coiled muscle.

"Ravensworth!" The word, barely audible, escaped Briony's lips on a moan.

The silence, to Briony's taut nerves, seemed to stretch unbearably, and into her numbed mind came the thought, quite inconsequentially, that Denby would be outraged to see his master's neckcloth in such disarray.

"Ravensworth—at your service," he replied ironically in a voice carefully devoid of expression and altogether at odds with the cold glint of steel in his eyes. He took a quick stride toward them and Briony reacted without thinking. She snatched her hands from Caldwell's frozen clasp and threw herself between the two men, her arms held before her as if to ward off a blow. The gesture snapped the last shreds of Ravensworth's self-control. With a bloodcurdling oath, he seized one outstretched wrist and flung her out of his path then fell with demonic fury upon Caldwell.

Briony stumbled against the table and sprawled on the floor in a heap. When she raised her head, she saw Caldwell on his knees. Ravensworth had him by the throat in a choking grip and was beating him savagely about the head and back with his crop. Briony cried out in protest, but he was deaf to her pleas. She staggered to her feet and flung herself across Caldwell, taking the lash of the whip against her shoulders.

"You dare to protect him?" Ravensworth raged, and he grasped her by the arms and sent her reeling.

"He won't fight you!" she screamed. "He won't defend himself. Don't you understand? He is a Quaker. He'll let you kill him before he'll strike back."

The words seemed to check Ravensworth momentarily. Then the full force of his anger turned against Briony. His fingers fastened upon her arms, digging into the soft flesh and she flinched with the pain of it. He looked at her with loathing.

"Slut," he hissed at her, and he shook her as if she had been a rag doll.

"It's not what it seems," she gasped through chattering teeth, then in sudden outrage when the import of his words had penetrated her intellect. "How could you even *think* it? Let go of me, you foul-minded, unholy fiend! How dare you imply such a thing, you brute!"

Ravensworth administered one last, rough shake but it was evident that her outburst had dulled the edge of his anger. She made no move to escape his punishing grip, but inclined her head slightly toward Caldwell.

"John, go! I beg of you! He won't hurt me. I promise." Caldwell, at Ravensworth's back, was still on his knees, clutching his bruised throat. He swayed to his feet and put a shaking hand to his head.

"No . . . no."

Ravensworth half turned as if to renew his assault and Briony grabbed for his sleeve. "Hugh, listen to me! He is a Quaker! A Quaker! You cannot strike a man who won't defend himself! For God's sake, listen to reason! Let him go!"

His lip curled in derision and he bent a look of smoldering fury upon his adversary. "You, sir, are a contemptible specimen, the sorriest excuse for a man that it has ever been my misfortune to encounter. Coward! Don't think to hide behind my wife's petticoats. Nothing can save you from my wrath now."

To this impassioned speech Caldwell responded by shaking his head in denial, too shaken by the thrashing he had received at Ravensworth's hands to attempt a rejoinder.

"Have you no pride?" Ravensworth demanded hotly. "Why don't you fight me like a man?"

"Quakers are different," said Briony, trying desperately to make him understand. "We abhor violence of any description. Let him go, Hugh. I can explain everything to your satisfaction."

Briony had little hope that these propitiating words would mollify Ravensworth's exacerbated temper, nor did they. Her use of the word "we," if anything, incited him to a renewed fury.

"A pacifist?" he expostulated as though the word stuck in his gullet. "A pacifist! Do you stand there and tell me that I cannot defend my honor—that I'm to be denied the pleasure of calling him out and putting a bullet in his detestable hide?"

"Not if you wish to be acknowledged as the man of honor you esteem," replied Briony, conscious of the first faint glimmerings of hope.

Ravensworth thrust Briony from him and began to pace the floor like a caged tiger. "A Quaker, a pacifist, and I daresay, appearances to the contrary, a man of conscience to boot." He laughed mirthlessly. "By God, it had better be so, Caldwell, for you have fallen into the hands of a man of honor. I don't scruple to tell you that if you have not played the gentleman with my wife, I shall put a period to your miserable existence."

Caldwell manfully struggled to gain command of his voice. "Do with me as you see fit," he said in a strained tone, striving to speak levelly. "But I pray you, do not vent your anger on Briony. You must believe that no harm would come to her through me. I regard her as a dear sister. It was wrong in me to let her help me, but you must believe that we are innocent of any impropriety."

"Innocent? Innocent?" roared Ravensworth. "Is that what you call it? What *should* I believe when I find you alone, in he middle of the night, snug in this cosy love nest?"

"Hardly that, sir," said Caldwell, looking around the disordered interior with a deprecating half smile. Briony quaked at his temerity and hastened to draw off Ravensworth's wrath to herself.

"John is not to blame. This was my doing. How did you find out?"

Ravensworth riveted her with a fierce glare, ignoring the question. "I might have known that your deplorable scruples would be behind this outrageous folly. Briony, will you never learn to curb your desire to do good whatever the consequences?"

"I should like to make a clean breast of this . . . misadventure," began Caldwell, shifting uncomfortably where he stood.

"Later," said Ravensworth curtly. "Go back to the house. I shall deal with you at my leisure."

Caldwell made as if to say something but Ravensworth was in no mood to listen.

"Good God, man, tomorrow is time enough to put your affairs in order."

"You do not understand, sir—"

"Leave us, I said," thundered Ravensworth.

Caldwell hesitated, then seeing the appeal in Briony's eyes, bowed stiffly in her direction and took his leave of them, walking unsteadily through the open door. In a moment, the muffled drum of hoofbeats could be heard retreating. Ravensworth advanced on Briony and encircled her throat with his hands. She stilled in his grasp, scarcely daring to breathe or look up at him.

"Hoyden! Jade! Doxy!" he growled at her.

"That's a lie! And you know it!" she cried out, rallying. Her eyes flew to his face and met his hot, smoldering gaze and she was held by what she read in his brooding expression. For a long moment, she found the will to resist his silent, eloquent message.

"Oh no . . . . Hugh! Please!" she said weakly, shaking her head in dawning comprehension.

He gave no sign that he had heard her entreaty, but like a man under some strange compulsion, he brought his hands up slowly to remove the pins from her unruly hair. A mane of blond silk fell across her face and shoulders. He pushed back some stray strands with a tender, sensuous motion. Briony cowered.

"Please Hugh, I want to go home," she mewed like a kitten.

"Do you refuse me, Briony?" he asked softly, implacably. "Have you concocted another excuse to avoid the inevitable?"

Some instinct for survival gave her courage. "I'm not afraid of you, Hugh Montgomery," she flung at him, and forced herself to look boldly into his face, scrupulously avoiding his eyes. A smile played about his lips. It gave her the confidence to continue in a more conciliating tone. "Hugh, I can explain everything. You won't like it, but it's not as bad as it seems."

"I don't doubt it!"

"Please, Hugh!"

"Afterward. Tell me afterward," he murmured, his lips brushing her temples.

"After what?" she demanded, wrenching herself out of his grasp. "If you think for a minute that I'm going to let you take me . . ."

She realized almost immediately that she had made a fatal mistake. The fury flared in his eyes at her sudden rejection. He reached for her and the impulse to flee overwhelmed her. Briony took to her heels.

In one quick stride he was at the door and had barred it. Briony changed direction and ran for the stepladder to the loft and scrambled up as quickly as the heavy skirt of her riding habit would allow. She heard his low, mocking laugh as he followed her at a leisurely pace.

It took a few moments for her eyes to become accustomed to the gloom. A pale shaft of moonlight lit the interior. She saw at once that there was nowhere to hide—no escape from him. She groaned when she observed the stack of straw pallets against the wall and on the rough floorboards. The fates, or Providence, had conspired against her.

She heard Ravensworth's step at her back and she whirled to face him. He made no move toward her, but stood immobile like some huge, menacing shadow of doom, filling her small world.

"Hugh . . . I'm afraid," she whispered on a sob. He held out his arms and she threw herself into them, weeping uncontrollably against his shoulder.

"Hush now! You must know that I would never do anything to hurt you."

His arms cradled her until her incoherent outburst had spent itself and she wept softly against his chest. For a wild moment, she lost her bearings and half fancied that she was back in time, caught in the ferocious storm, and Ravensworth her only sanctuary.

But on this occasion, he was both sanctuary and storm. There was comfort in his arms but a terrible threat also. He acknowledged her fear, understood it even, but set it aside as being of no consequence.

"I was a fool to let you keep me at bay all these weeks," he said gently as he undressed her till she stood shivering in her shift. "I love you, Briony, and there is nothing to fear in the natural expression of the love that exists between a man and his wife."

He pulled her down to lie beside him on the soft pallet and she lay passive, trembling at the aura of masculine sensuality which threatened her. He quickly divested himself of his garments and turned back to lean over her, the broad shelter of his chest rising above her. She felt his hands warm against her flesh, deliberately brushing against her thighs and breasts as he slowly removed her shift, and Briony heard his breath choke in his throat as he gazed at her nakedness.

She felt vulnerable, totally defenseless, and she turned to him in a gesture of appeal, but he gently restrained her, his eyes heavy with passion as they drank in every feminine contour. His hands moved possessively over her in a slow, intimate exploration of her body, and Briony weakly protested.

"Briony!" His voice was low and hoarse with longing. "Don't deny yourself to me."

His ragged breath against her lips was warm and tantalizing, coaxing her to open to the invasion of his tongue. Briony became aware of the soft mat of hair on his chest as it grazed her breasts. She gasped and he penetrated the softness of her mouth, thrusting his tongue deeply, and the last remnants of her resistance were swept away.

She gave herself up to his desire, accepting every new sensation which his gently caressing hands and mouth aroused, yielding herself trustingly to his ardent possession until her low moans of pleasure filled the small room. And then she wanted him, wanted to abandon herself to him, wanted him to guide her through the terrifying unknown until she was throbbing with the anticipation of it and fear was left behind.

She moved instinctively beneath him, arching herself against his hips, pressing her soft curves against his hard length, enticing him with her soft sighs until she heard him groan her name.

He moved over her and took her gently, schooling himself to control the rising tide of passion which her surrender to his lovemaking had unleashed. But the pain of his possession made her fearful and she tried desperately to recoil from him, sinking her teeth into his shoulder in a vain attempt to force him to release her. She heard his gasp of pain, but he refused to withdraw. He deepened the embrace, holding her close until she quieted. And then the pain was gone, and the fear of it, and only the experience of some wild, elemental force remained until Ravensworth released her from even that, and she lay shuddering in his arms.

Chapter 22

When Briony received the intelligence, early the following morning, that Mr. Caldwell had made himself scarce and that neither hide nor hair of the delinquent gentleman was to be found from the bowels of the Oakdale cellars to the celestial heights of its attics, she did not bat an eye. Ravensworth had come striding into her chamber, a frown of irritation clouding his broad brow. He ran an abstracted hand through his crop of ebony hair, spilling his locks in careless profusion.

"The young jackanapes must have taken himself off in the middle of the night. His bed has not been slept in. I must have put the fear of death into him. How could he even *think* I meant him harm?"

"What could possibly have given him *that* idea?" asked Briony pertly, throwing back the coverlet of the bridal bed she had shared with her husband. She stretched leisurely, a feeling of well-being spreading deliciously through every fiber of her being, and she cocked a lazy eye at her lover, a self-satisfied smile lingering around the corners of her lips.

"You look like a cat who just had a bowl of cream," he said lightly, caressingly, a soft smile curving his lips. The sight of her rumpled nightgown and one tantalizing half-exposed breast gave his thoughts a new direction.

She sighed languidly and grinned up at him. "A cat should be so fortunate!"

Ravensworth's smile broadened. "Bold words, madam wife, from a maid who—was it only yesterday?—ran from me like a terrified rabbit."

"And no wonder! Can you blame me?"

She swung herself unhurriedly out of the wildly disordered bed and slipped into a quilted dressing gown. "I thought you meant to do us murder. And Caldwell thought so too. But don't tease your mind about that resourceful young man. If I understand his scheme correctly, he will be safely on the high seas by now and on the first leg of his voyage home to America."

She was at her dressing table, brushing the tangles from her hair. Ravensworth came to stand behind her as she twisted the heavy strands into the coil which he preferred.

"The high seas? America? What are you talking about, Briony?" He sounded puzzled.

Briony swiveled on the stool, turning to look innocently up at him. Her fingers were deftly clamping pins into her head. "He couldn't very well hang around here without papers with the county constable on the lookout for an escaped American. You needn't worry about him. I assure you, he knows what he is about. His escape had been planned down to the last detail by his Quaker friends." She dropped a pin and bent down to retrieve it. When she glanced back at Ravensworth, she was taken aback at his look of frozen incredulity. "I thought you knew," she faltered.

"No," he said evenly, "how should I? I know only what you told me. I thought that you might be concealing something, but I deduced that Caldwell and your brother were under the hatches and had come into Kent to outrun the duns. Was I wrong?"

Briony hesitated.

"Well?" he demanded impatiently. "What do you have to say for yourself?"

Briony felt a sinking feeling in the pit of her stomach. His eyes, which a moment before had been warm with re-membered intimacy, were now coldly impersonal, their blue fading to an icy transparency. She began haltingly, and a little desperately, to explain the circumstances of Caldwell's predicament and how she had thought to aid him without involving her husband.

"I didn't *want* to lie to you, you must see that," she finished lamely, "but at the time, knowing how you felt about the war with America, it seemed to be the only solution. How could I turn Caldwell away? You yourself once told me that the end justified the means. Under the circumstances, I felt compelled to set aside my scruples."

His look of withering contempt brought her to a faltering halt.

"What about your conscience, Briony?" he asked scathingly. "Did it give you leave, with impunity, to tell a ferrago of lies to your husband?"

"No, of course not!" she went on miserably, a guilty flush staining her cheeks, "but what else was I to do? This was an emergency."

"You could have told me the truth, taken me into your confidence, trusted me, for God's sake," he said accusingly. "I trusted *you* implicitly, and see how I have been rewarded! But I should have known how it would be when I took you to wife." He balled one hand into a fist and brought it ferociously down into his open palm. "Damn your feckless soul—mouthing glib platitudes about conscience and scruples—and damn me for swallowing your lies whole. I was prepared to overlook your farouche behavior. I had hoped that, in time, you would grow into the role of my consort, that I could tame some of your wilder excesses to fit you for your future rank as my duchess. But I was wrong. I should have married a woman of my own station as I always intended, a lady of refinement who knows how to conduct herself under any circumstances. But above all," he went on more fiercely, "a wife who would give her first loyalty to me— her husband. By God, what a fool I have been—to marry for love!"

He turned away as if the sight of her disgusted him and Briony sat in miserable silence, the truth of his bitter words tearing at her till she could bear it no longer.

"What can I say?" she said to his rigid back. "My conduct is inexcusable, I know it. But Hugh," she continued with a desperate note of appeal in her voice, "can't you find it in your heart to forgive me, to understand the dreadful dilemma that beset me? Can you not at least try to make allowances for my wretched state of mind?"

But Ravensworth was in no mood to be forgiving. He had placed Briony on a pedestal. Dammit she had perched there herself without help from him, and she had stepped down and destroyed his most cherished illusions.

"Make allowances? When did you ever make allowances for me?" he demanded wrathfully, rounding on her. "When I think what I have been through this last month trying to *earn* your love and respect. Did you give a thought to *my* wretchedness when you spurned me? You made me feel like a worm. I've been a blind idiot— playing the part of the wise and beneficent lord of the manor—burying myself in this godforsaken backwater, keeping myself on a tight leash because I believed that you were too good for me! Too good for me! That's rich!" He threw back his head and unleashed a torrent of angry laughter.

Briony bit down on the fingers of one hand to stifle her rising panic. She was losing him, she knew it, and it was no more than she deserved. "Hugh, I'm s-sorry," was all she could manage in a tight, little voice.

"I thought you were different from other women," he went on heedlessly, "that your love was worth winning. But you played me for a fool."

"Hugh," she pleaded, her voice breaking, "don't say any more now. You're not yourself. When your anger has had time to cool a little, we'll discuss it further. This is just your pride speaking."

"You mistake if you think I am not myself," he retorted coldly. "I am more myself *now* than I have been this long age."

He swung on his heel and strode purposefully toward the door.

This could not be happening, she thought wildly as she started to her feet. It was a nightmare, and in a moment she would waken from it. "Where are you going?" she cried out, her voice rising in panic.

He halted with one hand on the doorjamb and turned to look at her with a sneer. "Back to my former existence," he replied cuttingly, "where, thank God, virtuous ladies are few and far between.

"B-but, what about last night?" she asked, her voice fading to a whisper.

His exaggerated bow was meant to be slighting. "Don't refine too much upon it, my dear. One swallow doth not a summer make." He dragged the door open.

"B-but when shall I see you again?" Briony persisted.

His eyes swept over her in an assessing, insulting appraisal. "Would 'never' be too soon, my love?"

The door slammed behind him and Briony recoiled as if he had struck her. She fell back on her dressing table stool, her mind numb with pain. She had lost him forever and she could not blame him for his desertion. What a fool she had been to jeopardize her only attraction for him—her unassailable virtue. She could never retrieve it. Damn her virtue! she thought bitterly. Why can't he love me for myself?

"Harriet? Oh my dear! Is it really you?"

At the patent distress in Briony's tremulous voice, Harriet stood arrested. She paused, the skirts of her cutaway, dusty rose redingote gathered in one hand as she prepared to alight from the Viscount Avery's crested carriage, which only a minute or so before had pulled into the drive of the Ravensworth mansion. Her head came up with a jerk and she was instantly struck by the vision of a woebegone Briony who, unmindful of the soft spray of drizzling rain, had stationed herself on the marble steps of the main entrance to Oakdale Court. Harriet's hand tightened on Avery's strong grip as she assimilated her cousin's careless appearance.

"Good God, Briony!" exclaimed Harriet, appalled at the spectacle of her fastidious cousin's neglectful aspect. "What in the world has happened to you?"

At the note of solicitude in her dearest friend's voice, Briony gave a strangled sob and hurled herself down the steps and across the drive into Harriet's outstretched arms, dislodging the pink confection of feathers and ribbons which was perched jauntily atop a cluster of flaxen curls.

"There, there!" commiserated Harriet warmly as she righted her lilting bonnet with one hand. "Cousin Harriet is here to look after you." She shot Avery a withering "I told you so" look over Briony's bent head which had him shrugging his elegant shoulders in mild perplexity.

Harriet held Briony at arm's length and examined her closely. "Good grief, girl! You look positively ill! What has that brute of a man done to you?" she demanded with feeling.

"N-nothing! I've brought it on m-myself," stammered Briony with a watery, self-pitying sniffle. "Please don't blame Ravensworth."

"Where is he?" asked Harriet, her lips drawn tightly together and her glittering eyes scanning the house and horizon for a glimpse of the absent malefactor.

"G-gone, a sennight since, to London. He n-never wants to see me again."

Harriet's small but shapely bosom heaved in hot indignation. "Nor shall he," she intoned in outraged accents, "for I shall send Avery to call him out for this infamous perfidy."

Into the shocked silence which followed these impetuous words broke Avery's smooth drawl, elaborately casual. "Shall we find shelter from this deuced drizzle, my dear, before we are soaked to the skin? Why don't you take Briony into the house and make yourselves comfortable while I see to the horses and baggage? Perhaps, on calmer reflection, we shall contrive to resolve this muddle without resorting to violence." He threw his wife a veiled look of warning.

"Oh please," said Briony, with appealing sincerity, "you mustn't be angry with Ravensworth. I failed him, you see. I betrayed him. I am not the innocent girl I once was!"

A look of sheer horror passed over the Viscount's normally saturnine visage. "Good God, Briony! This is shocking!"

"Don't be a clothead, Avery!" observed Harriet with a faint smile which divested the retort of any real rancor. "Briony exaggerates! Now go about your business and join us in an hour or so." She put a protective arm around the smaller girl's waist and ushered her up the short flight of stairs to the Ravensworth mansion, clucking soothingly and quite incomprehensibly as she went.

After two large goblets of Ravensworth's Madeira, reserved "for special occasions only," Briony's spirits began to revive. Nothing ever seemed so bleak when she had her cousin's capable counsel to guide her. The news of Harriet's nuptials she greeted with the first rush of unimpaired happiness she had experienced since the morning Ravensworth had taken himself off. But no sooner had she uttered the conventional rhetoric, "I wish you happy," when a fresh outburst threatened to overcome her.

"There, there! Tell Cousin Harriet everything," said Harriet with such motherly concern that Briony's barely controlled trickle of tears became a veritable deluge. By dint of a little coaxing and a great deal of persistent questioning, Harriet at long last unraveled the mystery of Ravensworth's iniquitous desertion.

"Well, I don't see anything to be so glum about," she said bracingly after Briony's near incoherent recitation had come to an end. "It's just a lovers' quarrel."

Briony was not impressed with this logic. "It's no use, Harriet. I've ruined everything. Don't you see? He fell in love with my innocence, my virtue, and they are lost to me forever. I've destroyed his love."

"Pooh!" retorted Harriet dampeningly. "What gammon! If you had even a peck of worldly wisdom, you wouldn't be in this fix now." She deposited her empty goblet on the low, leather-topped table flanking her high-backed tapestry chair and began to rummage in her reticule. After a moment, she withdrew her hand and extended a diamond-studded, gold filigree snuffbox.

Briony gazed at the exquisite trinket in gratifying admiration. "It is perfection," she breathed.

"Avery's wedding gift to me," said Harriet shyly. "Do you care to partake?"

Briony's pleasure gave way to incredulity. "Do you say

that Avery thinks it proper in his wife to take snuff?" she asked, diverted for a moment from her unending troubles.

"Certainly! Avery is no prude. He is a broad-minded fellow and he likes his wife to cut a dash in society." Harriet's breast puffed up with exaggerated pride. "Don't tell me you've given it up?"

Briony extended her fingers and retrieved a pinch of the aromatic powder. She rubbed it delicately between her fingers close to her ear in the acceptable manner and sniffed delicately. "No. But Ravensworth does not permit it."

Harriet gaped at Briony in astonishment. "Does not permit it? I cannot believe my ears! That my cousin should be so lacking in gumption! I never thought to see the day when you would let anyone bully you, least of all a man of Ravensworth's kidney."

Briony's spine stiffened at the unwarranted censure she heard in her cousin's curt tone. "I permit no one to bully me, Cousin Harriet," she responded in quelling accents. "And I take exception to your remark about my husband. Lord Ravensworth is a far better man than you give him credit for. If you only knew how much he has exerted himself to put the estate in good heart these last weeks. I admit that his temper may be a trifle unsteady . . . very well, ferocious then," she amended on seeing Harriet's elegant eyebrows elevate in scepticism, "but in this instance," she went on earnestly, "acquit him of wrongdoing, if you please. The fault must be laid entirely at my door."

Harriet looked thoughtfully at her cousin. "If you say so, dear. Then if you had to do it over again, you would tell Ravensworth that Caldwell is an American and let him hand him over to the authorities?"

"No, of course not! How could I?"

Harriet persisted. "Then how did you do wrong? Are

you saying that you are damned if you do and damned if you don't?"

"Yes! I don't know! What does it signify?"

"Only this, my pet. You have tumbled into many scrapes but, to my knowledge, never until now have you permitted the irascible Lord Ravensworth to have the last word. Right or wrong, you always stood up to him. And he admired you for it! Now look at you! You are like a whipped dog with its tail between its legs. Not a spark of the former bold hussy who netted the sought-after but oh-so-elusive fleet-of-foot lord."

"I? A bold hussy?" queried Briony, laughing at the nonsensical soubriquet for a demure Quaker miss like herself.

"Who changed her appearance like a chameleon, Miss Truly Virtuous one minute and Flagrant Femme Fatale the next?"

"Well, yes, but I had good reason!"

"Whose reputation was in tatters because Miss Truly Virtuous walked as bold as brass before the eyes of the whole ton into the opera box of London's most notorious courtesan?"

"Harriet, that's not fair. I was only doing my duty, and you know it!"

Harriet calmly disregarded her cousin's heated avowal. "A sleeping beauty," she went on coolly, "who had the temerity to catch forty winks in a Bed of Dalliance which every wellbreeched rake and roué in town was hot to procure."

"But not when I was in it!" said Briony horrified. "It was Harriette Wilson they coveted, not the bed. Besides, how was I to know?"

"That doesn't signify," responded Harriet primly. "Think of the scandal if the story ever got about. But that's not all by any means."

"Oh?" said Briony noncommittally, her lips thinning.

Harriet was not discouraged by Briony's obvious lack of interest in pursuing the subject. "No! Far from it! Who, I ask you, was practically ravished by an amorous lord and ran for protection to the arms of a *naked* gentleman, and who was discovered by her unsuspecting friend behind the locked door of this same gentleman's bedchamber?"

"He wasn't *completely* naked!" Briony protested.

"Oh wasn't he?" Harriet asked, her voice coated with disappointment. "Then I have been sadly misinformed. But to continue . . ." At this point she bent a very knowing look upon her cousin, who had folded her arms warily across her chest. "Who was given a slip on the shoulder by no less than the heir to a dukedom who could have his pick of any Covent Garden lightskirt or titled lady of questionable virtue in the realm?"

Briony gasped. "How did you know?"

"Avery, of course," drawled Harriet without the slighest show of remorse for oversetting her cousin's fragile composure. "My dear, these little peccadilloes do not happen to gently bred, milk-and-water misses. Would such a specimen hide a handsome young gentleman on her husband's estate and sneak off in the middle of the night to keep a secret tryst with him? Now I ask you!"

Briony hung her head in shame. "Put like that, I can see that my conduct has been highly irregular. No wonder Ravensworth holds me in such disgust. You are right, Harriet. I am a bold hussy and quite unfitted to be his mate."

"Haven't you been listening to a word I've said? Ravensworth don't want a well-bred, spineless, pattern card of rectitude for his wife. That sort would bore him to tears in less than a sennight. Contrary to what the misguided Marquess may have told you, he admires your spunk. Don't kowtow to his wishes. He doesn't really, in his heart of hearts, want to tame you. Believe me, Briony, I know about such things." At this point, Harriet smiled enigmatically at some private reminiscence.

Briony opened her mouth to deny the truth of Harriet's reasoning but a sudden, blinding flash of enlightenment surged through her brain and she fell back against the cushions of the settee in breathless wonder. "It's true! It's true," she said as if she could not believe it.

"Well of course it's true. What did you think?" asked Harriet prosaically. That he fell in love with your Quaker principles? Oh, I'm not saying that that wasn't part of your attraction, but as I recall, at your first encounter you swept the gentleman off his feet in a runaway carriage and we all know how *that* got started."

"No, no," said Briony, her dimples flashing. "That was our second encounter. The first time I met him, he kissed me."

Harriet's jaw dropped and she gazed at her cousin with an expression of mingled respect and horror. "The deuce he did! Briony, how could you let him?"

"How could I stop him?" countered Briony with a faint blush and, to cover her confusion, turned away to rearrange a posy of fragrant yellow rosebuds which decorated an end table at her elbow.

"Well I never! No wonder he was mad for you notwithstanding your dreadfully prudish airs and graces. He must have seen behind that sober front you present to the world! Lucky for me, Avery has no real notion of the tear-away character behind that prim exterior. But never mind that now! What we need is a plan of action, a strategy, a campaign to bring the battle to a speedy and successful conclusion."

The two damsels sat deep in thought completely absorbed in the perplexity of the problem which Lord

Ravensworth presented. After a comfortable interval, Briony broke the silence. "Harriet, what am I to do? I cannot pursue him all over town like a jealous, cast-off wife. The whole of London would soon know of our estrangement."

"I'm thinking," mused Harriet reflectively. The ormolu clock on the oak mantlepiece chimed the hour.

"Briony, I don't mean to pry into what does not concern me, but am I right in thinking that you are full of juice—I mean, independently wealthy?"

"I have the income from my capital which I may dispose of as I wish. Why do you ask?"

Harriet beamed. "In other words, you are as rich as a nabob and need not look to your husband for every bauble or gown you take a fancy to. Are you willing to squander a few thousand to lure him back?"

She had Briony thoroughly interested. "Need you ask?"

"Good. Then I have the perfect solution."

Avery poked his head around the door. "May I come in?" he asked affably, "Or should I beat a hasty retreat to Jericho?"

"Darling," Harriet breathed, her heart doing its usual flip-flop at the sight of his dear features. She glided gracefully toward him and his arms came out to encircle her in a possessive, lover-like gesture. "You'll never guess what Cousin Briony plans to do for us?"

"I can hardly wait to hear," Avery responded with exaggerated gravity.

Harriet's eyes sparkled. "Briony has taken it into her head to throw a ball in our honor. Isn't it kind in her?"

Avery inclined his head politely in Briony's direction. "Too kind by half, Cousin Briony. May I ask where this ball is to take place?" He noted the quick questioning look which Briony threw at his bride. He cocked a cautionary brow at Harriet and the arm on her waist increased its pressure.

"Why Avery! Where else but here at Oakdale Court?" she asked artlessly.

"Harriet!" His voice was low, half pleading. "Have a care what you are about."

"Avery, trust me in this, please?"

He felt a slight, momentary flutter of unease, but the appeal in the sweet face turned up to him was more than he could resist. He stifled his misgivings and answered with commendable fortitude, "My dear, you know that I do."

It was all that she needed. "How many guests can Oakdale accommodate for a house party, Cousin Briony?" Her mind was already engaged in refining the strategy of the forthcoming skirmish.

Briony did a quick mental calculation. "Fifty comfortably, I suppose."

"Good! Then we shall invite a hundred."

Lord Avery greeted this outrageous suggestion with unshakable tranquility. "Only a hundred?" he countered. "Tch! Tch! Coming it too brown, Harriet dear, if I may make so bold an observation. However, I know better than to throw a rub in the way of what you two damsels have hatched for my absent friend's welfare. I take it that Ravensworth is to be invited to his own ball?"

"Ravensworth? Oh I don't think we need send him an invitation!" said Harriet irrepressibly. "What do you say, Cousin Briony?"

Briony sat with a slightly abstracted air, pleating the folds of her crushed gown. She looked serenely up with unclouded gray eyes at her companions. "Invite the host? I should say not! What an impertinence!"

Avery took pains to explain patiently, and with unimpaired good humor, a circumstance which the ladies had obviously overlooked. "But once he gets wind of it, nothing on earth will keep him away."

"Precisely!" said Lord Avery's lady. She withdrew from his sheltering arms and curtsied deeply to her cousin, a smile of triumph playing around her cupid bow lips.

Chapter 23

When Ravensworth took himself off in a towering temper, he had only one purpose in mind—to embark on a night of such frantic debauchery that the pervasive image of the fair charmer who had stealthily taken possession of his heart and mind till he had no notion of whether he was coming or going would be forever banished, rooted out, exorcised, and he would be free of the awful knot of pain which seemed to have lodged itself in his chest. Ten hours later, having made a remarkable dash to town and ensconced the indispensable if taciturn Denby in his rooms at the Albany, Ravensworth was off like a shot on a walking crawl of his clubs.

That was his first mistake, for after a little desultory gambling and a good deal of indiscriminate imbibing, he was engulfed by a rush of maudlin sentimentality which left him with a thorough disgust at his unmanly weakness in continuing to desire a sanctimonious bitch who was up to all the rigs and who held him in such low esteem that she had put the interests of a veritable stranger above those of her own husband. It was not so much the treason to her country which inspired his bile, although that was serious enough, but the treachery to him personally was an offense which set her beyond the pale.

Although Ravensworth was on a winning streak, he

churlishly cashed in his winnings over the protests of his boon companions, and pushed into St. James Street, purposefully making his way downhill, skirting St. James Park until, fifteen minutes or so later, he reached the environs of the Abbey. He stopped before a shuttered house on the corner of a modest street and rapped discreetly on the side door with the handle of his ivory cane. The door was opened almost on the instant, and Ravensworth entered. That was his second mistake.

The Marquess of Ravensworth was no stranger to the establishment of Madame Rainier and her ladies of pleasure. In his salad days, what he was now pleased to call "life before Briony," he had been a regular and valued customer and had spent many a pleasant hour or two in the company of one of the barques of frailty who graced Madame's crimson saloon. He nodded civilly if a little forbiddingly to the odd male acquaintance who happened to catch his eye in the intentionally subdued lighting of the main saloon and tried to shake off the vague feeling of guilt which oppressed him. As he settled his long frame in the damask Sheraton armchair, one booted foot crossed over the other in an assumed posture of negligence, he uncorked the bottle of claret which a flunkey had been commissioned to bring for him while the madame of the establishment floated away to fetch the paphian who was to entertain him for the night. The place, he noted absently, was as noisy and crowded as he remembered it, with much coming and going on the stairs. Somehow, he found the artificial gaiety of the atmosphere rather depressing, although the smiles of the girls in their diaphanous gowns never faltered for an instant. He did not care for those arch smiles, nor was he partial to the heavy French perfume which assaulted his nostrils and was quite unlike the clean fresh scent of Briony's herbs which filled the rooms of Oakdale Court. At the memory of Briony, Ravensworth's jaw clenched and he made heavy inroads into his claret.

A shadow fell across his face and Ravensworth looked up, his eyes narrowing to take in the feminine form which swayed toward him. Behind the obscenely grinning madame, he caught a glimpse of a girl with blond hair coiled demurely at the nape of her neck.

"This is Angèle, your *arnie de la nuit*," intoned Madame Rainier in a confidential undertone and drew the blond forward till her knees grazed his lordship's thighs invitingly.

Ravensworth choked on his wine. The girl was the image of Briony! He gave a roar of rage and threw the bottle in his hand to the empty grate, where it shattered into a thousand pieces. There was a stunned silence in the saloon and then all hell broke loose. Ravensworth was on his feet hurling insults at the madame at the top of his lungs for luring innocent girls into a house of debauchery and, at the same time, berating Briony's look-alike, a very popular member of the establishment among the gentlemen if Ravensworth had only known it, for being so lost to decency that she permitted herself to be displayed like a common harlot in a den of iniquity.

Since this was exactly the case, and everyone present knew it, Ravensworth was at first mistaken for a Methodist minister heaven bent on reforming a world which did not wish to be reformed. As his diatribe continued unabated, however, it soon became evident that his colorful language and obscene expletives gave the lie to this erroneous impression. So intimidating was this vulgar and violent outburst that the terrified madame lost no time in summoning her minions, three brawny ex-boxers, graduates of the Southern Circuit, who made short work of the inebriated Ravensworth and threw him out on his neck with the greatest of relish.

How he managed the long walk home in his drunken stupor, Ravensworth could never remember. A tight-lipped Denby put him to bed in frigid silence, not a word of condolence for the pair of shiners which disfigured his lordship's handsome face nor for the indeterminate aches and pains which Ravensworth bore with stoic fortitude. Such was the attachment of a retainer who had been in his open-handed employ for a good ten years, noted Ravensworth with a stifled groan of pain as his uncharitable valet tightly bound his master's bruised ribs for all the world as if he had been a saddle of mutton being trussed by the butcher for Sunday's dinner.

It took the Marquess a full sennight to recover from the effects of the beating he had suffered and in that time he neither ventured out of his comfortable rooms at the Albany nor received any visitors. For some inexplicable reason, he had no wish for even a whisper of the shameful circumstances surrounding his misfortune to be carried back to the delicate ears of his virtuous wife. When, therefore, a suspiciously solicitous Denby gently recommended that a sojourn in the country might be expedient and beneficial, Ravensworth rejected the suggestion out of hand since he considered that it would be disastrous to return to Briony with his tail between his legs.

The period of enforced inactivity had provided him with a time for quiet reflection and assessment of his situation, and his lordship found himself in a bit of quandary. He grudgingly conceded that other women held no interest for him; that life before Briony was not all he had cracked it up to be; that he had, in fact, given it all up without a pang of regret; he was even willing to admit that he could not live without her, but damn if he would allow the chit who had made game of him to call the tune. Briony Langland must be brought to a sense of her iniquity. Let her stew in her own juice for a week or two until she was thoroughly chastened. Then, when she was willing to sue for terms, he would deign to accept her unconditional surrender.

The pleasant prospect of a return to Kent improved his spirits considerably and he dashed off a note to Briony informing her, noncommittally, that he would return by the end of the week to attend to some estate business which he mentioned in vague terms. This epistle was carried by personal messenger. When his groom returned late the next day, Ravensworth could not conceal from himself his disappointment that there was not one word of greeting from the callous girl. By engaging the unsuspecting groom in casual conversation, however, he elicited the intelligence that her ladyship was fully occupied in the preparations for the coming house party. Ravensworth was nonplussed, but had the presence of mind to conceal from his curious lackey that he was in ignorance of any celebration which was to take place in his own house in the near future.

That same evening, while he was striding along Piccadilly mulling over what he had learned from his groom, he was accosted by an old school chum on horseback who shocked him to the core by thanking him for the invitation to his ball and informing him that he would be down Thursday. Ravensworth responded with tolerable composure but as soon as his pal had taken himself off he did an about-turn and made straight for Albany House in search of Denby.

Denby had heard from Lord Grafton's man that they were to leave on the morrow for Oakdale Court for a ball that was to be given to celebrate the nuptials of the Viscount and Viscountess Avery. He had taken the liberty of repacking his lordship's valise and it only remained for his lordship to say the word and they could be quit of London on the instant. Ravensworth gave the word.

When Ravensworth's curricle pulled into the gates of Oakdale Court, he found the drive and stable bustling like any public hostelry on the King's highway. Grooms and footmen in diverse liveries were coming and going among the newly arrived carriages which disgorged a profusion of passengers and baggage upon the front steps and lawn. Ravensworth had never seen the likes of it—at least, not at Oakdale Court—and he wondered a little irritably if Briony had any conception of what it would cost to house and feed so many prime bits of horseflesh, not to mention the multitude of retainers who were needed to service such a crush of humanity.

Before his thoughts could become settled in this unhappy direction, however, he found himself hailed on every side and came under a deal of good-natured ribbing by some of his unattached familiars for having deserted their fraternity for the parson's mousetrap. He took it all in good part, even going so far as to recommend the estate of matrimony to the most skeptical of his old cronies, who shook their heads in unfeigned disbelief at the incomprehensible fall from grace of what they had come to believe was the most confirmed bachelor of their ranks.

He entered the great hall where long tables had been set up, buffet style, laden with every sort of delicacy to tempt the appetite of the most fastidious gourmet, many of whom were availing themselves quite liberally of his hospitality. He scanned the throng of faces in the gallery above and caught a glimpse of Avery and Harriet, who gave him a friendly wave but made no move to detach themselves from the group which held their interest. Of the hostess, there was no sign.

On applying politely for her ladyship's direction to the unfamiliar majordomo who was ably directing the proceedings, he was informed that she had taken a small party of the guests to admire the gardens. Ravensworth did a double-take. He had heard that soft, slow drawl before. He looked sharply at the broad-shouldered giant who towered over him and inquired rather frigidly, "What part of the colonies do you hail from, my good man?"

Ravensworth was rather taken aback by the bold scrutiny which he was given in his turn.

"Canada, sir," said the retainer stolidly, then, quite brazenly, winked at his lordship before turning away to attend to the queries of the latest party to arrive.

She wouldn't, couldn't do this to him a second time! The Marquess turned on his heel and made for the door. No need to tell him where to find her ladyship. The herbary was the only garden, in her estimation, worthy of that name.

She was in her old smock and straw bonnet serenely laying forth to an interested audience of ladies on the culinary, medicinal, and cosmetic properties of all her prize weeds. Ravensworth watched in fascination as each lady in turn, high sticklers every one of them, was induced to sample the plethora of leaves and twigs which Briony held in her arms.

"Good God," he thought, momentarily stricken, "she's as dotty as m' father! What kind of inheritance am I passing along to my heirs?" Surprisingly, the thought of his folly, far from exacerbating his unpredictable temper, put him in a more mellow mood. Then he remembered the bold scrutiny of a tall, broad-shouldered retainer with a colonial drawl and he came to his senses.

Their eyes met and held, and again his lordship was stymied, for Briony's glance was as clear and unabashed as he had ever seen it, and she gave him back stare for stare. It took her a few minutes to disengage herself from her companions, and when she came toward him, it was without the least show of embarrassment for being discovered in an ensemble that even the lowest scullery maid would be ashamed to sport.

"Ravensworth, are you here?" she asked him pleasantly as she took his proffered arm. Then in the next breath, she said, "If you are going to complain about your bedchamber, I am sorry for it, but you must see that there is nothing to be done about it under the circumstances."

"What about my bedchamber?" he demanded, his suspicions roused.

"Oh! You don't know? Well . . . I hope you won't take it amiss, but I've quartered Freddie Fielding and—oh, I forget their names—in your room, hearing, you see," she went on calmly, "that you were *fully* occupied in town." His close scrutiny drove down her thick eyelashes like fans against the curve of her cheeks. Ravensworth wisely forbore to press her on the source of her information.

"Then I shall move in with you," he said in a tone that forbade argument.

"That's just it, you see," argued Briony. "Thinking that I had become a grass widow"—she gave him an accusing look—"I made room in my chamber for some of the unattached ladies. I am afraid I rashly invited over a hundred guests to this ball for Harriet and Avery and we are shockingly pressed for space. But everyone has taken it in good part and I daresay we shall scrape by for the day or two that remains.

At the mention of "ball," Ravensworth was recalled to a sense of his grievous injuries. "I would have thought, madam wife, that it was fitting in you to apply to me before undertaking the expense of such an extravagant party. For all you know, I might have whistled my fortune down the wind at the gaming tables in the fortnight I have been in London."

"Gaming too?" Her unexpected rejoinder brought a guilty stain to Ravensworth's neck but she met his tormented eyes with a limpid expression and Ravensworth sucked in his breath. If he did not know his wife better, he would stake his life that the minx was toying with him. Briony's lashes fluttered down and Ravensworth's worst suspicions were confirmed.

"Briony," he said in a warning tone.

She ignored his crushing grasp on her fingers. "It would appear, my lord," she began coolly, "that you have gone from one den of iniquity to another. Are you purse-pinched? You need only say the word and I should be happy to stand buff for you. As for the expenses I have incurred for this ball for Harriet and Avery, think nothing of it. I never intended for you to bear the burden of my whims. I am, as you well know, a woman of independent means."

There was much that Ravensworth would have liked to say to these provocative remarks, but since he was unsure of how he stood with his wife and how much she knew of what had transpired in town, he thought it prudent to ignore an area in which he knew himself to be highly culpable. They had turned the corner of the house and were in full view of the main entrance and the eyes of any number of inquisitive spectators. He pulled her into the cover of a clump of flowering rhododendron bushes.

"Of course I am not purse-pinched, but never mind that now! I have something of a more important nature to discuss with you. Tell me about this latest acquisition of yours—the giant who is directing traffic in the great hall."

"Oh! You've met him?" she asked with a guarded expression, and she reached out to pull a violet bloom from the bush by her shoulder. "What a pretty color," she said inconsequentially, and held it to her nose.

This was too much for Ravensworth. He grasped her by the shoulders and turned her to face him squarely. "The truth, madam wife! Who is he and where did you find him?"

"What you don't know cannot hurt you, my lord," she replied with infuriating calm. "The story is that he is Mrs. Rowntree's nephew home from Canada—she is our housekeeper by the way."

"The story is . . . . the story is!" expostulated his lordship fiercely. "I am your husband. I want the *truth*, dammit, not some tale you've concocted to fob off the county Constable. Now is he or is he not the American seaman who escaped detention some weeks ago?"

Briony was silent and Ravensworth administered a rough shake to loosen her tongue. "Tell me, damn you!"

"No, no!" she replied with a shake of her head, looking at him regretfully. "I am not at liberty to tell you more, and I *won't* lie to you. Give me credit for that much at least. I am sorry to disoblige you in this instance but the story was told me in confidence."

His hands clamped tightly on her shoulders and after a moment Briony was constrained to say, "Ravensworth, you are hurting me."

He let her go immediately and she took a leisurely step away from him. One quick glance from under her lowered lashes confirmed his hurt expression and she sighed inaudibly.

"Ravensworth, my dear, won't you simply trust me in this matter if I promise *not* to undertake anything foolhardy without advising you of my intentions? You must see that my one wish is to protect you from any unpleasantness."

Her contrite tone visibly softened the grim lines

around his lordship's mouth. "You idiotic girl!" he retorted vehemently. "It is *you* who needs protecting! Why don't you trust *me*? Do you think that I am utterly without scruples, that I would betray your confidence under any circumstance, whatever my sentiments? What kind of man do you take me for? But that there should be secrets between you and me is something I will *never* tolerate in a thousand years."

"Never? I'll hold you to that, Hugh Montgomery," said Briony, laughing boldly into his eyes and savoring the depth of loyalty his words had conveyed. Ravensworth eyed her warily, and she put out her hand to him. "Come, sir, a truce for the present. I give you my hand on it. We shall return to this subject later, if you wish it, but our guests await our pleasure. We have duties which we are obliged to perform. I must return to the house. Pray excuse me."

He made as if to say something then thought better of it. His expression softened, and he sighed in resignation. "Briony! Briony!" he chided softly. "You incorrigible girl! What am I to do with you? Don't think to escape the authority of your husband. I shall require a full accounting from you later, you may depend on it. But you are right. This is neither the time nor place. Take my arm and permit me to escort you to the house." He extended one elegant arm clothed in finest superfine.

Briony took in the perfection of his Weston tailoring and the pristine folds of his spotlessly white, starched neckcloth and her eyes twinkled in perverse amusement.

"With pleasure," she responded, striving, though not very successfully, to suppress the laughter she felt bubbling to the surface. "But would you mind taking me to the *kitchen* entrance?"

Ravensworth raised one aloof, inquiring eyebrow as she laid her hand lightly on the back of his arm. "A mannequin and a scarecrow!" she confided between hoops of laughter. "The Sublime and the Ridiculous."

Ravensworth grinned appreciatively. "You should deal famously with m' father."

"So I've been told," she replied amiably. "But satisfy my curiosity, if you please. Your neckcloth—I don't think I recognize the knot. It looks new and terribly complicated. It must have taken you an age to achieve."

Ravensworth turned to look at her with sparkling eyes. "It is and it did," he responded with exaggerated gravity, fingering the object in question. "I call it 'à la Briony.'"

There was a moment's silence as she assimilated his meaning. "Do you know, Ravensworth," she asked at last in wide-eyed innocence, "when you are good, you are very good indeed, but when you are bad, you are horrid?" But the smile which flickered at the corners of her mouth disarmed the remark of any ill humor, and when she saw his answering grin, her head went back and she laughed in unfeigned delight.

Chapter 24

Later that evening, when Briony emerged from the chamber which she shared with two of the younger un-attached ladies of the house party, she had every expectation that the unaffected elegance of her new, French-styled gown would throw her obdurate husband for a loop. One quick glance at Ravensworth's expressive face under the brilliant blaze of flickering candlelight confirmed her wildest hopes. His lordship was completely bouleversé.

She moved in a slow, graceful glide toward the head of the main staircase, where Ravensworth, magnificent in full evening dress, was in conversation with their guests of honor. Harriet observed Ravensworth's frozen smile and turned to view the object of his intense regard. When she caught sight of her cousin, she beamed with undisguised approval, and at her whispered aside, Lord Avery nodded and glanced ruefully at his immobile host, who appeared to be oblivious to everything save the fair vision who advanced steadily upon him.

Briony, in a shimmering satin gown of Quaker gray which no Quaker damsel would ever have been caught alive in, became aware of the intense regard of three pairs of eyes, and demurely lowered her lashes, but at the sight of the pale, unadorned expanse of bosom swelling above the low square neckline of her frock, she quickly averted her gaze. Perhaps she had gone too far, she thought belatedly, as she read the martial glint in her husband's eyes.

She had trustingly put herself into the hands of her new dresser, Fifi, a French émigrée, and a counterpart for Denby. Briony's instructions had been concise and to the point. "Dress me as befits the consort of the Marquess of Ravensworth, but above all, bear in mind that I am a virtuous lady who esteems simplicity in all things." The results had been more than gratifying. Her ensemble was simplicity itself. Fifi had advised against any ornamentation with the exception of pearl drop earrings with matching combs placed strategically in the smooth coil of hair at the nape of Briony's neck. To counteract the severity of this uncompromising knot which Briony insisted upon since it was her husband's unequivocal preference, Fifi had teased long tendrils of hair to lie provocatively against Briony's neck and cheeks. White kid gloves reaching well above the elbow and matching slippers and reticule completed the ensemble.

Briony allowed her eyes to rove over the assembled guests in the great hall below, and the kaleidoscope of glowing colors reassured her. In comparison to the peacock finery of the other ladies present, she was as demure as a dove. She put up one hand to touch the smooth blond swathe at her neck, and lifted her chin a trifle— a gesture which was not lost on her husband.

As she moved at a leisurely pace along the gallery to take Ravensworth's arm, she became aware that the silk of her skirt was clinging tenaciously to the outline of her legs in a most unladylike fashion. She pulled at it unobtrusively to no avail. Ravensworth's keen eye swept over her, missing nothing, but his whispered comment, when it came, was crushing.

"Where is the rest of your dress?"

Briony looked into his scorching glance and found that she could not keep a straight face. "How like you! You hypocritical reprobate! The day that you tell me I look charming, I'll know for a certainty that I look like a nun! Now stop frowning at me and say something pleasant for a change. What do you think of my hair?"

"It's different. Have the pins fallen out? It looks to me as if it is coming undone."

"Nonsense," said Harriet in a matter-of-fact tone. "It's all the rage. I'll wager Briony's dresser took hours to tease those wayward locks into this tantalizing disarray. You look ravishing, Briony."

Ravensworth forbore public comment, but as the four began their slow descent of the grand staircase, he inclined his head toward Briony and said in a soft undertone, "If you don't do something about that dashed skirt, that's exactly what you'll be—ravished. Every baronet, viscount, and earl is shamelessly ogling you."

"Not to mention marquess," Briony interposed smoothly, smiling with disarming coquetry into her husband's grim face.

"Look at Grafton," Ravensworth went on with rising ire as he spied the offending Earl. Lady Adèle, attired with habitual flamboyance verging on the vulgar, was hanging on his sleeve. "What the devil does he think he's about, gaping at my wife in that moonstruck fashion? It's that dress, of course. I shouldn't blame *him!* It's meant to heat the temperature of any red-blooded male to boiling point!"

Briony laughed. "Don't be nonsensical. I am the plainest-attired lady in this entire assembly! Not a person here sees in this unremarkable getup whatever it is that you think you see!"

Ravensworth answered her fiercely. "Don't gammon

me! *As* if you didn't know! It's that damned dewy innocence which you project so convincingly which that—neckline and—oh, the sum of all the different parts give the lie to. Why you look like—like . . ." Here his lordship paused to find the right words of condemnation.

"Like a common harlot displaying her wares in a house of debauchery?" finished Briony, a polemic gleam kindling in her eye.

Ravensworth froze and his knuckles showed white against the bannister. "Briony, where did you hear those words?" he asked, the color draining from his face. "Was it Grafton?"

"I have my sources," replied his lady with cryptic evasiveness.

"I can explain everything," Ravensworth exclaimed. "It's not as black as it seems. I beg of you, Briony . . ."

"Pray, don't put yourself to the trouble," returned Briony, suppressing an urge to giggle. "You warned me how it would be when you went up to town." At this she turned a luminous look of reproach upon the stricken lord.

"But *I didn't;* I *couldn't;* Briony, you know I *wouldn't!* I am *innocent,*" he ended on a note of desperation.

His Marchioness gave a slight shrug of her shoulders. "So say you," she intoned with pitiless unconcern for his protestations of innocence.

Ravensworth would have said more, but the orchestra began the first bars of the opening waltz and he was obliged to change partners with Avery. As he led Harriet out to the middle of the great hall to open the ball with the guest of honor as custom and precedence decreed, he bent a look of acute supplication on his Marchioness, who gave nary a sign that she understood his eloquent entreaty, and the portraits of long-forgotten Montgomerys on the oak-paneled walls smiled down stiff-lipped and unblinking at his misery.

It was a grand ball, the most spectacular gala event that had been seen in the district in living memory. Every neighbor for miles around had been invited, swelling the number of residents at the house to more than twofold. A marquee had been set up on the south lawn to accommodate the guests for supper and many were drifting away from the great hall to avail themselves of the culinary delights of the French chef whom Briony had especially imported from London for the occasion.

Briony was in high alt. She had basked unashamedly in the flagrant compliments which had come her way. She was an original; one of a kind; she was a great gun and Ravensworth a lucky man to have attached the Incomparable Miss Langland. And she had savored the dark, smoldering glances which Ravensworth had directed at her as she had danced the night away in the arms of every man but him. She had brought him to the point of surrender, she was sure of it, and at the thought, a ridiculous smile of anticipation played about her lips.

Avoiding the unwelcome attentions of Lord Grafton, who had been blatantly pursuing her all evening, Briony threaded her way resolutely through the crush of dancers to the east wing, making her way to the downstairs library, only a stone's throw from the noisy throng in the great hall. She cast a lingering look over her shoulder and her eyes briefly met those of the ever-watchful Ravensworth, whose attention was almost immediately claimed by the persistent Adèle. Briony saucily tossed her head and surreptitiously snatched a glass of champagne from the tray borne aloft by one of the innumerable lackeys who waited on her guests with unabated good humor. A gala evening in the servants' quarters was planned for the following evening, by which time, it was to be hoped, many of her ladyship's guests would have departed for greener pastures.

She heard the faint strains of the orchestra as it struck up for the second waltz of the evening—"a wicked waltz," as Nanny would say—and Briony smiled reminiscently as she recalled the ball at Broomhill House, so long ago, when she had first met the darkly handsome, hot-at-hand Marquess of Ravensworth. Well, she had learned the trick of managing him, she thought sagely.

She plumped down on the settee flanking the fireplace and took one sip of champagne before laying aside her glass. From her reticule, she withdrew a small mother-of-pearl snuffbox, a gift from Harriet. The practiced flick of her left wrist was meant to open the lid in one easy motion, but by some mishap the object in Briony's hand fell to the new Aubusson carpet and rolled under the massive oak library table which stood against the window.

Briony dropped to her knees and crawled under the table, groping with arm outstretched to retrieve it. She found it hard against the wainscotting and sat down, knees drawn up, to complete her favorite ritual, but before she could begin, she heard the door open and a masculine tread came striding into the room.

A pair of white silk stockings encased in black patent shoes stopped directly in front of Briony. She hesitated only fractionally then reached forward to mischievously pinch the elegant calf so invitingly displayed to her view. In a moment, a laughing Briony was hauled from her hiding place by two strong, masculine arms and she was caught in a crushing embrace.

At the first clear glimpse of her captor, Briony groaned, "Oh no! No! No!"

"Yes! Yes! Yes!" The Earl of Grafton, bleary-eyed and somewhat the worse for wear from champagne, bent his head to ravage Briony's lips.

"Well, well, well! What have we here?" My Lord Ravensworth, leaning with indolent grace against the closed door of the library, arms languidly crossed over his broad chest, surveyed the dramatic action with a sardonic eye.

"Do you know, my dear," he addressed Briony, "I have the strangest feeling of déjà vu?"

"Broomhill House," offered Briony helpfully as she disengaged herself from Grafton's ardent embrace. In one hand she still clutched the mother-of-pearl snuffbox. Without a flicker of embarrassment, she deftly opened the lid and withdrew the smallest pinch of snuff and put it delicately to her nostrils. "Delightful," she said as she exhaled.

"I was thinking of our . . . honeymoon cottage," mused Ravensworth aloud, frustrating her deliberate attempt to throw him off stride.

"I've been meaning to talk to you about that," said Briony prosaically as she brushed past the Earl of Grafton as if he had been a statue carved in marble. "I've had it done up, you know—the cottage, I mean—new roof, new furnishings, new bed." Her eyes flickered to Ravensworth and flicked away again. "Thing is, your man of business came to see me earlier this evening. I have overextended myself, Ravensworth—the ball and everything else, you understand. You, um, couldn't let me have a little something on account? I'll gladly pay you back out of my next quarterly interest."

Much to Grafton's amazement, my Lord Ravensworth smiled fondly at his wife. "My dear, on your lips, there are no other words I'd rather hear—almost. But I fear we are embarrassing Grafton here with our domestic chatter."

The Earl, recalled to a sense of his jeopardy, began to mumble a disjointed apology but Ravensworth held up a restraining hand. "No need to apologize, old chap, I assure you. It happens all the time. You don't mind my asking, but you're not a Quaker by any chance? No, no, I didn't think you were. Not that *that* signifies in the least! Put it down to idle curiosity. No need to name seconds or anything of that sort. I trust you don't think I'm shirking my duty as a man of honor, but such niceties don't weigh with her ladyship, you see.

"No, no! You haven't taken advantage of my hospitality. I won't hear of such a thing! Lady Ravensworth tumbles into these little scrapes all the time, don't you dear?"

He opened the library door and stepped back a pace. "I'd be most obliged to you if you would grant me a small favor. Lady Adèle is waiting for me in the yellow saloon off the main drawing room in the west wing. Would you be so kind as to convey my apologies to her? Just tell her I am otherwise engaged. What? Oh, nothing drastic. I'm merely going to box my wife's pretty little ears." He spoke with such imperturbable affability that Lord Grafton was sure he had misunderstood the last remark. He retreated through the open door with much bowing and scraping and offers of abject apologies until Ravensworth was constrained to say, "Yes! Yes! We understand. Just go!" And with a helpful hand on the shoulder, he propelled the befuddled Earl backward into the hall and promptly shut the door in his face. He thereupon locked it, and pocketed the key.

"What about our honeymoon cottage?" asked Ravensworth, striving without much success to repress the look of triumph flashing from his eyes. "Whom do you intend it for?"

Briony self-consciously fingered the pearl drop at first one ear and then the other. "Whom do you think?" she prevaricated.

He gave her a slow "à la Ravensworth" smile. "What a remarkable woman you are. Who would have believed that you would have such foresight? You were very sure of yourself, were you not, Briony?"

"Very!"

"You knew that I would return?"

"Of course."

"And you had the cottage made ready so that we might be together?"

"That goes without saying."

"But my dear, it really wasn't necessary."

Ravensworth advanced toward her, and Briony, reading his intent, evaded his grasp and swiftly ranged herself behind the back of the sofa.

"I take leave to remind you that there are still no drapes on the windows," she reproved in quelling accents.

"As though I care a fig for that," Ravensworth rapped out, and vaulted the obstacle which barred him from his quarry. In one easy movement, he encircled Briony's waist and pulled her roughly against him.

As he bent to kiss her, she twisted her head to the side and gasped, "Before we resume our relationship, Ravensworth, I think we should come to an understanding."

His hands roamed possessively, caressingly down the length of her. "I agree," he concurred, his warm lips tantalizingly coaxing her mouth open. "Unconditional surrender on both sides."

"That sounds reasonable," managed Briony before she was adroitly tumbled to the floor in a bear hug. After several minutes of pleasurable lovemaking, she finally mused, "I thought you were going to explain about that den of iniquity."

Ravensworth's head came up. "What would you say, my love, if I said that I shall forget about all the explanations *you* have to make if you forget about all the explanations I have to make?"

"Mmm. That sounds reasonable," moaned Briony as Ravensworth's hands touched a sensitive spot.

"Tingling?" he asked at length.

"What do you think?" she sighed hoarsely as her impatient fingers worked to undo his "à la Briony" neckcloth. She slipped her warm hands into his open shirt to stroke the soft mat of hair curling on his chest.

Ravensworth groaned, "Briony Langland, try to remember that you are a virtuous lady." And then the unscrupulous lord did everything in his power to make his Marchioness forget that she was indeed a lady.

Please turn the page for an exciting sneak peek of
Elizabeth Thornton's
TO LOVE AN EARL
coming in September 2004
from Zebra Books!

Chapter 1

My Lord Rathbourne's indolent gaze flickered indifferently over the crush of noisy diners in the White Swan's public parlor and came to rest on his silent companion.

"I beg pardon, Wendon, I wasn't listening."

Viscount Wendon, of an age with his friend although of a more pleasantly boyish aspect, was at that moment leaning hard back in his dining chair, which was balanced precariously on only two legs. He brought it slowly down to rest squarely on the carpeted floor and leaned his elbows on the white damask of the covered table.

"I merely remarked, Gareth, that out of regimentals, to all intents and purposes, we veterans become indistinguishable from the rank and file. I have been attempting this age to attract the notice of our estimable landlord, to no avail. I own that the poor fellow may have good reason to be so hard pressed with every man and his dog taking refuge from the elements, but dash it all, don't he recognize Quality when he sees it? Here we are, a couple of peers of the realm, not to mention heroes of the Peninsular Campaign, and we are passed over as if we were a pair of negligible country bumpkins."

This good-natured complaint brought a ghost of a smile to the Earl of Rathbourne's pensive countenance. "Speak for yourself," he said in an amused baritone. He turned slightly in his chair, bent a riveting glance from glittering amber eyes upon the harried landlord, and raised one hand imperceptibly. In a matter of moments, the landlord was at his side with mumbled apologies, and Lords Rathbourne and Wendon had given their order for the best nuncheon the inn had to offer.

"Boiled brisket! I ask you!" said Viscount Wendon in discust when the landlord was out of earshot. "I swear we did better under Wellington. Well," he amended on noting Rathboume's incredulous expression, "there were occasions."

"Yes, but very few and far between," averred Rathbourne as he leaned across the table to fill his friend's glass from the opened bottle of Burgundy which stood at his elbow.

Wendon lifted the half-filled glass to his nostrils and savored the bouquet. "The real thing! I wonder . . . do you think that they ever went without anything or gave us a thought whilst we squandered the best years of our lives on those squalid treks across the Peninsula hunting down Boney's elusive armies?"

"Not *always* elusive," responded Rathbourne, his face taking on a grimmer aspect. "We are lucky. We came back in one piece. Thousands didn't."

"Do you miss it at all?"

"Do I miss what?" There was a shade of disbelief in the Earl's voice. "The near starvation? The utter exhaustion? The executions? The needless savagery? The loss of friends I've known since school days? What do you think?"

"Then why didn't you resign your commission?" Wendon persisted.

Rathbourne took a moment or two before replying. He relaxed the imperceptible tension across his shoulders and settled back in his chair. "Who knows? Youthful idealism? Loyalty to one's comrades? Duty to King and Country? It seems such a long time ago now, I hardly remember. It becomes a habit. Sometimes I have to remind myself that the war is over, that I'm not the autocratic officer whose every command must be instantly obeyed. I suppose it will take time to adopt more civilized ways, to resume my former existence. I have little practice in the role of chivalrous gentleman."

Viscount Wendon gave a shout of laughter, and heads turned to look disapprovingly in his direction. He lowered his voice. "Gareth, you scoundrel. You . . . chivalrous? Never! I've known you most of your thirty years, since we were both in short coats. Being autocratic comes naturally to you! You didn't learn it in the army! Good God man, when we were at school, at Harrow, who commandeered the best bunk in the lower school dormitory, drawing the cork of no less a pugilist than George Gordon, the present Lord Byron? And that was only the beginning of your scandalous career! And after that, when we were newly up at Oxford, who cut out all the other hopefuls with the fair Griselda, the wife of our illustrious dean—yes, and fought a duel with the poor old codger who was only trying to protect his own?"

Rathbourne suppressed a shudder. "Some episodes in one's life are best forgotten and that is one of them. Can you imagine? He didn't know one end of a pistol from the other! He might have killed himself, poor devil! If I cut you out with the lady, I am sorry for it, but I did you a favor, albeit unconsciously."

"Think nothing of it," said Wendon magnanimously. "I couldn't afford her. My father, the old skinflint, kept me on a very tight leash. I hadn't a feather to fly with from one term to another. You, on the other hand, were never short of the ready." He fell silent as he belatedly recalled that Rathbourne, as an undergraduate, was wont to laugh away his affluence by intimating that his widowed mother bribed him to stay away from the ancestral home. The joke had been too close to the truth for comfort, as he remembered—something to do with a falling-out between mother and son after his younger brother had lost his life in a climbing accident.

A bold-eyed serving maid brought an ornate platter with their dinner, and the two gentlemen fell silent as she set it on the table before them. Her roving eyes darted from one to the other in open appraisal, eliciting an inviting smile from the friendlier of the two gentlemen, but her glances were for the handsomer although austere Rathbourne, who gazed steadfastly out the window until his companion addressed him.

"Nice," said Wendon appreciatively.

"I didn't think you cared for boiled brisket." There was a twinkle in the Earl's eye.

"Never mind," Wendon shook his head. "You were telling me about your sister—the reason for this trip to town, as I recollect. Or could it have anything to do with the darling of Drury Lane, Mrs. Dewinters, who, as I hear, has taken up residence in Chelsea—in one house among many of which you are the acknowledged landlord?"

"Absent landlord," said Rathbourne emphatically as he carved a generous portion of beef. He offered the platter to his friend. "How very well informed you are, Wendon. We could have used you in Intelligence, if only we had known of your penchant for listening to gossip."

"Not I," retorted Wendon with some vehemence. "Your methods are not compatible with my gentle turn of nature. I suppose somebody had to do the dirty work, but . . ." He fell silent, realizing the implied insult in his words.

It was only the merest chance that he had ever discovered that his companion was not all that he seemed to be when they served together in Spain with Wellington (or Wellesley as he then was). Wendon had been on a recon-

noitering mission with a detachment of cavalry when he
had been captured by the French and taken to their
headquarters for questioning. The Earl had walked in on
that interview, but posing as a French officer. If he was surprised to see the Viscount, he covered it well, much better
in fact than Wendon did, who almost gave the game away.

It was the Earl who saved Wendon's hide when things
turned ugly and it appeared that he would be summarily
shot. Rathbourne had spirited the Viscount away before
anyone was the wiser. In so doing, he had almost blown his
cover. Wendon supposed that he owed his life to the fact
that his acquaintance with the Earl went back to the playing fields of Harrow. He wondered whether Rathbourne
would have risked so much for a perfect stranger. He very
much doubted it. Once safely back behind British lines, he
had been sworn to secrecy and had in fact been close-
mouthed about the Earl's clandestine activities during the
war since then. Until recently, he recalled, with an uncomfortable flash of memory. Still, the war was now over.
Rathbourne was safe from a French assassin's hand, and
his confidante was someone who could be counted on not
to betray his confidence and who posed no threat to the
Earl. Nevertheless, he wished he had kept his mouth shut.

He threw a quick glance at his companion and was relieved to note the amused quirk of one dark eyebrow.
"Woolgathering?" asked Rathbourne quizzically. Avery
recovered himself quickly and rushed into speech. "Forget the war! Old Boney is Emperor of only a pile of rocks
on Elba. England is safe from attack, and we are military
men no longer. Tell me about your sister."

Rathbourne shrugged his shoulders. "There is nothing to tell. Now that Caro is eighteen, my mother wishes
her to make her come-out. My presence will simply add
a little countenance to all the parties and balls which she
is bound to attend. What the devil is this?" he asked

distastefully as he removed the lid from the vegetable tureen. He brought up a ladleful of soggy, dark green leaves.

"Boiled cabbage. What did you expect at an English tavern? Here, put it on my plate. It is the perfect accompaniment to boiled brisket. Yes, and I'll have some of those boiled potatoes too, if you would be so kind."

The Viscount's appetite, apparently, was not impaired by the quality of the food. The Earl, of a more fastidious palate, confined himself to the Burgundy and the Stilton.

"Do you happen to know anything of an Armand St. Jean?" he asked casually after an interval. "You are in town more often than I. I thought perhaps your paths might have crossed."

"I haven't been in town this age, but yes, I know of him," Wendon replied, looking speculatively at his friend's carefully impassive countenance.

"And?"

"He's a young hothead—no more than twenty, I should say. His propensity for gaming is legion, as are his women, and he hardly out of leading strings. Shocking, ain't it? He's half French, of course. There's an older sister in the wings somewhere who exercises not the slightest restraint upon him. He's a charming devil though. Come to think of it, he's a bit like you were in your salad days. But your cousin, Tony Cavanaugh, can tell you more than I. He's taken him under his wing, so to speak, and has tried to restrain some of St. Jean's wilder impulses—to no avail, I'm sorry to say."

A smile flickered briefly on Rathbourne's lips. "Now I know we should have seconded you to Intelligence, Wendon. The war would have been over in half the time if we'd set you loose behind French lines. You have a veritable talent for gathering information."

Wendon laughed self-consciously. "Well, I do go about

a bit. I can't settle into running my estates as you seem to have done. The war has made me restless, I suppose. Perhaps I should find myself a wife and secure the succession as my fond mama keeps telling me."

A thought suddenly struck the Viscount. "Good Lord! St. Jean isn't angling after Caro, is he? He's got nerve, I'll give him that!"

Rathbourne demurred but Wendon continued as if he had not heard the denial. "Be careful, Gareth! He's a dangerous cub with a demon temper! It don't matter to him whether he dispatches you with foil or pistol. He's blessed with cool nerves and natural talent, you see, a deadly combination."

The Earl spoke in a soft undertone, humor lacing every word. "The prospect terrifies me! A callow youth, you say? I'm thankful I never met the hellion on the battlefield. I'd have been tempted to put him across my knee and paddle him."

"You'd be a fool to underrate him," Wendon went on pleasantly. He cut himself a thick slice of brisket which he proceeded to attack with relish. "I've done my duty. If you don't wish to take him seriously, that's your lookout. Don't say I didn't warn you."

The door to the parlor opened and the chill draft of that cold, wintry morning ruffled the covers of their lordships' window table. Rathbourne looked to the door, his brows knit together.

Two women stood on the threshold. The elder was smaller in stature and hung back as if unsure of the propriety of entering the inn's public dining room. The Earl's eyes became riveted to the younger woman, and his fingers tightened on the stem of his wineglass. She stood with head held high, one hand securing a green mantle which hung in loose folds from her shoulders, her clear eyes coolly assessing.

He would have known her anywhere! Five years seemed to slip away as he absorbed every lovely feature, every soft contour, every endearing detail which had been a constant memory since their last encounter. Yet she was different—no longer the fledgling, but a woman with the bloom of promise fulfilled. He felt the constriction in his chest—a reminder that the sight of her classic beauty had always set his pulse to an erratic tempo.

His hand went absently to finger a small faded scar on his left cheekbone. He had hoped for a different setting in which to make himself known to her. No matter. He was not one to cavil at Providence. Better sooner than later.

She removed her high poke bonnet to reveal the thick burnished braids at her nape. He could almost feel their silken smoothness between his fingers. His hands itched to unpin the heavy skein of spun gold and wrap themselves in the curtain of hair that he knew would fall to well below her shoulders. He smiled as she pushed back a stray tendril from her smooth, high forehead in a familiar gesture of impatience. She flashed an encouraging look over her shoulder at her companion then took a halting step into the room, a small smile of anticipation curving her generous mouth, as if she was enjoying every minute of the novelty of finding herself in the White Swan's public dining room.

Her eyes traveled around the interior, lighting with undisguised interest on the various occupants, and Rathbourne had the sudden urge to rob her of that fragile composure, to drive down those thick, dark lashes in confusion and bring the blush to her creamy complexion. He had the overpowering desire to make her as disturbed by his presence as he was by hers.

Her eyes alighted on Wendon momentarily, and he saw the smile on her lips deepen. Then her eyes met his and Rathbourne held them, inexorably, unwaveringly. He was conscious of the startled lift of her dark eyebrows, the defiant tilt of her head, the sudden shock of recognition in the depths of green eyes widened in alarm at the unexpected sight of him, and still he held her.

He knew she was breathing rapidly, fighting him off with every breath, as if they were locked in mortal combat; he knew that she was remembering in vivid detail, as he was, that other time so long ago when she fought him with every ounce of strength which she possessed, and he was determined that, in this contest, he would not be the loser. His smoldering gaze captured her, compelling her to yield to him. The blush on her cheeks deepened, and a slow smile touched Rathbourne's lips. He would have continued the contest, but someone moved between them, and when he sought her eyes again, they were carefully averted.

"Who is she?" Wendon asked softly as she allowed the landlord to seat her at a table, her back turned resolutely against Rathbourne.

"Someone I once knew, a long time ago," said Rathbourne noncommittally.

"Don't think I ever met the lady." Wendon could hardly contain his curiosity. "Don't seem as if she cares to renew the acquaintance."

He looked at his friend expectantly, but Rathbourne's only comment was, "Shall we have coffee and brandy?"

The Earl tried to catch the landlord's eye but he was unsuccessful, for the girl in the green mantle had at that moment crooked her index finger and he was hastening to her side. Rathbourne saw the flash of an emerald ring and he smiled enigmatically.

"If that don't beat all!" exclaimed the Viscount with mingled astonishment and chagrin. "How shall we ever live this down, Rathbourne? To he outranked by a slip of a girl with only a pretty face to recommend her! Look at our host positively drooling over her!"

"Yes, it is a bit of facer, isn't it? But console yourself with the thought that if she were a man and could be persuaded to accept a commission in His Majesty's service, she would quickly rise to the higher ranks."

"Oh?" Wendon intoned encouragingly.

Rathbourne's thoughtful gaze took in her straight spine and squared shoulders. "Defensive strategy would be her forte, I should say." After a moment or two's reflection, he added, "But this is one occasion when she shall not outmaneuver me."

He felt in the breast of his dark frock coat and withdrew a scrap of lace from an inside pocket. "Mrs. Dewinters's," he explained with a hint of apology. The stale perfume of carnations was in the air, and Weadon grimaced.

"What do you mean to do?"

"What else? Merely renew an acquaintance of long standing."

The Earl pushed back his chair and rose to his feet in a leisurely manner. There was something in his expression which provoked the Viscount to exclaim, "Good God, Gareth, she's only a slip of a girl! Have a care, man! What on earth was her offense that you look so blasted . . . punishing?"

Rathbourne evinced surprise. "Punishing? You are mistaken, Wendon. Say rather 'determined.' If you will excuse me?"

Deirdre sensed his approach rather than saw it, and her shoulders tensed, but her conversation continued unabated, and the smile on her lips became fixed. She saw her aunt's surprised glance become focused on a point above her head, and she carefully half turned in her chair to look dispassionately into the familiar face which had persistently tormented her waking and sleeping hours since he had flung away from her on their last, never-to-be-forgotten encounter.

He loomed over her, a menacing masculine presence, and Deirdre had to force herself not to shrink from him. His eyes, coolly polite, met hers briefly then he ignored her as if she did not exist.

"Rathbourne at your service, ma'am," she heard his deep baritone say gravely to her aunt. She had forgotten how husky and liquid his voice could be—soft, soothing, or seductive, as he chose to make it. "I believe this article of feminine apparel belongs to you? You dropped it as you entered, I collect."

Deirdre's aunt, Lady Fenton, examined the friendly gentleman who stood towering over her. His presence compelled attention. His dark hair shot with auburn was cut long on the collar; broad shoulders encased in restrained black superfine; the flash of white teeth in a deeply tanned face; but it was his eyes which arrested her—amber eyes, flecked with gold—tiger eyes, but gentle as he waited patiently for her response.

"Thank you kindly, sir, but it does not look familiar." She turned it over in her hand to examine it more carefully. "Perhaps some other lady . . . Deirdre, is it yours?"

Deirdre's nostrils detected the stench of stale scent on the lace handkerchief and her eyes flickered in annoyance. "I think you should try some other lady," she said coldly and pointedly.

Her aunt glanced sharply at her niece with questioning eyes, but Deirdre looked steadfastly at the shining, silver cruets on the table.

"Then I apologize for the intrusion, Miss . . . ?" He waited expectantly.

Deirdre preserved a stony silence, but her aunt, now startled by her niece's lapse of good manners, hastened into speech.

"Permit me to introduce my niece, Miss Deirdre Fenton. I am Lady Fenton."

"Charmed," responded the Earl, raising Lady Fenton's fingers to his lips. "Miss Fenton? I recall that name. Yes . . . come to think of it, I believe I had the pleasure of making your acquaintance prior to my embarking for Spain. That would be about five years ago. Your mother, as I recall, was undertaking your come-out at the time." He captured Deirdre's hand and brought it to his lips. "And who could ever forget the dazzling emerald? You still wear it, I see."

Lady Fenton was conscious of the charged atmosphere. Deirdre, who had been sitting throughout as if frozen in her place, her pale cheeks as white as the linen covers of the table, brought her head up and looked at the Earl with a flash of temper.

"I regard it as my good luck piece," she said, snatching her hand away.

"Indeed?" The Earl deliberately fingered the scar on his cheek and Deirdre's defiance seemed to crumble. Her gaze reverted to the cruets. "Superstitious, Miss Fenton?"

"Hardly that, sir. I wear it because it was my late father's. That is all."

"Touching, I'm sure. But I have already taken up too much of your time. Lady Fenton, I hope I may call on you in town? Miss Fenton, your servant, ma'am."

It was the longest hour that Deirdre could ever remember. Hardly aware of what she ate, or the pleasantries she exchanged with her aunt, she concentrated on keeping her back turned rigidly against him, checking her unwilling eyes from roving from table to table. She knew when he took his leave, for her aunt's smiling eyes followed him out and she nodded her head in silent salute. Deirdre breathed more easily again, relieved to be rid of his threatening presence.

BOOK YOUR PLACE ON OUR WEBSITE AND MAKE THE READING CONNECTION!

We've created a customized website just for our very special readers, where you can get the inside scoop on everything that's going on with Zebra, Pinnacle and Kensington books.

When you come online, you'll have the exciting opportunity to:

- View covers of upcoming books
- Read sample chapters
- Learn about our future publishing schedule (listed by publication month *and author*)
- Find out when your favorite authors will be visiting a city near you
- Search for and order backlist books from our online catalog
- Check out author bios and background information
- Send e-mail to your favorite authors
- Meet the Kensington staff online
- Join us in weekly chats with authors, readers and other guests
- Get writing guidelines
- AND MUCH MORE!

**Visit our website at
http://www.kensingtonbooks.com**